DOUBLE CROSSED

DOUBLE OR NOTHING BOOK 1

ADORA CROOKS

Join my newsletter to get a free romance!
https://adoracrooksbooks.com/gift/

AUTHOR'S NOTE

Helen's gold (legend or otherwise) does not exist. The mysterious city near Türkiye where Gabe's mission occurs does not exist. The top-secret Wolfpack Special Ops Team (as far as I know) does not exist, nor do any secret societies or government entities mentioned here. This book is not meant to be a reflection of the US Navy in any shape or form.

Trigger warnings and sensitive material include violence, characters dealing with PTSD, spicy group scenes, bondage, dvp, consensual degradation, let's-tie-her-to-a-tree-and-do-naughty-things-to-her, gun play & knife play in the bedroom, an awkward Thanksgiving dinner, and very bad dad jokes.

Read safely and enjoy responsibly.

XOXO, Adora

1

JACK

You can tell a lot about a man from what he drinks.

Unhappy husbands order cheap, tasteless beer. Businessmen in knockoff suits drink to impress—gin on the rocks, top-shelf scotch. Regulars—like Mort, in his car-oiled stained jeans—get the same thing every time. Miller High Life. The champagne of beers.

The Pink Pony isn't exactly known for being classy.

I like that about it. I like rickety tables. I like the patch-work booths. I like the duct tape that holds the bar together.

It's a piece-of-shit place that knows what it is. It doesn't pretend. Honesty like that gets far with me.

Which is one of two reasons I picked this place to moon-light as a bartender.

I say *moonlight* because this isn't me. I play the part—dark jeans with a brown belt and a tight black T-shirt. But my other job—my real job—buzzes at my hip.

There are only three people at the bar, and they're all glued to the stripper rounding the pole to Mötley Crüe's "Girls, Girls, Girls," so I palm my cell and check the text.

[Anders] *Got a job for you. Details pending.*

It takes a lot to shake my calm. Two tours in Iraq, there's not a hell of a lot that gets to me anymore.

But boy, does that text make my heart skip a beat.

I respond: *Copy that.*

I'm so deep in my imagination—wondering what the job might entail—that I don't notice the tune change tracks. It's a wolf whistle that cuts through my thoughts, and then I hear it. Beyoncé is blasting, asking the question: "Who run the world?"

The answer: girls. Always girls.

I lift my gaze, and I see her. Lady Liberty—that's her stage name. Big, pouty lips, hazel eyes that peer out from dark eyebrows, and a heart-shaped face under thick, wild brunette hair. She's wearing an emerald robe and a pointy crown—Lady Liberty indeed. She works her coy smile as she saunters onstage and plays the crowd. She's not the best dancer, but what she lacks in flexibility she makes up in attitude.

She's reeled in every warm-blooded person in the club —hook, line, and sinker. The patrons in the back suddenly wake up with shouts and hollers. She flips her hair back and teases a long leg through the slit in her robe, and already they're throwing cash on the polished stage. I've seen her do this dance a hundred times, but even I start to salivate.

Mort taps his dirty nails against his empty. My eyes don't leave Lady Liberty as I crack open another beer for Mort and slide it across the bar.

"Jack," Mort says, "check this out."

He's pushing his phone across the bar, but I hold up a palm to stop him.

"Not now."

Mort's yellow eyes follow my gaze to the stage, and he nods. "Right. Can't miss the Liberty Bell, am I right?"

He's right.

Liberty is winding down now—grinding her clothed pussy against the pole and arching her back in a lead-up to the final crescendo. Then, in a feat of pure gymnastic talent, she leaps up the pole, crosses her legs around it, and drops her body down. The music cuts with a gong sound as she swings her upside-down body from side to side, her bare tits on full, mouthwatering display.

That's her move. The Liberty Bell.

The men go wild. They throw money at the stage in crumpled bills. I clock a particularly enthusiastic table of businessmen. They're a couple of rounds in, they've already ordered two rounds of shots, and I know they're past their limit. I make a note to keep an eye on them.

I let Mort distract me this time. He wants to show me a video that's gone viral on Facebook—it's an agitated cat, wide-eyed and making humanlike noises. We chuckle and shoot the shit for a little bit while my eyes flicker frequently to the stage and to the hanging beads that separate the back room from the bar. Finally, I see Lady Liberty exit through the shuddering wall of beads. She's wearing a robe over her green slip. The second she enters the bar, one of the businessmen—a short guy with a fake Rolex—approaches her. He corners her and talks with her. I can't hear what they're saying, but I can see their body language. She smiles, but she shrinks away from him. Meanwhile, he's getting closer. More insistent.

Mort wants to show me a video of a dog reuniting with his army-bound owner. I tell Mort, "One second," and I quickly wind around the bar. When I get close to them, I can hear the businessman pestering Liberty. "—C'mon, just one drink. You can sit on my lap if you want, princess..."

And then he puts his greedy hand on the bare flesh of

her shoulder and squeezes. That's it. I grab him by the front of his shirt and slam him against the wall. It happens so fast he can't catch his breath, and his eyes go wide.

If we were in Iraq, I would eat this soft boy for breakfast. I'd floss with his fucking femur. I'd break every bone in his hand that touched Liberty. But here, in plain clothes, I'm not allowed to do that. Instead, I twist his shirt in my hand and lean close so I can growl in his ear, "Can. You. Read?"

"What?" He's sputtering, eyes bugging out of his head. His "friends" go quiet suddenly, shuffling awkwardly around the table.

No one wants to step in the line of fire for this mongoose of a man.

I jab my finger toward a sign on the wall, then read it for him. "*Don't touch the girls.* You touch them, I touch you. And I won't be gentle. Got it?"

I want to feel his shoulder pop out of its socket. I want to damage him. But he doesn't put up a fight. Instead, he just whimpers and squirms like a fish on the line. "*Please,*" he begs, "I'm sorry, man. I didn't know. We'll leave. Right now. No hard feelings."

"Whoa there, Tiger." It's her voice—not his—that convinces me to release the idiot. Lady Liberty puts her hand on my bicep. "I think we've all learned our lesson for the day. How about you fix a girl a drink?"

I don't want to let him go. But for her, I do. I release him and let him scurry back to his pack of overgrown frat boys. Then I turn to her and ask, "The usual?"

She smiles. "You know it."

I return to my post behind the bar, fix her a seltzer and lime, and then call the business-dicks a taxi—because I'm a nice guy. I overhear her talking to Mort. "So? What'd you think of the set?"

"Eh." Mort shrugs. "Don't like that song."

"What? It's Beyoncé, what's not to like?"

"Gimme something classic, honey. You kids don't know good music anymore."

She laughs. It sounds like Christmas ornaments clinking together.

"Jack," she says to me, "walk me to my car?"

"Yes, ma'am."

I'd walk her to her car even if she didn't ask. Just like I always do. Outside, the shell of man-sweat and stale beer falls away. The air is crisp. Nice. Tastes like fall.

At her car—a burnt-orange Chevrolet—she twirls around and puts her hand on my chest. "When do you get off?"

"Three."

She groans, "So late."

"Uh-huh."

She's wearing too much glitter, and her face sparkles in the dark. I want to ruin her glossy lip balm. I don't, though. When we officially got together about six months ago, her boss had "that talk" with her, warning her against PDA with her new boyfriend. Said it was bad for tips.

I follow the rules. She doesn't.

She leans forward on her tiptoes, and her mouth grazes mine. Her lips are sticky and taste like strawberry, and I want to hike up her skirt and raw her right on the hood of her death trap of a car.

"Don't be late," she purrs when she pulls back.

Oh, I won't.

I wait until her car has started up, that dying *chug-a-lug-a-lug* that always makes me wince and pray, and watch her headlights peel off down the road before I go back inside. There are a few new patrons leeching off the bar already, loudly grumbling about the slow service. One man isn't complaining—that's Anders. He's a human tank at the end of the bar with his arm in a sling, spotted with tattoos, who never got the memo that the "pornstache" went out of style in the '70s. One tattoo in particular connects us—on his forearm, he wears a wolf head with an Ontario MK 3 Navy Knife sticking out of the top of its skull. I've got the same ink on my bicep. All Wolfpack boys have them.

It's the one thing that connects us. That, and an undying loyalty to country and brotherhood.

"What's the story, Jack?" he says, his voice low and gravelly.

"The lone wolf has bite, but the pack has might," I tell him.

I fix him his drink first—a Tom Collins—and slide it over. On the house. A man saves your life, he gets to drink for free as long as I'm behind the bar. I take care of the other barflies before settling back beside Anders, leaning my elbows against the table.

"Where's your girl?" he asks.

"You just missed her."

"Damn shame," he sighs. "She's got the tightest ass here. You're a lucky dog."

He's the only one who can talk that way about my girlfriend and still keep his teeth. I just grunt an acknowledgment, pour two shots of Jack, and clink mine against his before downing it.

"What happened to your arm?" I nod to the sling.

He shrugs. "Broke it in two places."

"No shit." Genuine concern. "What'd the doctor say?"

"Stay out of those places."

We share a laugh. He's a corny shit with bad puns, but believe me when I say those bad puns were better than painkillers some days when we were pinned behind enemy lines, mouths full of blood and sand.

Anders spends more time chatting with me than he does fawning over the half-naked girls. We don't get any more excitement for the night, and I cut off the bar promptly at three. It takes another hour for everyone to file out before I can close out, and I'm aching to get home.

Anders lingers with me, and after a while, it's only the two of us. I let the music play on—Def Leppard—and close the register. I left him the bottle of Jack, and he's done a fair job of killing it.

Now that we're alone, he can speak freely. "So. Up for a new job?"

"You know it."

He grins. "Knew I could count on you."

A little background about the Wolfpack: Wolfpack is a privately funded mercenary agency filled with the toughest vets you've ever met. We get paid to do the jobs that the government can't be caught doing. In layman's terms: I'm a hired gun for the good guys. I'm honored to be a part of the Wolfpack, but we're not your typical family. It's not the tight-barracked army life. Wolfpack men work alone and in the shadows. We don't exist. I report to Anders. He gives me my jobs. I never have contact with the buyer. It's a closed loop.

Which is fine by me. I'm a hired gun. Nothing less. Nothing more.

The organization is sprawled across the world. I have no idea who most of my Wolfpack brothers are. Anders is the exception. We have history. We did a tour together, and he found me again when I was back on American soil. I was at my lowest, a shell of a man barely held together with liquor and bad memories. He brought me into the Wolfpack. Gave me a purpose.

That breeds a loyalty that goes deeper than blood.

He takes a swallow straight from the bottle, and when he sets it back down with a clank, his mouth is a serious line. The warmth has gone out of his tone now—he's my commanding officer again, and he's readying me to take my orders.

"Target's name is Gabriel Madsen," he says. "Last seen in the Keys."

I wait. He passes a manila envelope across the table. It's lumpy. I know the contents already—a silencer, unregistered. Maybe some information about my target, but probably not a lot. I don't need to know what I don't need to know. I'm a weapon. That's it. Anders tells me *who, where, when*, and I take care of the *how*.

And when it's done, he'll fill up my bank account, and I can go a few more months before I get called on again.

When my fingers touch the envelope, however, Anders adds, "He's a Code Black."

Code Black means two things: 1) my target has military experience—which means he'll be tougher to take down than most—and 2) he's a traitor. A switch. Someone who was on our side but defected to the bad guys. Code Black is reserved for the worst of the worst, and I've been tasked with cleaning it up.

"Understood," I say. I tuck the envelope away and pack up for the night.

I walk Anders to his car. I offer to give him a ride home, but he shakes his head. He gets in and rolls down the window.

"Take care of yourself," I tell him, patting the hood of the car.

"Hey, Jack." There's that Halloween-pumpkin grin. "What's the story?"

"The lone wolf has bite, but the pack has might," I recite the Wolfpack mantra.

He revs up his car and howls loudly before zipping out of the parking lot. I shake my head. Nine-life'd crazy bastard.

I toss the envelope in my passenger seat and get in my car. I always keep a duffle bag in the trunk. It's filled with the essentials—a couple of pairs of clothes, a small first aid kit, my passport, and a few thousand in cash. If I need to make a quick exit, it's all there. And I could. I could leave right now from the darkened Pink Pony and gun it the 722 miles it'll take to get me from Georgia to the Florida Keys. I could take care of this *Gabriel Madsen* business and get back by Friday —maybe Saturday if I pull over and sleep at a welcome center on the way back.

But I have a stop to make first.

I drive a Land Cruiser with a hybrid engine—an electric car because 1) the environment is dying, and we have only ourselves to blame and 2) it's quiet, and you'll never find a better car to do recon with. My ears ache from the club's pounding bass, so I cut the radio and wind the car down I-85, onto the sprawling highways that never sleep. I leave behind the fast-food joints, nail salons, and strip clubs, drive through the twinkling, towering Atlanta skyline, and finally enter the calm, quiet, destitute East Atlanta neighborhood. It's suburbia with a city bite—parks overrun with dealers, a church transformed into an Airbnb, hippie coffee shops, and cottages and family homes nestled together. The Chevrolet is in the driveway (her house, her dibs), so I park on the street.

I leave my duffle bag in the trunk—she has a rule, no guns in the house, and I respect her rules, except when it comes to her safety. She doesn't know about the Colt I've stashed in her fireplace or the pistol taped to the toilet—and, hopefully, she'll never have to know.

I step through the squeaky wire gate, over the cobbled steps, and through the small, overrun garden. A wooden, hand-painted sign hangs over the porch that reads: WHAT'S SAID ON THE PORCH, STAYS ON THE PORCH.

If I was a settling-down guy, this would be the kind of house I'd settle down in. And she'd be the kind of girl I'd settle down with.

In the interim, we play house. I've even spoken to her parents over video chat. They live in North Carolina, but they pay her rent. They'd pay for her law school, too, but Kennedy's pride has limits. Her father has called me a "stand-up guy." I like it, even though I've never really understood the expression. As opposed to a sit-down guy?

A stand-up guy.

I unlock the door and see her there. She's stripped Lady Liberty—her green robe, spandex, wig, and undergarments are thrown over chairs and on tables. And now she's just...

Kennedy. My Kennedy.

She's fallen asleep on the couch, stuffed into an over-sized sweater—I got it for her as a joke for her last birthday; it says "PROPERTY OF A SEAL," and she hasn't taken it off since—with a quilt half draped over her. The table is littered with empty Smarties candy wrappers, her studying feel-good food. Her glasses have slumped down the bridge of her petite nose, and she's facedown, drooling into her Con Law textbook.

She's a walking cliché—third-year law school student who pays for her classes by moonlighting as a stripper—and I told her as much to her face, back when we were first getting to know each other. She scrunched her nose up, scoffed, and educated me on how exotic dancing has a long history in feminism. "Political activist Susan Stern shook her goods for cash," she lectured, "because she *liked* it, and people gave her shit for it then, and they give women shit for it now because God forbid we exude sexual confidence and a functioning libido."

Hell, I think I fell in love with her right then and there.

Seeing her like this now—not the stripper version of her, the one she puts on for show, but my Kennedy, warm and sleep-soft and cuddled up with her least favorite book… it makes my heart thump and my cock swell. I step beside her, remove her glasses from her face, and cup her warm face in my hand. There's an indent in her cheek where the book marked her. She doesn't open her eyes, but she moans softly, those full lips pouting. I want to unzip my pants and wake her up with my hard dick between those pouty lips, but I'm a gentleman, so I murmur, "Kennedy."

At the sound of my voice, her eyelids flutter open. And she smiles, drunk with exhaustion. "You're late," she says.

"Sorry."

She twists, stretches her arms over her head, and her sweater hikes up, revealing her soft tummy, bare legs, and cotton panties. "Is it time for bed?"

"Yes." *Yes.* It's definitely time for bed.

I scoop her up in my arms—the book thuds loudly to the ground—and carry her to the bedroom. The house is nice, cozy enough for Kennedy and me, just far enough away from the hum of the city to be inexpensive. Her bedroom door is wide open, and I shut it behind us. Her clothes are on the bed—Kennedy lets things clutter. She can't help it—no one ever made her do two hundred push-ups because her sheets weren't tucked around the edges of her mattress just right. I shove the mess to the floor and lay her on her back.

Her kisses are sweet, sleepy, but mine are not—I'm a live wire of pent-up energy, and I think she senses that because she chuckles softly against my mouth. "Have you been thinking about me all night?"

"Yes," I growl. I want her so bad my throat contracts and makes my voice low and husky.

She bites her lip, and her slender little fingers dance across my belt, tugging it free. "I've been thinking about you, too..." she says. "My strip club knight...so quick to come to my rescue..." She turns serious suddenly, her mouth pursed in a frown, and she moves her hands to either side of my face (no, back on my belt, need your fingers *lower*).

"Jack," she says, and when she says my name, I listen. "You know it scares me when I see you like that. You get so... cold. Different. Dangerous."

A knot of guilt in my chest. "I know." I can't help it. I can't help that I'm dangerous. I can't help that I'm a living, breathing, walking weapon.

"But..." She shudders. "The truth? It also...turns me on." Then she takes my hand and guides it between her thighs. I stroke her swollen lips over the soft cotton, and she spreads her legs wider, wanting. I dip my finger underneath her panties and sink it into her sweet sex and—

Fuck. She is wet. She's furnace hot, dripping, and she gasps loudly when I tease her. I fondle her slippery lips and her hardened pearl until her thighs tremble.

"Please," she gasps.

"Ask for it."

"I need you, sir."

Sir. All my blood immediately goes south.

I peel off her panties and toss them aside. My clothes go next, and I rip them off until I'm naked over her, cock growing even stiffer at the sight of her open, ready sex.

Her fingers are cold as they trickle down my broad chest and play the muscles of my abdomen like piano keys. She bites my lip coyly as she wraps her hand over my cock. She doesn't stroke me; she just holds it, and I taste her smile. "You're throbbing," she says with this sweet wonderment. She squeezes my thickness, and I groan, ache wrapping and tightening around my dick like wire, pulling at my balls and making my abdomen clench.

But she does this—she likes to tease me until I can't take it anymore, until my patience breaks and I mount her like the animal I am. And it works. I grab a handful of her thick hair, and she yelps in surprise—and delight. I flip her onto her stomach and grip her hips, hoisting her to her knees, and—

Yes. I am an animal. But she is an animal, too, and she lifts her ass and wiggles it invitingly. I take her by the hips and plunge into her wet heat. She cries out, and I pivot deeper inside of her and twist a handful of hair, and she shouts louder—she's shouting my name now—and I fuck her in a rapid-fire clip. The metal of my dog tags clicks together with each thrust. We're sliding and panting and rutting—harder, faster. I need this—I need my muscles to coil and I need my sweat to sting my eyes and I need to pound something into submission...even if she's definitely not submitting, she's shouting for more, *more*, don't stop, oh God, don't stop...

Her headboard knocks against the wall, her shouts fill the room, and she clutches my cock with her orgasm once, twice, and still I don't stop. I feel her arch and contract around me, I hear her moan with sloppy pleasure, and I think about the loaded gun waiting for me in the trunk of my car, and I blow. Hard. I fill her, and she whimpers and shoves her ass tightly against my pelvis, taking my come in, deep. She grinds against me until she's taken all of me—I'm hers. I have nothing left to give her. I roll onto my back, and she cuddles against me and puts her head on my chest. We pant. We sweat. The adrenaline high buzzes and glows in my veins.

"You really were thinking about me all night, huh?" she says and flicks my nipple playfully.

"Really, really."

We get quiet now, her legs tangled up in mine. This is the eye of the storm. The dead calm after a firefight. She's soft again, warm, like a kitten, and I scoop my arm around her to hug her closer.

"I have a job," I tell her finally, popping the bubble of our docile silence.

"I know," she hums against my chest.

I shift my arm so I can look her in the face and furrow my brow. "What do you mean, you know?"

"I mean, I *figured*. You get...different."

"Different how?"

"It's like...you wake up or something. And. You fuck me *like that*."

"Guess I'm not as stealthy as I think."

"Not with me." She growls playfully and nibbles my jaw. "Is it dangerous?"

I shake my head. "Anders's cat is stuck in a tree."

This is a game we play—she knows what I do. Kennedy is the *only* person who knows that I make my living doing questionable work for a government contractor. She doesn't know the gritty details, but she's not stupid. She knows it's dangerous.

People die. Every day. Why do I have to tell her that I'm the trigger finger behind a population decrease or two?

So we play this game—she asks, I make up a dumb story.

I'm not incredibly creative, but it gets her to smile anyway. "Good thing you're good with pussy," she says.

She's playing with me, but I see the concern in her eyes. When I kiss her again, it's a soft, sweet kiss, an *I'm coming home* kiss, and I slide my thumb over her cheek, and she sighs into my mouth.

I TAKE A SHOWER. Never know when I'll get one next, so I take advantage of it. I rinse off—letting my sweat, the stench of the club, and Kennedy's come roll off me and slide down the drain. I suds up, and my brain drifts to my mission.

It's not the first time I've had a one-man hit. In my two years of belonging to the Wolfpack, I've seen my share of bad guys. Madsen is ex-military. That won't be easy. I have to keep the element of surprise on my side. A hunter can tell when he's being hunted.

Unfortunately for him, I'm the biggest cat in the jungle.

The water's gone cold, and I have to go.

I dry off and exit the bathroom. Kennedy is still sprawled out in bed, naked, face pressed against the pillow, eyes closed. I have a single drawer—Kennedy cleared the bottom drawer of her dresser for me. I've barely filled half of it. Her clothes spill out from the open dresser drawer, and I have to shut them and crouch down so I can pull on a shirt.

"When will you be back?" Kennedy mumbles, no longer pretending to be asleep.

"Soon enough."

I get up and kiss her. She's warm, and her lips are pillow soft, and I know that if I climbed into bed right now, she'd melt into the crook of my body and fall asleep on my chest.

She makes a noise when I break the kiss. "Stay," she

whines. And it's tempting, with her arm stretched out toward me like a wanting child.

I love Kennedy. I really, really do.

But the cold, hard truth is, as much as I love Kennedy...

My devotion to the Wolfpack will always win.

After all, Gabriel Madsen isn't going to pull the trigger on himself.

I pet her cheek. "Go back to sleep," I tell her.

And I'm gone.

2

JACK

The Cruiser sails like a bullet down the seven-mile stretch of overseas highway that separates Florida from the Keys. I've been on the road for eleven hours, had four Red Bulls, listened to one audiobook (John Grisham's *Rogue Lawyer*), and three Tool albums before I finally pass the welcome sign: WELCOME TO KEY WEST, PARADISE ISLAND.

Fall in Key West isn't fall at all. It's summer with pumpkins, and the ghoulish Halloween decorations look out of place hanging off of palm trees and boat lines. I crack open my window, and the moist, warm air slaps me in the face like the sweaty belly of a sumo wrestler.

I need sleep. It's noon—not an ideal time for a hit. I pull into a pelican-pink motel, give a fake name, and pay in cash. They give me a key with a palm tree hanging off it, my room number scribbled in Sharpie on the blank side of the rubber tree.

There's a rogue chicken wandering the parking lot, and it escorts me from the reception desk and down the narrow concrete walkway to my room. Her feathers are chewed up, and she's got a red puff on the top of her head like a mohawk. She's a little off and lilts to the left, head bopping with each step.

"Thanks, Clucky," I tell her. She clucks in response (cheery bitch) as I slot the palm tree into the keyhole. My room contains a twin bed, a stubby dresser, a round table with two rickety chairs, and a bathroom. Beggars can't be choosers. All I really need is the mattress anyway. The motel is so close to the coast that there are seashells in the parking lot instead of gravel, so I expect the smell of sea salt to waft in when I open the window, but I get the cough of car exhaust and motor oil from the neighboring marina. Clucky is eating rocks. I close the window and pull the blinds.

I drop my duffle bag on the table. Then I go into the minibar, find a tiny tequila, and unscrew the cap. Not my go-to drink, but I feel like embracing Florida. They have a baggie of salt next to it, and it takes me a moment to realize it's not cocaine. Cute. I fill a plastic go-cup, sit at the table, and take the envelope Anders gave me out of my bag.

I rip into it. Eager as a kid at Christmas.

Inside is a 9mm Glock pistol, an attachable silencer, and a full clip. And the only information I get about my target—a couple of photographs of Gabriel Madsen. Dark hair, dark sunglasses, leather jacket, and black pants; does he know any color besides black? Even in the fuzzy images, I can see his lean, panther-like physique. No question about it—he's a Navy boy.

I pull my computer out of my duffle bag, plug it in, and start it up. Kennedy makes fun of me for holding on to my Windows instead of following the sheeple devoted to their Apple products, but she doesn't understand that a PC can do things a Mac can't. When I insert my scrambler into the USB drive—for example—I can access my own secure internet connection without worrying about the FBI stalking my search history. Since I know he's Navy kin, it's a place to start, and I go into the directory and hunt for a *Gabriel Madsen.*

He isn't hard to find. SEAL. One tour overseas. I expect to find something about him going AWOL—*Code Black*, Anders had warned me—but nothing comes up.

Doesn't matter. I don't need to know who he is. I need to know *where* he is. Nothing about Gabriel Madsen anywhere else, no social media accounts, and I've hit a momentary dead end.

He's in hiding. Obviously, he won't make it that easy to find him. I review the pictures again. He's supposed to be in hiding, but there's something about the way he stands— shoulders slanted, lips turned in a crooked smile—that rubs me the wrong way. He's not on the run. He's dressed like he's modeling for the front cover of Bad Boys Magazine. He's cocky.

I move my attention to the background. He's standing in front of a bar called the Hook. So I look up the bar. It's in the Keys. I'm getting warmer. I scan through the list of people who've liked the page and stop at one.

Gabe Smith. Bingo.

His Facebook page is private, so there's only so much I can see. His profile image is of a fish with a hook in its mouth, so not a lot to glean from that, except that, like everyone else on the Keys, he passes away the dull stretches of nothingness with fishing. Banner image, the American flag (obviously). There're a couple of public posts from him —corny political memes, feel-good videos of dogs getting rescued, dogs befriending odd animals, dogs excitedly greeting their masters when they come home—okay, you're a dog person, I get it.

But then I hit the jackpot.

He's checked into the Hook for trivia night *every* Thursday, without fail, for months. And it must be my lucky day because today is Thursday, and the Hook is advertising trivia night at 9:00 p.m.—*no registration required*.

I pull the USB, tuck my computer back in the duffle bag, and shove everything back in the envelope, except for the gun. That, I stick under my mattress. Then I strip down to my briefs, fold my clothes on the nightstand, and fall into bed.

I've got four hours until go time, so I set my alarm for 7:00 p.m., and sleep takes me immediately.

THE HOOK IS SANDWICHED in the middle of a bustling marina—sailboats swaying on either side, fishing boats bobbing. The shack is propped up on stilts and located out on a pier. The only way in and out is a narrow, plank-wood walkway.

In short: it's a terrible place for a stakeout.

I park my Cruiser down the street, kill the lights, and watch people filter in and out. I washed up, shaved my five-o'clock shadow, and donned a festive Hawaiian shirt and a pair of khakis to blend in, but now I get the feeling that I've overdressed. Most of the people filtering in and out of the Hook are salty dogs—older men with full beards and scraggly locals.

I linger in my car, waiting.

I crack open an energy drink in my console. The sound prompts a confused *cluck-cluck?* from the back seat.

"What the fuck—?"

I swivel around to find Clucky bopping in my back seat, skinny neck outstretched, curiously eyeing my drink.

"No. Out. *Scram.*"

I pop open the car door. What follows is a flurry of feathers and an outraged *cauh-cah!*

I'm in the middle of forcibly booting Clucky out of my car when I see him.

I thought swagger was something made up by pirates and pretty boys in '90s movies, but Gabriel Madsen fucking *swaggers* when he walks. His dark hair dusts his shoulders— he's letting it grow out; interesting choice—but otherwise, he looks exactly like his pictures. Black jacket over black T-shirt and black jeans—does this guy *own* any other clothes, and who the fuck wears so much black in *Key West*? The last item of his ensemble, however, is an enigma to me. He wears a black fanny pack strapped around his hips, like a tourist dad at Disneyland. It doesn't seem to fit his *bad boy* chic, but what the fuck do I know?

Maybe theme park dad is what the kids call *cool* these days.

Madsen walks, so I imagine that either his cliché motor- cycle is in the shop, or he lives nearby. Since I plan on taking him out in the comfort of his own house, I'm banking on the latter.

He's a smoker, and he kills his cigarette while chatting to the guy outside who looks half-man, half-barnacle. Eventu- ally, Madsen crushes his cigarette under the toe of his boot and vanishes inside.

I check the clock on my dash. It's quarter till. Since I have no intention of playing trivia, I give it another half an hour before I exit the Cruiser. My shoes crunch on the shell gravel, and I walk the plank. There are big lights pointing down at the turquoise water below, and it's so clear that I can see the giant, foot-long groupers wiggling back and forth. I saw *Jaws* at a too-young age, and it left an impression, so I feel better once the pier ends and the Hook begins.

There are maybe thirty people here—which I take is bustling for a place like this. The décor includes such highlights as a 2013 Baywatch calendar and a big-titted mermaid statue. Oars litter the ceiling; all of them look hand-painted. A bald man in a straw hat sits at a table in the back and calls out questions and heckles the audience over the sound system.

I pull up a stool at the bar. The bartender is part of the team at the end, so it takes a good five minutes to get his attention. I haven't had anything to eat but bags of chips and gas station food, so I order a fried chicken sandwich with a side of waffle fries and a Corona.

A rooster saunters into the bar. They really give new meaning to *free range* out here.

I salute him and say, "Compliments to the chef."

He cocks his head and glares at me.

The roosters are rude. I miss Clucky.

I pop my lime in the beer and take a swallow. From my position, I can see Madsen out of the corner of my vision, though I mostly try to keep my back to him. He's sitting at a table of four men who look like they have at least twenty years on him, and they've got a pitcher of beer between them. Madsen is, apparently, part of a team that calls themselves *Nine Inch Males*. Figures.

If there's a theme for tonight, it goes over my head. The questions seem to bounce around from subject to subject—sports, music, TV, and entertainment. Name two female artists in the 1980s with seven number-one hits (Whitney Houston and Madonna), listen to this TV theme song and guess the show (it's *Cheers*), and what football team was founded in 1946?

Once the answers are in, Madsen shouts a chant for the Miami Seahawks, and his team cackles. They're the loud table. For a man supposedly on the lam, he's bad at keeping a low profile.

I finish my sandwich, wipe tartar sauce off the edge of my mouth, and toss the napkin onto the plate so the bartender can take it away. I ask the bartender to box up my fries to go. A man with a doggy bag is inherently less suspicious than a man without one.

The MC announces the end of the second round, and they take a music break. Madsen & Co. have already drained the pitcher, so Madsen leaves his table and makes his way to the bar. The chain attaching his belt loop to his wallet jangles with each step, announcing his approach. The bar has mostly cleared out at this point, but even though he has a whole empty stretch of island top, he fits himself between the chairs one over from me. He parks his elbows on the polished wood, lifts a hand, and requests another round from the bartender, whose name is apparently Jason.

A Guns & Roses song bounces off the speakers above us. As the bartender fills his pitcher, I toss a glance Madsen's way. I notice something the spy cameras missed. He has the prettiest eyes of any man I've ever seen. Tropical island blues with long, brush-soft eyelashes.

I get it now. The leather jacket. The unshaven jaw. The I-don't-give-a-fuck slouch. High school must've been hard for him—always typecast as pretty boy Peter Pan when he really wanted to be Captain Hook.

My stomach knots strangely. I belch to relieve the pressure.

I'm a grown-ass man. I can belch in public. I can do whatever the fuck I want.

I've caught his attention now, and he swings his body around, those eyes hooking into me.

"Nice bass," he compliments.

"Thanks. First-place champion."

"Where's that—Iowa State Fair?"

He's fishing for my hometown—some clue as to why I'm there. I don't give him what he wants. I play this little game we have going with. "World champion, actually."

"Not every day you meet a celebrity."

"I'll autograph your tit if you'd like."

"Careful, I might take you up on that." He has a smile like a movie star—rows of perfectly pearly white teeth. Then he sticks out his hand. "Gabe."

"Arthur," I lie and take his hand. It's warm, smooth, and strong in my own. The next time I touch his hand, it will be cold, limp, and lifeless.

"What brings you to Key West, Arthur?" He's immediately pegged me as an outsider. He's not as stupid as he looks.

"Work. Just passing through."

"What kind of work?"

You ask a lot of questions, Madsen. One would think you're paranoid. I smile politely through his interrogation. "Extermination."

"Must be some pretty big rats if they've called in an out-of-towner."

"The biggest."

Madsen doesn't flinch. When his pitcher comes over, he refills his empty pint glass and says, "I hope you catch the bastards."

"I'll drink to that."

We click glasses—his pint, my Corona.

"You like trivia?" he asks. "We could always use an extra brain."

"I'm not into team sports."

"Suit yourself, buddy." He pats my shoulder and gives it a squeeze so tight I feel it in my coiled muscles. "You know where to find us if you change your mind."

I won't. It's one thing to drink with the enemy—a whole other ball game to play trivia with him.

In the smudged mirror behind the bar, I watch Madsen make his way back to his table. Instead of sitting with his team, however, he goes to the next table on the left. It's occupied by only one man. He's a dark-skinned man in a sharp, caramel-colored suit and polished shoes. He looks mid-fifties, clean-shaven, and he's sipping a gin and tonic.

In short: he's way too well-dressed for a dive bar like this.

Madsen flops down into the booth across from The Suit. He takes up too much space with his body, splaying arms and legs like an octopus. They chat, but even in the duty mirror, I can clock the tense posture of The Suit.

This doesn't look like a friendly meeting. This is a negotiation.

I sip my Corona and watch on.

Sure enough, Madsen takes off his fanny pack. He slides it across the table to The Suit.

The Suit doesn't move to take it. If anything, his limbs turn to stone. Actively refusing it.

Interesting.

The Suit takes another swallow of his drink, says a few words, and then stands. He passes me as he leaves. He even smells like nice shampoo. Definitely not from around here.

I check Madsen in the mirror. He stares at the empty

seat for a moment. Then he snatches the fanny pack back and snaps it back on.

His gaze swings over to me suddenly. I swear, he's glaring at me.

I avert my eyes and kill my drink.

Madsen rejoins his team. He seems to have shaken off his bad mood, and he's all smiles with them. The game starts up again, and I close out my tab, collect my doggie bag, and leave. I want to be seen leaving first so when the cops start asking questions, the bartender and other witnesses can truthfully say that they saw me at the bar from 9:15 p.m. to 10:45 p.m. I load into my car, drop my bag in the passenger seat, and get comfortable in the dark. I pull my Glock out from the dashboard and check the clip. Fully loaded. The silencer comes next, which I screw onto the barrel. With each twist of the silencer, the tension leaves me like steam from a teapot. In the bar, I was clunky and awkward and out of place. Here, in the dark, with a gun in my lap, my senses cat-heightened, I'm in my element.

It's a waiting game now. To kill time, I check my phone briefly. Kennedy has texted. Multiple times. Heart emojis and *I miss yous*. I want to text her back, but I don't. I pocket my phone instead. My hand itches where Madsen touched it, so I rub it over my khakis to feel the rough scratch of linen against my palm. I watch the door of the Hook and wait. An hour passes before people start filtering out of the bar. I recognize Madsen's teammates. They walk out together, give each other brotherly hand-grips and back-pats before hollering their good-nights. His teammates head out to their own individual cars. Madsen, on the other hand, walks alone.

Bingo. I stick my gun in the back of my pants and exit

my car. I nearly nail Clucky in her dumb head with my car door. She's eating the gravel underneath my tire and starts to trail behind me.

"Not tonight. Shoo."

I nudge her back with my boot, and her wings flutter briefly in protest before she skips backward.

I don't have time to babysit poultry.

I follow Madsen at a safe distance. It's nighttime but never truly dark in Key West. The full moon casts a spotlight on the ocean below, and neon signs advertising restaurants and motels flicker. A spark of light emanates from Madsen as he lights up a cigarette as he strolls along the boardwalk. He steers left when he comes to a marina and fumbles in his pocket. He taps his key card against the gate and then lets himself in.

So Madsen owns a boat. Which is probably how he's able to stay relatively off-grid. I lessen our gap and wedge my foot in the gate entrance before it closes behind him. Quietly, I follow behind him.

We're off the beaten path now. Dock lights illuminate the marina, but it's quiet here, except for the occasional chime of ropes knocking against masts as the sailboats bob side to side. The breeze blows up a taste of salt water and the char of barbeque. I lose sight of Madsen momentarily, and then I see it—down the dock, the door to a barn-sized boathouse jangles shut.

I follow behind. I slip through the door as quietly as I can and close it behind me. The boathouse is wide, stuffed with dock boxes, boat parts, and loops of rope. A dry sailboat stands on stanchions to the side, and it's weird to see a boat out of water like that—unnatural. The place is dark, and I scan the room for signs of Madsen.

My pulse slows. My vision pierces through the dark. I listen for everything. The unnerving creak of the stationary boat. The chime of mooring lines outside. My own boots, stepping quietly across the concrete floors.

Movement. Out of the corner of my eye, I see it.

I swing my muzzle to the shadow and almost pull the trigger.

Not Madsen. *Clucky.* Fucking Clucky.

I told her not to follow me.

Then I hear it. The click of him thumbing back the safety on his gun. The point nuzzles the back of my skull.

"Wrong cock," Madsen says.

Son of a bitch.

He's so close I can feel the heat of his breath on the back of my neck.

"You should've walked away," Madsen continues. "I'm sort of a peace and love guy these days, but you're really fucking up my night."

"If you're *peace and love*, why the gun?"

"Because it was only a matter of time before someone took the bait," Madsen muses.

I think about his check-ins. I think about the profile picture of the fish on the hook, and I think, *Jack, you dumb motherfucker.*

He's been waiting for someone like me. *Fishing.*

He set the trap, and I walked right into it.

"Who are you with?" Madsen asks. "CIA? Special Ops? Guess it doesn't matter who claims your brain matter. Where's your gun?"

"My pants."

"Aw. And here I thought you were just happy to see me." I can feel Madsen's breath against the back of my neck as he takes the gun from the back of my pants, removes the clip, and tosses it. "Sorry, buddy," he continues. "It's not personal. You just made the mistake following me here."

"You've made a mistake, too," I tell him.

"How's that?"

"You're standing too fucking close."

In a single move, I whip around, grab the barrel of his gun, and shove it downward. He fires off a couple of shots anyway, but the bullets just bite into the floor. Every sound echoes loudly in the tinny boathouse. The last thing I want is to draw attention to us, so as we struggle for the gun, I slam him up against the wall. It's enough to make him release his grip, and the gun goes skittering to the floor.

Madsen is a flurry of limbs—I get an elbow in the face and a knee to the stomach before I can untangle myself from him. I dive for the gun, and he makes a run for it. I hit the floor, snatch the weapon up, and fire in his direction, but I miss. Instead, he vanishes up the side of the dry sailboat. I take off after him. He's yanked the ladder up as far as it will go, so I have to improvise—I climb up the thick ropes that dangle from the wall and launch off that to grip the ladder. The boat shudders when I make contact with it, and for a second, I fear that the thing is going to roll off the stanchions, but it holds.

I climb up to the deck and hold my gun cocked as I hunt for Madsen. He's a fox, and I'm going to sniff him out—it's not an *if*; it's a *when*. I stalk across the deck, gun cocked in front of me, and my breath feels short in my chest.

I've made it halfway across the dock when I hear a sound behind me. I whip around, gun aimed and ready, and I see Madsen by the steering wheel. He's got a rope in his hand, and he yanks, and suddenly, the long metal arm of the boom comes whipping around and slams me in the chest. My gun clatters to the ground. I have no choice but to grab the boom and hold on for life as it groans and swings me straight off the boat. Suddenly, I'm holding on to the branch-like pole, my legs dangling, nothing but a twenty-foot drop underneath me. My biceps strain and ache as I fight gravity.

"Well, buddy," Madsen's voice rings out. "I hate to leave you hanging like this. But then again, you did try to kill me first. So." From over the long arm of the boom I'm clutching, I can see Madsen salute me, and I hate the smug bastard. He hops down from the ship and starts to make his exit. I make some quick calculations. With my body weight, there's no chance I'll be able to swing my body back to the safety of the ship. I could try to climb the boom and shimmy over, but the sail cover is slippery, and I'm already losing my grip.

Sail cover. *Sail.*

I have a pocketknife in my shoe. I ball the sail cover up in my fist, and my bicep and abdomen burn like all hell when I drop a hand to reach below. My fingertips scrape the leather of my shoe, then underneath, and brush against the hilt. My arm muscles are spasming with the weight of me—I'm not going to be able to hold on much longer. But I fish out the knife, open the blade, and start sawing at the straps around the cover. They pop off—one, two, three—and I fix the blade between my teeth.

I pant and taste metal, and I can hear Madsen dropping off the ladder, his heavy boots clomping victoriously toward the door. I'm slipping as I grab onto a clump of the white, waxy sail underneath. There's a rope here, and I wind that around my wrist. I don't get much time to formulate a plan before gravity does it for me—the last of the straps snaps, and suddenly, I'm tumbling.

I am fucking Tarzan of the country club.

I swing off the side of the boat, the main sail billowing like a cape behind me.

I only get a brief glimpse of Madsen's wide-eyed surprise when he swivels around and sees me sailing through the air toward him before the soles of my shoes hit the ground and the cover flutters around the both of us. It's swallowed him whole, and I have to shove my way through the heavy material before I come to him. Madsen is on his knees, his inky-black hair dripping down his face, but when he lifts his head toward me, his mouth opens to form words.

He doesn't get to. The rope bites around my wrist where it's double looped, and I hook it around his throat now. I pull him taut against me—his back to my front, the rope around his throat—and he flails as he tries to breathe, and the sail is very, *very* annoying, fluttering around us, the static clinging.

His hands reach for the rope, attempting to yank it from my hands, but to no avail. His shirt rides up his torso, baring a tattoo on his midriff, and a chill washes over me. On his hip, a wolf snarls on an Ontario MK 3 Navy Knife. It's the same tattoo I wear on my arm. The same tattoo all of us wear.

I recite, "The lone wolf has bite."

He wheezes a laugh. The veins in his throat stick out like chords. "But the pack has might," he chokes out.

I tighten my grip until he goes limp. The instant he does, I loosen and check his pulse. He collapses in my arms, but there's a beat at his throat. He's not dead. He's just unconscious. Finally. There's quiet.

I need quiet. I need to figure out my next move.

My body is throbbing, but the real pain lives in my chest.

I feel punched. Like I swallowed a live snake and now it's wriggling around in my stomach.

Anders sent me to kill a brother. And for the first time in my life, the *who*, *where*, and *what* aren't enough. I need to know *why*.

And I need to know now.

3

GABE

I wake up.

This—really—is in itself a massive surprise. I should be dead. I've been brought down by two hundred pounds of Terminator-style killing machine.

And yet...

Yours truly lives to breathe another day.

Not the first time I've been snatched out of the jaws of death. There was Yemen. The bar fight in New Orleans. My mother's cooking. That one girl I dated from New Jersey. But it's always a surprise.

Tough Guy (that's what I'm going to call him now) paces across from me. He stops when I groan and shift in my seat. We're still in the boathouse, but he's lit an oil lamp, and it sits on the floor beside us. It casts strange shadows over the mess we've left on the ground—a chewed-up sail cover, a pile of ropes. My hands are bound tightly behind my back, and there's no way I'm squirming out of it.

"What is this, a double knot?" I ask. "Half hitch? If I knew you were into bondage, we could've worked something out."

Tough Guy doesn't laugh. *C'est la vie.*

He has a pocketknife, and he's whipping the blade in and out.

I try conversation again. "What should I call you?"

No response.

"Clearly, your real name isn't Arthur. I could call you *Hot, Edgy Military Boy*, but it's a little long."

His jawline deepens. Hmm. Perhaps I can't flirt my way out of this one, but it was worth a shot. Tough Guy steps forward and unsheathes his blade, and I flinch when he presses it to my belly. But he doesn't pierce skin. Instead, the tip of his knife licks my skin and comes to rest at my belt, right above the fanny pack, pressing against the tattoo at my hip.

"Explain this," he tells me.

"What—my affiliation with the super-secret mercenary team *Wolfpack*?" I ask innocently. My eyes flit over to the matching tattoo on his bicep, and I bare my teeth in a smile. "I didn't think I'd have to explain that one to you, *brother*."

"Why do they want you dead?"

There's real fire burning through his coal-dark eyes, and the press of his blade makes me shiver. I lick my lips, then sigh. "That, unfortunately, is a rather long story."

"You've got ten minutes."

"Or what?" I laugh and regret it. Laughing hurts—my throat feels like it's filled with pine needles. "Or you'll kill me? Get in line. You, Wolfpack, and about half a dozen others want my head on a stick."

"If anyone's going to kill you," he growls, "it's me."

That...shouldn't arouse me. But it does. *Would that these were different circumstances.*

What can I say? I like my men possessive.

Or maybe the lack of oxygen is making my thoughts drift.

"Why," he repeats, "does the Wolfpack want you dead?"

I chew on my explanation. "How many men have you killed for the Wolfpack?"

"That isn't—"

"You asked a question, I get to ask one, too. It's a simple number. Unless you've lost track."

He doesn't budge.

"Twenty?" I try. "Thirty? Am I in the ballpark?"

"Sure."

"Okay. And in those twenty or thirty times that you've been handed the envelope with your gun and your target, have you ever asked *why* they wanted said target dead?"

"It's classified. It's not my job to know."

"Oh, what a *good boy*." I can't help the venom that seeps out of my lips. "I can see why they like you. Pretty machine, no thoughts of his own."

He snaps the blade shut. Then he turns around and opens a dock box.

"What are you doing?" I ask as he starts to rummage around in it.

"Looking for something to break your fingers with," he states.

A bead of sweat drips from my forehead and crawls down my neck.

"Listen," I tell him. "We Wolfpack operatives, we take orders from the boss man because we trust what he says implicitly. We trust what we're doing is good for the country. But if there's a break in the chain—if, in fact, the boss is not providing us with missions for the good of the country and instead providing missions for the good of his pocketbook, then...well. Things could get tricky."

He stops rummaging and narrows his eyes at me. "What are you saying?"

"I'm saying your friends are corrupt, and you're working for the bad guys."

He growls, "That's a hell of an accusation."

"Yes," I say plainly. "The kind of accusation a man might get killed over, don't you think?"

He watches me warily. He's not a good actor—he wasn't at the Hook either. I spotted him as an assassin right off the bat, just as now I can see the wheels turning behind his eyes. He's thinking, debating, and then—

The wool falls over his eyes again, and he snaps at me, "Or you're a coward on the run."

He's pulled a hammer out of the dock box, and my fingers curl into my palms. None of them want to break today. Still, as he approaches me, I steel off my insides, feeling my bones strengthen, my ribs tighten. "Look me in the eyes," I tell him, unshaken, "and tell me that I look *afraid*."

He's a couple of feet from me now, hammer dangling from his fingers. But he hasn't hit me with it yet. He's paused, considering...

Then his eyes widen. Before I know it, he launches forward and grabs the legs of my chair, throwing me back.

I hit the ground hard, and the breath is knocked out of me. The red laser dot that must have been on my forehead is now on the side of the boat, and a bullet meant for my brains immediately cracks through the fiberglass. A flurry of bullets follows, machine gun spitting against the boat. Tough Guy and I are both on the ground, and the chair breaks underneath me.

"One of your friends?" Tough Guy shouts at me. He's flat

on the ground, palms pressed to the dirt as debris flies over us, and he glares at me.

"No," I tell him, "one of *yours*."

The ropes have finally loosened enough, and I wiggle my arms free.

I would run if my way wasn't blocked by machine gun fire.

I look at Tough Guy. Suddenly, we're less interested in killing each other and more interested in who is trying to kill us.

"Madsen!" he calls my name and points to the barrels of fuel in the corner. One has been punctured, and now it's dribbling fuel onto the floor. It's wetting our shoes...and heading straight for the oil lamp in the center of the room.

I launch toward the lamp, but then the firing starts up again, and I'm forced to retreat back behind the body of the ship. A bullet ricochets off the oil lamp, and it tips...

Fucked. We are fucked.

Tough Guy is on his feet, but we don't have time. I put my hand to his chest, shove him back against the wall. A line of upside-down canoes hangs over us, and I yank a rope, undoing one.

"The rope!" I yell. Tough Guy gets it—yanks the other rope.

A canoe comes crashing down over us, just in time. We crouch underneath it as the rest of the boathouse is swallowed in a fiery inferno. I shut my eyes and feel the blast of heat wash over the shell of the canoe. I hear the explosion and the roar of flames.

When the blast has cleared, smoke begins to seep underneath the canoe. I lift our protective shell up. What was once a boathouse is no more—the entire place is swallowed in flames. Things that are wood are cracking; things that aren't are popping and burning.

"Let's go!" I shout to Tough Guy. We have to get out of here before this whole thing comes crashing down on us. But Tough Guy—he's silent.

He's a limp heap on the floor, eyes closed, blood leaking from his forehead.

Well. He did try to kill me.

I could run. I should run. I should leave him here in the cracked, burning hellfire he created.

But when I take a step to go, I hear a cough behind me.

He's barely conscious, but he groans, and his eyes flutter.

My heart hiccups in my chest. I can't leave him. Not like the last time I left a man behind—

The memory is a cold stab in the back, and it pushes me into motion.

I crouch down and grab his shoulder. Tough Guy is huge, full of muscle, and he's not going to be easy to carry on my own. "Come on, we have to go," I urge him. A beam yawns and crashes down behind us. We're going to be trapped in here within seconds. I throw his arm over my shoulder and use all my remaining strength to lift him off the ground. He's half-alive now, stumbling with me, and I yank us to the door and throw us outside...

Just as the boathouse gives its last shudder and the roof caves in, collapsing.

We fall to the cool gravel outside. The small stones bite into my back, but here I can spit ash and try to catch my breath. My gaze drifts passed the inferno, and I see, in the distance, a man. He's carrying a sniper rifle, cloaked in darkness. We're hidden enough because he doesn't return to finish the job—instead, I see him hop into a Jeep and take off.

I crouch and work on pulling clean, clear air into my lungs. Completely unperturbed by the burning building, a chicken bobs passed us. It comes to a stop at my feet and pecks at the ground, clucking happily as it eats bits of gravel.

4

JACK

Trees slice across my vision like fan blades. Sun glare. Tree. Sun glare. Tree.

The window feels cold against my cheek. Parts of me hurt. My forehead throbs, my body feels bruised and battered. Even my goddamn lungs hurt. I squint against the light and shift in the car seat.

Madsen is driving us. Where, I don't know. He's got one hand on the wheel, and his other hand dips periodically into the Styrofoam box on his lap to take a fry...

Are those my fucking leftovers?

His blue eyes flicker to me. His smile is crooked. "Rise and shine, sunshine." He shoves the cold fries in my face. "Hungry?"

I groan and turn away from him. The smell of mayonnaise makes me want to hurl. "This is my car," I comment.

"Mmhm. Not easy to drag you in, let me tell you. You banged yourself up pretty good there."

"*I* banged myself up?" It comes out as a growl. "You hit me in the head with a fucking canoe."

"And saved you from becoming extra crispy. You're welcome." He pats me—*pats me*—on the thigh.

Normally, I have a lid on my temper. I'm cucumber cool. In control. But Madsen gets under my skin like nothing else. If he wasn't in the driver's seat, I'd finish the job I started right now.

He tosses a fry in the back seat. Clucky walks across the seat and pecks at it happily.

That's it. I'm concussed. I have serious brain damage.

"So." Next to my leftovers, he has my wallet on his leg. He flips my wallet open and reads. "*Jack Crossed.* Crossed. What kind of name is that?"

"Polish."

"It doesn't sound Polish."

"They changed it at Ellis Island."

He blinks. "Seriously? That's fucked-up."

What's fucked-up is this conversation about fucking surnames. I redirect.

"Where are you taking me?"

"Away." Those eyes flicker from me, then back to the road. "Key West was nice while it lasted, you know? I was really looking forward to a warm winter. But since you burned that safe house—literally—it looks like we're going north this time."

"*We?*"

His tongue catches a crumb on his upper lip. "Mm—well. I thought about leaving you in that smoldering hellfire, but the way I see it, you'll probably just keep coming after me. And a tough guy on my side is better than a tough guy on *their* side."

"Who says I'm on your side?"

"If you were going to kill me, you would've done it already."

He packs up the leftovers and tosses the bag onto my clean floor. "Don't count it out yet," I mutter.

I have to catch my bearings. I feel groggy still, like I'm half-submerged in fog. I see a sign for Tuscaloosa, Alabama. He must have been driving for hours.

I try to reel my memory back in. The boathouse. His wolf tattoo. Burning. "Who were those guys?" I mumble.

"Which guys?"

"The guys that tried to kill us."

"Wolfpack would be my guess."

"*I'm* Wolfpack. Why the hell would they send someone after their own man?"

"Maybe they didn't trust you to finish the job."

"I finish every job," I growled.

"Sorry to stain your perfect record." He flashes me another smile.

This doesn't make sense. None of this makes sense. My head hurts, and I want to go back to sleep and wake up with Kennedy in my arms, tucked away in our Georgian cottage house, in an alternative universe where I never accepted this job, never got stuck in this mess, never had a sloppy punk rubbing french fry grease in my fucking car.

"What makes you so special?" I ask him.

"You mean besides my perfect teeth?"

I want to strangle him. "I mean, why does everyone want you dead?"

"I could tell you, but then I'd lose my value. And I like being...well. Valuable."

My eyes fall to his fanny pack, still strapped to his hips.

I remember the failed trade at the Hook. Whatever is going on here—it has something to do with what's in that pack. *Valuable.*

I cough, and my lungs burn. He picks up a water bottle

from the cup holder, handing it out to me. "Here. You took in a lot of smoke."

I unscrew the cap and sip it slowly. It helps. A little. I'm feeling a little more like myself. "What happens now?"

"Here's the good news—Wolfpack thinks we're dead. I saw the guy who fired at us. Hoodie-type, maybe six feet. Sound like anyone you know?"

I shake my head. He continues.

"Anyway, we've got a couple days' head start until they figure out there aren't any skeletons in the debris."

"And then?"

Madsen isn't smiling anymore. "And then they go after you, your family, and everyone you've ever held dear."

"They wouldn't," I force out. "I've been loyal—"

"*Been.* Past tense. You've *been* loyal. Until you threw your lot in with me."

I scowl at him. "I'm not *in* with you."

"It's going to look like you are. *We* left the boathouse. Together. You're Code Black now, buddy."

We're coming up to a gas station. "Pull over," I tell him.

"We have to make it to the state line—"

"Pull over!" I snap.

He does. I take my wallet from his lap.

"If you're longer than five minutes, I'm leaving you," he says before I slam the car door behind me.

I stumble into the gas station. It's pre-dawn outside, and the clock on the wall says 6:23, but there's an attendant behind the desk. No bulletproof glass. Southern hospitality. The attendant still looks at me warily (I don't blame him) as I limp across his tiled floor and over to the counter. I pick out a Snickers bar, pull my wallet out of my pocket, and place a $20 on his counter. "I need to use your phone."

He points me to a phone hanging on the wall by the

cheap earbuds. I pick up the receiver, dial a number I know by heart, and rip into the candy bar. It rings three times before Anders answers with "Sunny's Laundry and Dry Cleaning."

"The kid's asleep," I tell him. Code for: *the job is done.*

There's an inch of silence on his end. And then: "Jack?"

He sounds surprised. *Why does he sound surprised? Unless...*

Unless he thinks I'm dead. Unless Wolfpack sent a hit on me.

The Bad Feeling is creeping on strong. I've known this guy going on six years. Why is he acting cagey *now*?

"Mm" is all I give him. "Surprised?"

"It's just..." He fumbles for words. "Fast."

He doesn't fumble. Anders *doesn't fumble.* This is bad, all wrong.

"It was easy," I lie.

"Okay," he says. "Good job. Well, when you get back, let's talk."

"What about?"

"Special job. I can't go into details."

Right. You can't go into details because there is no special job.

I'm *the special job.*

I feel like I've swallowed dry ice. The chocolate sticks in the back of my throat. All my years of service, of loyalty, and now...

Now the very men I'd give my life for want me dead.

"Okay," I tell him.

"Take care of yourself, Jack—"

I end the call. My hands are shaking. I dial a second number, Kennedy's. I get her voicemail. *Hey, you know what to do.* I've seen her screen unknown calls, so I fish out my cell phone and try her again there. The same smoky voice: *Hey, you know what to do—*

Fuck.

The door jangles behind me as I race out of it. Madsen is still there, car still running. I jump in.

"We need to go to Georgia," I tell him.

"What's in—?"

"Jack," I say. "My name is Jack. I'm thirty-six. I served two tours. I came to Florida to kill you, but that doesn't matter anymore. What matters is the only woman I care about is in Georgia, and if we don't get to her first, they will."

Those ice-blue eyes shimmer on me, and then he nods and shifts the gear into drive. "Then we better gun it."

Even as we break the speed limit, the Bad Feeling chases me down the highway.

5

JACK

Madsen drives most of the way, but we switch outside of Georgia. We only have about thirty miles to go, but my head is throbbing, and I nearly nod off three times before we make it to East Atlanta. It's truly a fucking miracle we don't get pulled over. The first stop I make is a couple of blocks from our house. I don't go inside, though. Kennedy's car isn't there, but a new car is. An unfamiliar SUV parked across the street. Black. Tinted windows. Waiting. I peel out before they notice us.

My next stop is the Pink Pony. It's only 5:00 p.m., but Kennedy sometimes squeezes in odd hours, especially when I'm out of town. She's told me before that she wants to move someplace smaller—that the house feels too empty when she's all alone.

If we get out of this alive, I'll get her a smaller house. I'll get her whatever she wants. That's what I'm thinking when my Cruiser rolls over gravel and into the parking lot.

"Your girl works here?" Madsen says. I ignore him.

"You're coming in," I tell him.

"Twist my arm."

I don't entirely know what to make of Madsen yet—I don't trust him, but I don't *distrust* him either. I just want to keep him in my sight. We exit the car, and I double-check my gun is loaded before tucking it away. I changed out of my charred Floridian clothes in a Shell station bathroom, and now I've got jeans, a black shirt, and a denim jacket to cover my side holster. We walk into the Pink Pony, and—as anticipated by the empty parking lot—there's next to no one here. Mort is hunched over at the bar. A couple of other men are pregaming in the corner by the stage.

Cassidy Lane (part-time bartender, part-time dancer) is working the bar tonight, and she folds onto her elbows and perches her tits on the bar when we come in. "What can I do you for, boys?" she asks.

"Liberty in the back?"

Cassidy Lane nods.

"Stay here." I squeeze Madsen's shoulder.

"Aye, aye, boss." Madsen winks at Cassidy, and I swear, her nipples pop on the spot.

Roxy Rocket is Roxy Rocketing across the stage to "Do You Wanna Touch Me?" and I push through the wall of beads that separates the main floor from the backstage.

Their "backstage" isn't much more than a large mirror, a couple of cubbies, and some toilets. A girl in a leopard-print robe and little else plays Candy Crush on her phone, but my eyes lock on Kennedy behind her. Half-Kennedy, half-Liberty—she's bent over the counter, dabbing green makeup over her face. She's only got half of it done, but Leopard-girl casts me a glance and then says dully, "Liberty, package for you."

Kennedy jerks upright, looks at me, and her mouth falls open. And I want to kiss that mouth. She's wearing nothing but jean shorts and a bra, and the curves of her body look like home to me. My heart is so goddamn full right now because it feels like ten years since I've seen her last.

"Jack!" she squeaks in delight and bounces over to me, throwing her arms dramatically around my shoulders. It hurts, but it's worth the pain, and I scoop her up and hold her warm little body against mine and press my lips to hers. I savor her—the warmth of her, the *life* in her—because a very large part of me was afraid that Anders or *someone* from the Wolfpack would've gotten to her before I did. But she's here, and she's alive, and she's mine, and I want to make her mine—I want to press her up against the mirror and part her thighs and her lips and feel her heartbeat flutter around my cock.

But there's no time. I take her by the hips, push her a step back, and tell her, "Get dressed. We have to go."

"Your face." Her hands cup my face, and in the dim light of the backstage, her eyes go wide. "Holy shit. Jack. What happened?"

I can see my reflection in the mirror from here, and... crap. I do look bad. My left eye is busted, the skin black, the veins cracked, and there's dried blood from the gash in my forehead where Madsen dropped a fucking canoe on me.

"It's nothing," I try to tell her, but she's on her feet.

I glance at Leopard-print. "Can you give us a minute?"

She rolls her eyes, but she does, sashaying through the beads. I take Kennedy by the hands and sit her down on one of the stools. "Kennedy. Listen—"

"Sit," she says, pointing to the stool.

"Ken—"

"*Jack.* Take a knee," she says and points again. I do, because I'm a killer, former SEAL, badass alpha man who takes no shit, but I am weak for her.

I flop down onto the stool. The legs are uneven, and my

equilibrium tilts every time I move. Kennedy flutters around to the cubbies, and she has to stand on her tiptoes to drag the first aid kit off the top. She drops it open on the makeup counter, takes out a bottle of hydrogen peroxide, and wets a cotton swab.

"So," she says as she dabs the cotton ball against my forehead. It burns like a bitch, but I don't flinch. "That cat you had to unstick from a tree. A big cat?"

"A lion."

"What did you do with it?"

"I tamed it and brought it home." She squints at that. So I clarify: "He's sitting at the bar, actually."

She swallows at that, the wheels in her head turning. "What does that mean?"

"It means...we're in trouble."

"In trouble with *who*?"

"Wolfpack, for starters."

"Shit." She hisses in her frustration, and I don't think she's aware of it, but she starts absently scrubbing the blood off my face harder. "After everything you did for them... everything you've *done*..."

"It doesn't matter. I went against my orders."

"What about Anders? Maybe if you go to him and explain—"

"We can't trust Anders. We can't trust anyone."

"But if you tried talking to him..."

"Look." I change lanes. "There's a place. A safe house."

"Where?"

"Far enough."

"Well, how long will we be there?"

"Until I figure this out. A month, maybe two." I'm making up numbers, but I want to give her the impression that I have a plan.

"A *month*?" Kennedy gets off my lap and paces, raking her fingers through her hair. "Jack, I'm in my last year of law school. I can't just pick up and go—"

"We don't have any other options," I try to explain, my patience running thin. "They're already on our tail. They were staked out at our house."

"Our *house*? What does that mean? We can't go back?"

"Not yet."

"Jack, I have, like, $10,000 worth of textbooks back there—"

"I'll buy you new ones."

"And clothes—"

"*Kennedy*." I growl her name and grab her arm to still her. I don't mean my tone to be so sharp, but she's brought sensation back to my wounds, and I can't stop thinking about that car parked in our driveway, and *we don't have time for this.*

There's a breath of silence between us. She looks so wilted I have to say something. "I'm sorry I brought you into this." I forfeit. "This is my burden, my demons. You didn't ask to be involved in any of it—"

"Stop," she says suddenly. Her hazel eyes are soft. Her hands rest on my shoulders. "I'm in this. With you. End of story." She kisses me hard, and my heart tightens in my chest. Because there is no part of me that deserves Kennedy and her ride-or-die loyalty—especially when that loyalty could very literally get her killed. She breaks the kiss without pulling away, and she says with a definitive tone, "Okay."

"Okay?"

"Okay. Let's do this."

God. I want to kiss her lips until they bruise. I want to press my heart to hers and feel them beat in tandem. I want to push her against the counter and get on my knees and worship her with my tongue. My heart and cock swell two sizes larger, and *the things I would do* to this perfect woman if only I had the time.

But time isn't on our side. I settle for a hard kiss, and it sets off a small whimper from her. "Pack your things," I tell her.

She nods, pushes her hair behind her ear, and shoves everything into her fur purse. Her makeup, some clothes, her keys, her wallet. She yanks on a shirt and pair of jeans and then says to me, "Let's go. Before my boss catches us playing hooky."

The beads jangle as we exit. I catch Madsen at one of the circular tables, Roxy Rocket in his lap, hearts in her eyes. "Hey, boss," Madsen greets me, and his eyes take in Kennedy. "Is this her? Now I can see why you zipped halfway up the country like a bat out of hell."

I don't have time to beat his face in, so I say, "We're going."

"Aw. But things were just starting to get fun—"

"*Now.*"

Madsen lifts Roxy off his lap, then takes her by the hand and presses a kiss to the back of her fingers. "In another lifetime, ma chère," he says, and she makes a noise that only cartoon birds in Disney movies are supposed to make.

"Gabe," he says and shoves his hand out toward Kennedy.

"Kennedy," she says shyly.

"Door," I say, and we move toward it.

We burst through the door and are greeted by a blast of white, blinding light.

And Anders. We're greeted by Anders.

The door nearly hits him in the face. It's that close. The

other man blinks at me, frowning from behind his grizzled mustache. He adjusts to the sight of me. I adjust to the sight of him.

This is not a happy accident. This is an ambush.

"Jack," he says. His eyes flicker to me. To Madsen.

"Anders," I reply.

For a second, no one moves. His hand is close to the gun at his belt.

So is mine.

If he so much as twitches, he's a grease stain.

But then Anders smiles. "Let's not make this awkward."

"Why not?" Madsen pipes up. "Awkward is my specialty."

I say, "You don't have to do this."

"I don't want you," Anders counters. "I just want Madsen."

"Since when did we start eating our own?" I ask.

Anders's mouth twists into a jack-o'-lantern sneer. "Hand him over," Anders deflects, "and I'll tell you everything."

"Right. After you shoot me in the back."

"*Jack.*" When he says my name, it's a sharp chastisement. "How long've we known each other? You've been nothing but good for the Wolfpack. A good man. A good soldier. Let's call this...a minor lapse in judgment."

"I resent that," Madsen complains. "I'm at least a *major* lapse in judgment."

"Shut up," Anders and I both snarl, and he pipes down.

I've got my eye on his trigger finger. And I push, "Just tell me why."

"It's a need-to-know basis," Anders explains.

"I need to know."

"No. You don't. You need to leave this while you still can.

While you can still take Kennedy back home, safe and sound, and get back to life as you know it."

"Jack," Kennedy whispers. Her fingers clutch my bicep.

All at once, I wonder, *What the hell am I doing?* Like waking up from a bad dream, I see my friend—the man who I bled with and fought with—standing in front of me. Kennedy beside me. And this stranger—this pain in the ass, Mr. No One—I've somehow let him under my skin. I let him uproot my life and Kennedy's life. And for what?

For a gut feeling that something is very, very wrong here.

But I've sold my soul before. And this is no different. Only this time, I've got the opportunity to get off with a measly slap on the wrist.

"What's it going to be?" Anders asks, and I make up my mind.

I touch the small of Madsen's back. I click the snap. As his fanny pack falls off his hips, I catch it and lift it from him.

"Hey!" Madsen says, but I've already got it in my hand, and I lift it for Anders to see.

"This is what you want, isn't it?" I say.

Anders's eyes flash, cementing my theory.

I toss the pack to him. He catches it in a single hand.

"It's yours," I say. "Take it and call it even."

Out of the edge of my vision, I see Madsen's jaw go tight. "You dumb motherfucker," he mutters under his breath, all good humor gone.

Whatever.

Fuck him. Fuck all of this.

This isn't my battle.

Anders unzips the pack. When he sees what's inside, the edge of his mouth twitches upward. His eyes meet mine. "Do you know what this is?"

I lie. "I know all about it."

Anders lets out a sigh. "That's a shame." He shakes his head. "I was really hoping to keep you alive."

Before I can react—

Everything goes to shit.

"Run!" Kennedy screams as she simultaneously whips out her pepper spray and nails Anders in the face with it.

He howls and reaches to cover his face. We shove passed him. I toss Madsen the keys to the car—he catches them midair—and the three of us tumble in, Madsen in front, me and Kennedy in the back seat.

"Duck!" I shout. I grab her head and force her to down.

"Chicken!" Kennedy says.

"Caw-caw!" a startled Clucky squawks and flaps at the floorboards.

A bullet shatters the back window. The tires squeal as Madsen launches the car forward, and we speed out of the parking lot. A couple more shots go off, but Anders's vision is blurred, and his aim is off—way off.

The Cruiser eats asphalt, and once we're a safe distance away, I take Kennedy's face in my hands. "Are you okay?" I ask.

"I'm great!" Madsen chirps from the front seat. "Fine and dandy! Thanks for asking!"

Kennedy's eyes are huge, but she nods in the affirmative. "I'm...okay. I think. God, that was so close. I can't believe that...did Anders really think you were going to just hand him over like that? Like some...human slavery trade? He was always so nice...I had no idea there was so much...ugliness inside of him."

I'm stumped as to a response to that, so I just exhale a "huh."

She lets out a hefty groan and drops her head against my

chest. I pull her into my arms and kiss her earth-brown hair, feel her rapidly beating heart and the warmth of her skin. She is rabbit soft and precious.

Everything is upside down, and nothing makes sense.

But Kennedy is safe, and that's all that matters now.

MY SAFE HOUSE doesn't exist on the map.

It's a cabin in the north of Georgia that I bought straight off my second tour of duty. It's the only thing I've never wanted a return on investment, but here it is. Returning it.

I haven't been back here in years and never had anyone upkeep the place, so I'm honestly thrilled that, when we arrive, it doesn't look like the place has been overrun by a small family of bears.

I park outside. The car dies quietly outside the cabin, and as soon as the engine goes mute, I hear crickets. The sky is black. The stars are out. The windows are chilled like a frosted mug, and the blown-out window in the back does nothing to keep it warm. I need another jacket, but I didn't think to pack one to go to fucking Florida.

In forty-eight hours, I've essentially done a coastal road trip. My head hurts from all the caffeine and energy drinks. My ass has become one with the car seat. I need sleep.

My angel is curled up in the passenger seat, cheek against the window, her robe draped over her for warmth, softly breathing. Clucky is curled up in Kennedy's lap, legs tucked under her belly, fast asleep. Madsen was asleep in the back, but his eyes open the second the engine cuts. "This is a nice slice of bum-hick you've got here, Jack," he murmurs.

I put my hand on Kennedy's shoulder and squeeze. "Hey. We're here."

Her eyes flutter open. She makes a sleepy noise and tucks tighter into herself. "Cold," she mumbles.

I want to take all my clothes off and heat her up with my body. Instead, I say, "I'll get your stuff."

I get out, and the air bites. I pop the trunk, grab her drawstring bag from inside, and sling it over my shoulder. They get out as well and follow me to the house. There's a lockbox around the handle, and I punch in my code, grab the keys, and open up.

It smells like mold and mothballs—the stink of a sealed, unopened house. I flip on the light, and it blinks on, illuminating the slatted timber walls, spiderwebbed beams and hanging bald bulbs, dusty couch, barren fireplace. The memories of this cabin hit me like a fog, and I shudder.

"What is this place?" Kennedy asks as she enters behind me.

"Just a place I've kept. Just in case I needed it."

"Where's the Laura Ingalls room?" Madsen quips.

"It's *adorable*," Kennedy trills. Leave it to her to see the diamond under all that rough.

"Does the plumbing work, or do you have an outhouse?" Madsen asks. I point him to the bathroom, and he follows.

I turn on the heat and crank it up. The system coughs once and spits out the smell of burnt dust. Kennedy hops from room to room like an excitable child. She bounds through the living room, opens the fridge (empty), examines the drawers (a stack of small plates, couple of glasses), and shakes the trash (bottles clink, and I wince—*fuck,* I thought I'd gotten rid of the evidence).

Then she puts her fingers on something bad—there are

three entry wounds in the blue wallpaper, bullets buried somewhere in the walls.

"Whose house was this?" Kennedy asks.

"Used to be owned by a nice old couple. They died, and it went up for cheap."

"Seems like they got into some trouble."

I steer her attention away from the kitchen, the empty bottles, the bullet-ridden walls, and put my hand on the staircase knob. "Bedroom's upstairs. Want to check it out?"

"No skeletons up there? Bodies dissolving in the bathroom?" Kennedy steps close to me and rubs her hands over my chest. "Jack and his creepy, creepy cabin in the woods."

"You want me to double-check?"

That gets a little, tired smile from her. She has a bizarre sense of humor. "Is there a shower upstairs?"

"Yep."

"Working?"

"Only one way to find out."

Then she sways on her heels. Her voice drops to a shadow. "How long are we going to stay here?"

"Until it's safe." It's the only answer I can give. I press a kiss to her cheek. "Shout if you run into any raccoons."

Her eyes widen. "Is that a thing?" And then she dashes upstairs before I can tell her what to do if she actually finds any raccoons. She'd probably take the rabies-infected things against her chest and name them.

A low cooing reminds me of the fourth body in the house. I genuinely don't have a clue what to do with this crazy chicken that's followed us up the coast. I take a pillow off the couch and toss it to the floor.

"Make yourself at home," I say.

Clucky looks at me, tilts her head, and then ambles over

to the pillow. She scratches at it and, satisfied, flutters her feathers once and settles down back to sleep.

Good bird.

The house is covered in wood, and the floorboards creek under me as I go into the kitchen. The glasses aren't terrible, just a little dusty, and I rinse one out under the faucet before filling it with water and taking a swallow. The water is cool and feels good on my throat. I fill it again as the toilet flushes, and Madsen exits the bathroom. I straighten up and say, "I'll show you your bedroom."

"How hospitable," Madsen comments.

I walk him to the downstairs bedroom—floral-print wallpaper, a bed, a closet, a bedside table. A lot of empty space for Madsen to hang his leather jacket.

Across the domestic, old-school wallpaper is a single word, spray-painted in red: KILLER.

Madsen sits on the edge of the bed, and the mattress springs creek. "Cozy," Madsen says, staring at the graffiti.

I set the glass of water on his bedside table. "Do you need anything?"

"No." He pauses and then adds candidly, "I know things got a little...well. Fucking insane. But...I know you came to kill me. And your life would be a hell of a lot easier if you'd just done that. So...thank you. For not finishing the job."

"Don't thank me yet," I tell him. Then I take my gun out from the back of my pants.

Madsen's blue eyes widen. He lets out a hefty sigh and lifts his palms. "Buddy...if you're going to kill me, just do it. I'm too tired for this."

With the gun trained on him, I swing Kennedy's bag over to my chest and dig around inside of it. I hunt until I find the one thing she shoved in here that I knew would come in handy later...my fingers brush against metal. I tug out a pair of handcuffs. They're real—something Kennedy was adamant about, no *quick-release* gag for her. I hold them up and tell him, "I'm not going to kill you. But I am going to handcuff you. Give me your wrist."

Madsen blinks but does as he's told. He gives me his left arm. I set the gun down, snap one end of the cuffs around his wrist, and close the other end around the wooden slats on his headboard. Could he break through them? Yeah. Maybe. But at least this way, I'd probably hear him banging around before that.

I explain, "I don't know you. I don't trust you. I don't know why Anders wanted you dead. So until I do…I want to keep you in my sight."

He lets out a sigh, and we're close enough right now that the heat of his breath kisses my neck. "One of these days," he muses, "you and I are going to laugh about all this."

I tighten the cuff around his wrist and then step back. "Not today." I pocket the keys to the handcuffs. "Get some sleep."

Madsen's sky-blue eyes glare at me, thick mess of hair scattered over his forehead. When I pick up my gun and close the door behind me, he's still sitting on the edge of the bed, pouting, chained there. He can be mad at me all he wants, but it takes the edge off my anxiety to know where he is.

The pipes groan and hiss in the ceiling. Kennedy has found the shower. I climb the stairs two at a time.

The main bedroom has a king-sized bed, complete with wooden owls carved into the headboard, and a matching dresser. Kennedy's clothes are on the floor, and the bathroom door is open, steam billowing out. I peel off my clothes, fold them in a pile on a chair by the dresser, and step into the bathroom.

Kennedy's silhouette bleeds through the off-white shower curtain. I pull it back and step inside with her. The water makes her chestnut hair black. She turns and blinks droplets off her long eyelashes. She places a wet hand against my bare chest and draws it down. I wince when she traces bruises I didn't know where there—the one on my side is particularly tender.

"Hey, sir," she croons.

I cup her soft cheek in my hand, pull her against my body, and press her lips to mine. She opens up to me—her mouth, her legs—and she sighs into my mouth as she reaches between us to take my cock inside of her.

No condoms—that's her idea. I don't have a problem wearing them, wore them with all my other girlfriends. I have my scars (the jagged ridge down my throat to my clavicle, the dent in my left calve), and Kennedy has hers (the inch-long protrusion on her bicep where her birth control implant lives under her skin). She told me that she got it because it turned her on to feel my come drip out of her.

Come. It's not a pretty word. *Labia, petals,* even *pussy*—these are pretty words. These are the words that describe Kennedy because she is lovely and beautiful and feminine in all the right places.

Meanwhile, I have a hard *cock* and balls full of *spunk*—and none of those words are pretty because nothing about me is pretty. I am a killer, and my angles are sharp, and it's a miracle I don't cut her with my hips when I machine-gun pound her.

Yet she takes me. Again and again and again. My innocent, sweet angel is also a kinky sex kitten, and sometimes I just look at her, slick with my own sweat and my come and her *honey dew*, and I think—*fuck*, how did I get so lucky?

I've never won the lottery—not even a couple of bucks. I

suck at poker. I've never gotten out "by the grace of God" in any of my missions here or overseas.

But I hit the jackpot with her.

I back her against the tiled walls, and she hooks her arms around my shoulders, her thigh around my hip. I lick her bare skin, taste the water there. My dog tags hang between us. A gasp falls from her lips when I push deep inside of her. The heat of her shower-warmed skin, the sweetness of her kisses, her nails in my back—it's all proof that we're alive, and I savor it.

She's slippery with water and her own arousal, and we slide together in tandem, gripping and licking and clinging because as much as I try, I can't get *close enough* to this woman. She pants in my ear, and I can't even feel the pain in my side where her legs latch on because her pussy is too sweet and this feels too good and I can't stop, I don't stop, not even when she closes around me like a Venus trap. She grinds her clit against my pelvis, her toes curl against my leg, and she cries out, her head falling back, water falling down her shoulders, between her breasts. I release—pleasure bursting from me and into her—and we cling to each other for a long while, our hearts beating rapidly.

Kennedy starts to cry then, her tears mixing with the water and spooling down the drain. I hold her tightly, murmur that everything will be okay, and our fingers turn to prunes as the water goes cold.

6

KENNEDY

I open my eyes to a hundred little blue birds staring at me.

So I'm *totally* a sucker for the quaint-cottage-in-the-woods vibe, but whoever decorated this house (and I *know* it wasn't Jack because he doesn't have an interior-decorating bone in his body) had a very *Twin Peaks* aesthetic. The walls and ceilings in the main bedroom are blue and covered with images of the same two blue birds sitting together on a twig. It's super cute, but it's also a lot of beady eyes to wake up to.

This is all so surreal. Insane. Just yesterday, I was in law school, happy in my cozy Georgia house. My biggest problem was figuring out a nail length that looked sexy on Lady Liberty but still allowed me to rapidly type out bar study notes.

Today, I'm on the run from a secret agency with two super soldier men.

You know. *No big.*

But Jack is here. In bed. How often does that happen? Not often enough. I'm *never* awake before him, but he's been through hell and back again. He's dead to the world, asleep on his tummy, clutching one of the pillows and snoring into it. I play with the buzzed hair at the nape of his neck, trace my fingers down those broad, muscled shoulders, and he still doesn't budge.

My king needs his beauty sleep. Carefully, I unwind from the blankets tangled around my legs and slip out of bed.

I need to feel human, so I fish my makeup kit from my bag and start applying my face. *When you don't feel your best,* my mother used to say, *you can still look your best.* Granted, when I went to her as a teenager and told her I was depressed, I probably needed a therapist, not a new eyeshadow palette, but silver linings: I now find the beauty in the ugly feelings. I erase the tired bags under my eyes, paint my lips, and pin my wild hair back into a fishtail braid. I pull on jeans and a loose T-shirt, and I'm starting to feel like maybe things aren't *so* bad here.

A girl can conquer the world with a good cat-eye.

I leave Jack snoring into his pillow, grab his car keys, and go downstairs. Now that I'm well rested—bright-eyed and bushy-tailed—this place looks even dingier than when we got in. The wallpaper is yellowing, and it's definitely got the feeling of a place someone died in, their body dissolved in the upstairs bathroom or buried in the woods outside.

Should I be worried that Jack has a secret house that I knew nothing about?

In the six months that we've been together, Jack and I have gone from zero to sixty. I moved him into my house. We tell each other that we love each other. He knows me, down to my every atom. It's one of those impossible whirlwind romances that only happen once every century.

But there is one nagging foundation of our relationship…

Jack gets to know everything about me, but I only get bits and pieces of him.

His secrets have secrets, and I get the feeling I'm only beginning to scratch the surface.

There's nothing in the fridge (a blessing, honestly), and the cabinets are empty. The chicken (who, I've discovered, Jack has named "Clucky") climbs off her pillow bed on the floor and circles my legs like a dog. I open the door to let her out, and she chatters happily as she pecks at the grass.

I go back inside and knock on Gabe's door. "Gabe? Are you awake?"

"Come in," his voice calls out dully from the other side.

I open the door, and what I see makes my stomach twist. "Oh, shit. Did Jack do this to you?"

Gabe is slumped in bed, an arm handcuffed high up to the bedpost. He lifts it in a half wave. "Wouldn't be the first time I slept in handcuffs."

I sigh. "Hold on."

Fucking Jack.

I leave him for a moment, go back upstairs, and start rummaging around in the bedroom. Jack is like a squirrel. The more paranoid he is, the more he squirrels. I noticed it after he unofficially moved in with me. It was something that just sort of *happened* with us—he stayed the night once, and then he never left. Jack didn't have a lot to move in with, but what he did have, he burrowed around the house. A gun behind the toilet seat (pretty sure he still thinks I don't know about that one). A briefcase stuffed with clothes hidden at the back of my closet. A knife taped underneath my study desk. He *squirrels*—hides his things where no one can see them.

He might be a squirrel, but I'm a bloodhound. And when I go looking, eventually, I find what I'm looking for.

Bingo. I find a set of keys on the bedside table, underneath the base of the lamp. The minute my fingers touch it, however, Jack's hand grabs my wrist viper-fast.

"Ow!" I say—though it doesn't hurt, it just startles me. "You and your...freaky reflexes!"

He doesn't let go of me; he just shifts onto his elbow. The blanket slips off his shoulder and bare chest. "What're you doing?"

"Freeing our prisoner."

"No. You're not."

"*Yes*, I am." I yank my arm back, and finally, Jack releases me. "We're not keeping a man locked up in the bedroom. That's Jeffrey Dahmer shit."

"I haven't decided if I trust him yet."

"You haven't *decided*?" My mouth drops open. "We left our home, my law school, I pepper sprayed Anders, and you haven't *decided*?"

He sits up so he's on the edge of the bed. "It's not that simple."

I throw the keys at his chest, and they fall into his lap. "Put on pants. We're going downstairs and making a decision."

Jack narrows his eyes at me—like maybe he wants to argue or snap at me—but he can't hold my gaze long without his shoulders dropping back. He exhales a sigh, grabs the keys, and gets up. "Fine."

"Fine?"

"*Fine.*"

7

GABE

It was supposed to be my last job.

My mission—should I choose to accept it—was, more or less, like a handful of other missions I'd taken before. Go into some sandy, rural town. Find the bad guys. Neutralize the threat before they turned into *worse* guys.

So I packed my little manila envelope and some bug spray and hopped on the first plane to Turkey, tickets courtesy of the Wolfpack.

My instructions were to rendezvous on friendly territory, a Turkish hotel called Hotel Cyprus. I met the rest of my team, where we downloaded in the lobby in plainclothes and downed a pot of maybe the best tea I've ever had in my life.

My party was a small but mighty team of experts. Five guys, including:

Holt, a natural ginger and a wannabe cowboy.

Bridgeman, a tough, seasoned vet who could probably crush bullets between his teeth.

An archaeologist and translator, Omar Onasis, whose

job it was to identify the stolen goods, help us talk to the locals, and point us to the nearest bathroom.

The last one on the team—someone you might be familiar with—the infamous Troy Anders. Our team leader. Are the wheels clicking into place yet? No? Okay, we'll get there.

The download went something like this: we were to infiltrate a rural town on the border of Turkey and Iraq. Our job was a rescue mission. A terrorist organization had looted a handful of museums in the chaos, and they were now in possession of billions of dollars of stolen artifacts.

The cell had been located in the mountains. It was our job to neutralize the hostiles, reclaim the stolen artifacts, and return them to the rightful hands of the locals.

Since we were on friendly territory, the American government couldn't get involved, and it was up to the Wolfpack to go in and handle it quietly.

You know—one of those "this never happened" types of deals.

We drank until dawn, swapped war stories, and got a couple of hours of beauty sleep before rolling out.

It was something, watching the elaborate temples and bustling city dissolve into lush mountaintops and miles and miles of empty roads. We bounced over roads that were mostly rock and dirt and pulled into a village of tin-roofed houses and sullen, distrustful faces.

The locals wouldn't give us anything—not even to Omar, who had one of those kind faces that you couldn't help but spill your soul to.

He dressed like a professor, and he carried around a light brown satchel everywhere he went. I nudged the bag.

"Indiana Jones?" I asked.

He smiled at the reference. "I think I'm the guy Indiana Jones shoots at," he replied.

I couldn't argue with that.

Holt was the one to find the kid. He stuck out from the rest of the townspeople. He had short-cut hair, a runner's build, and crisp, expensive clothes.

When Holt pushed him inside his own home and shoved him to his knees, he didn't look like a dangerous criminal.

He looked scared. Young. Maybe eighteen.

The price of war. It'll really kick you in the nuts, sometimes.

Anders asked him where the artifacts were. Omar translated. Holt and Bridgeman took turns punching him in the face.

I stood guard in the doorway. Days like these were why I'd already decided on early retirement.

"I can do this all day," Anders said. He crouched to a squat so he could meet the other man, eye-to-eye. "But you can only take so many punches before even your own mother can't recognize you anymore. What'll it be?"

That's when the kid made a mistake.

His eyes fell to the prayer rug in the corner of the room.

Holt kicked it back. "Sir," he said. "There's something here."

There was a trapdoor cut into the floor, hidden under the rug.

Anders lit up. "Madsen, Onasis, move. Holt, if this fucker so much as twitches, blow his head off."

I opened the trap door and dropped down first, in case Charlie was waiting for us on the floor. But there was no one there. The air was thick and musty, and I flicked on my pocket flashlight.

"All clear!" I called up, and Omar lowered himself down the stairs, dropping beside me.

My little beam of light fell on stacked wooden boxes. We opened up one box, then another. They were filled with thick straw and crumpled newspapers for padding. Inside were old, rusted pots. Dull yellow ornaments. Thick, jeweled bracelets that needed a good shine.

My dumbass said, "All the trouble for a bunch of old shit? Vases and jewelry? You'd think they'd at least have a grenade launcher in here."

Omar lifted a single item out of the box. It was a thick gold necklace textured to look like rope with a knot in the center.

"This," Omar said, his voice quiet and reverent, "is more precious than any weapon."

"Lieutenant!" Holt's voice barked from above. "We've got trouble!"

I quickly climbed the stairs just in time to see the jeeps roll up dust as they parked outside our little hut.

The infantry had arrived.

All soldiers. All fully armed and fully prepared to defend their territory.

We were sorely outnumbered. But these were Wolfpack men, and we don't go down without giving them hell first. Bullets whizzed around like hornets. I could hardly see through the dust that the shooting whipped up around us, but what I could see, I aimed for and fired.

The whole firefight must've lasted five, maybe ten minutes.

And then, just like that, there was silence.

We counted our men. Holt had shrapnel stuck in the thigh, but otherwise, we were in one piece. All five standing.

"Let's roll out," Anders said, so we did.

It was dark when we made it back to home base.

After the excitement of the day, no one was ready to sleep. Holt had jimmy-rigged a tourniquet to his leg to stop the bleeding, and now he was ready to party.

Wolfpack guys. They're a different breed.

I went back to my room to shower off the sweat and sand. I pulled on a fresh shirt and, feeling like a million bucks now, went downstairs.

The team hopped in a jeep and rolled out to a local watering hole. It was this dimly lit place that slung cheap drinks and had a live string band. Anders was buying, so Holt immediately ordered a round of shots. Bridgeman broke out with some truly original dance moves that made everyone laugh. We were adrenaline-high and rolling around in our success like pigs in mud.

Everyone but Anders.

He Irish-goodbyed us. I only noticed because I'd exited the stifling heat of the bar to suck down a cigarette in the crisp night air outside.

He had a heavy look on his face when he left. One of those real tired, bulldog expressions.

"Tapping out already?" I asked with a tsk.

The moonlight made his eyes sag deep in his skull. "Just tired."

"Penny for your thoughts, boss?"

He stood in silence for a long moment, looking out to the cars parked in front of us.

"He was just a kid," he said. I knew he was talking about the boy we interrogated. I kept my mouth shut, and he continued. "The things we see...sometimes, I wonder why the hell we even try."

"Have another shot. It'll cheer you up."

He shook his head. "I'm done. I'm walking back. Make sure the jeep gets back in one piece."

"Copy that, sir."

I watched him walk down the cobbled street back to the hotel.

This life—it'll get to you. That's for sure.

We've all got our coping mechanisms. Holt drank until he couldn't remember his name. Bridgeman told old battle stories with a hero's bravado.

Me? I cope best with company.

Omar sat in one of the plush, black-leathered lounge chairs. He wore glasses with thin, dark rims that brought out the brown in his eyes. He wasn't drinking. His trusty satchel sat like a dog at his heels.

I sat down beside him. My leg bumped his, and he left it.

"Where can a guy get a proper tour of this city?" I asked.

His mouth creased into a frown. "In the hotel, I'm certain they can direct you—"

"No, not a tourist tour. I want to go where you go. I want to see the city through your eyes."

His lips turned upward, just slightly. He removed his glasses, tucking them neatly in the V of his shirt.

In case I haven't mentioned it yet, Omar was really fucking cute.

"Alright," he said. "Follow me."

"This is my temple," Omar said, "where I worship."

And:

"This is my university, where I teach."

And:

"This is my bed."

Omar rolled his own cigarettes. I watched the moonlight spill in from his window and silhouette his naked body as he worked, lithe fingers stuffing—but not overly stuffing—and rolling it up with such precision I could barely see the seam.

He lit it in his mouth first before putting it to my lips. I inhaled, tasting only him.

His bedroom was sparse: comprised of a small bed, a single dresser, and a prayer rug. No art on the walls. His rectangular window offered a view of the mud-brick house across the street and the darkened, star-dotted sky above it.

We completed the mission. We'd saved the day. We'd even rescued the bounty of priceless artifacts.

So why did something feel off?

I couldn't shake it. Even Omar's delicious cigarettes and the agarwood scent of his room couldn't distract me.

His satchel lay splayed open on a bench at the foot of his bed. It looked like a body at the morgue, its innards on full display. The necklace lay folded out on a velvet cloth. He'd recovered it in order to authenticate the find.

It looked different in his home. Stuffed in the boxes, it'd seemed muted. Devoid of color.

Here, it looked as though it was starting to wake up. The gold caught the moonlight's shine, shimmering like an open pond.

I couldn't take my eyes off it. The vision of it pounded in my temple like a low-grade migraine.

Neither could Omar, apparently. As I smoked and sank into his mattress, he stared at it thoughtfully. I watched his naked body as he rose to his desk, picked up a small magnification bead, and sat on the edge of the bed to study the necklace.

"What's something like this worth?" I asked.

"Eighty million US dollars," he said flatly, as though the price bored him.

That shocked me. "That much for a necklace?"

He smiled. There was a sad note in it. "Such an American."

"How's that?"

"So blinded by the dollar signs you don't see what's in front of you."

"Oh, I see what's in front of me."

I hooked my arm around his middle and licked my tongue up his spine. He shuddered deliciously against me.

"With the war...so much of our history has been lost. The war took who we are from us. This...it's reclaiming our identity. It's priceless."

"Talk history to me, baby," I crooned against the crook of his neck. We fell back in bed.

If I'd known what came next, maybe I would've paid more attention to the history lesson and less attention to the way he purred like a feral cat between the sheets.

BEING the great one-night stand I am, I went out to get us coffee and breakfast in the morning.

I clocked a café downstairs, across the street from his apartment. I thought I'd be stumbling over the language like an idiot, but mercifully, the barista knew English. I managed to score a scone and two cups of coffee.

As I waited, my eyes caught on a newspaper someone had left on their uncleaned table. On the front page, I saw something that made my stomach turn.

I shoved the paper at the (very patient) barista and asked

him to translate. It was a picture of the bar we'd been at last night. The image showed a car burnt to a crisp. An explosive had been wired to the engine. The car had blown as soon as they'd turned the ignition. Two casualties.

Both wearing dog tags.

My blood went cold.

I tipped him well, abandoned breakfast, and bolted back to Omar's place.

When I got there, the door was already open. The wood split around the handle, like someone had kicked it in.

I was too late.

Painfully aware that I was unarmed, I pressed my fingertips to the door and quietly pushed it open.

My heart felt like it was pounding through wet cement as I entered the apartment. At first, everything looked just as I'd left it.

Then I found him.

Omar's body lay splayed out on his bed. The dark, bruise-colored blanket covered his naked body. His eyes were wide open, though, staring emptily at a spot on the wall.

The shot was clean. A single red dot right between his eyes.

I touched his throat. He was still warm. But that pulse that had jumped so rapidly against my fingertips only hours ago was silent now.

My blood roared so loudly in my ears I didn't hear the sound of running water until it stopped.

The bathroom door opened.

Anders exited, towel in his hand.

Literally washing blood from his fingers.

He spotted me, and his feet stopped short. I watched as his eyes widened for a split second, and then he made his fatal error. His gaze immediately went to the necklace, which told me everything I needed to know:

1) Our mission was to rescue the necklace.

2) But Anders never had any intention of returning it to the people.

3) And now he'd neutralized everyone who could connect him to the necklace.

4) Everyone except me.

We both sat in that knowledge for a long, hard second before he came out with, "Madsen."

"Anders."

"You didn't stay with the crew."

"No..." I lifted my hands and dropped them in a shrug. "I'm a slut."

Anders sighed. "Damn."

I agreed. "Damn."

His gun sat on the top of Omar's dresser, next to the necklace. Anders dove for the gun, but I slammed my body against his first. We sailed into the kitchen, tumbling over chairs. The kitchen table broke our fall, and then we broke the table.

Anders had about fifty pounds on me, and all of that was muscle, so when he hooked me into a chokehold, I knew I was in trouble. I elbowed him, but it was like throwing my weight into a wall. I tried to get traction, but my boots just squeaked against the floor.

He had the upper hand.

But I had bottomless rage and a broken chair leg.

I hit him with the leg until he released me. When he raised his arm, I swung it like a bat and heard his bones crack.

He shouted, which was satisfying.

Before I could break it against his skull, he threw his head into my stomach and threw his weight forward.

He forced me backward.

And sent me flying right out the bedroom window.

I woke up sixty miles away, with a camel chewing on my hair.

The sun blared from above. Two farmers with leathered skin and deeply confused frowns took turns poking me and yelling at me. I couldn't understand the words, but I could understand the sentiment: *get the fuck out of the truck.*

In my fall out the window, I'd somehow landed in the bed of a truck carrying a huge supply of watermelons and accidentally hitched a ride out of the city.

In my hand, I was still clutching the golden necklace I'd managed to snatch off the stand before Anders drop-kicked me out the window.

I stumbled out of the truck and shook wet melon seeds out of my hair before they could call the local police.

By the time I made it back to the city, Anders had already vanished. I knew that as long as I was alive and as long as I had the necklace, I was a liability, and Anders wouldn't stop hunting me. So I left an anonymous tip so someone would find Omar's body. Then I booked a flight back to the States and went underground. I found someone I could trust in Florida. I hunkered down and left a trail of bread crumbs for the wolves so I could catch them before they caught me.

Then I ended up with you two, handcuffed to a bed with the word *killer* on the walls.

And, well, that's the morning news, Jack.

8

JACK

Silence permeates the walls.

"I know it's not an easy thing to hear," Madsen says, "so I'll put a point on it. Your man Anders went rogue. This mission was not a Wolfpack mission. This was his own personal vendetta. The Wolfpack sensed this and sent their man after Anders's man, aka you. Do you see what I'm saying? The man who tried to kill us at the boathouse was—"

"Wolfpack," I fill in.

"Exactly. Now, you have Anders after you for double-crossing him, and you have the Wolfpack after you because they think *you're* with Anders. The only way for you or I to get out of this alive is Aaron Schilling."

"Who?"

"The man you spooked that night at the Hook. He's a former Wolfpack member, now works in politics. He knows the full story. He'll give us sanctuary in return for the necklace, which he plans to deliver back to its home country. Oh —except some idiot handed over the necklace to Anders. So. Thanks for that."

I close my eyes. The negotiation at the Hook. The fanny pack. It's all coming together.

Madsen wasn't the "Code Black."

Anders was.

"Kennedy," I say. "Let's talk."

She nods, and we stand.

"I'll just wait here!" Madsen calls out from his spot, swaying his cuffed hands back and forth. "Unless you want me to get up, maybe make us some snacks? I'm great at a charcuterie board—"

Kennedy and I exit the room and shut the door on him.

"What do you think?" Kennedy asks.

I tuck my arms across my chest. "It's a story."

"I believe him," Kennedy says. I don't like that look in her eyes. It's electric, her honeyed irises practically neon with excitement. It's the same look she gets right before a big test or when she brings home a new XL sex toy.

"You can't be serious." I don't mean my voice to come out as a growl, but there it is. "An ancient necklace. Anders killing his own. It sounds like a comic book."

She bites her lip and—fuck, I hate it when she pinches her plump little lip between her teeth because it's so goddamn distracting. "I don't know," she says thoughtfully, then adds, "Anything's possible. Whatever it is, I believe he found something overseas, and some serious people are after him because of it."

"You mean the Wolfpack."

"For starters. I mean, who *knows* how high up this goes. This could be Area 51, Pentagon shit."

"Cool it, Scully."

She squints at me. "If you don't trust him, why'd you rescue him?"

The wolf tattoo. Long eyelashes. A gut feeling.

I say nothing. Kennedy rolls her eyes. She puts both of her hands on my shoulders, looks me directly in the eyes, and says, "Jack. Take a knee."

This is what we do. This is our code.

"Take a knee" is our way of entering a safe-space bubble. We both lower to our knee and look each other directly in the eyes. Now, we can say anything. Safely. Free from repercussions. "Take a knee" is where we go when we need to look each other directly in the eyes and *talk*.

Take a knee is sacred, so I follow her lead.

"I trust him," she says.

"I don't," I say honestly. "Not yet."

She nods slowly. She doesn't argue. Not in our safe space. "We can't keep a man chained to the bed."

"I agree."

"So we let him go."

"And...what? See what happens? This isn't some heckler at the Pink Pony. He's ex-military. Wolfpack. He's dangerous."

"Maybe. But you're more dangerous. And if he tries to run, you can break his neck and tell me I told you so." Her words are so violent, but her tone is calm. Those soft brown eyes are easy to get lost in. It's hard to maintain eye contact with Kennedy. All I want to do is kiss her.

"Okay," I agree.

She opens her palm, and I get to my feet first so I can help her up.

Madsen (still in the same spot) blinks up at her in surprise. She sits down on the side of the bed and leans over him as she unlocks the cuffs.

"So," she says, "here's the deal. The three of us are going to stay here for a while, probably, and lay low for a little while. So we're going to have to trust each other. We're going to help you out. In the meantime, you have to help *us* help you by not trying to run away. If you do run, Jack will hunt you to the ends of the Earth. Got it?"

Madsen's hands drop, and he rubs the red ringlets around his wrist. "Loud and clear."

"Great!" Kennedy smiles and claps her hands. "One big happy family."

~

I CAN'T SIT STILL. Not in this place.

So I put my hands to work.

The Cruiser needs help. I find tape and a drop cloth in the basement. Next, I go out to where the car is parked outside. The back window is a mess of glass. I punch out the rest of the window.

I'm cleaning the tiny, diamond-sized bits of glass off the back seat and the interior of the car when I hear someone approach.

In the open door, I see Clucky circling Madsen's boots. She pecks at his shoelaces, seemingly unconvinced they're not worms.

"Need a hand?" Madsen asks.

"No."

I smell the smoke of his cigarette. He's lingering.

"You want to tell me the truth about this place?" he asks.

"What do you mean?"

"We're stuck together. We're going to have to start trusting each other. Eventually."

I exhale. I use the cloth wrapped around my fist to brush more glass into the dirt. "There's nothing to tell. I finished two tours. Came home. Bought a house."

"In the middle of the woods. Where no one could find you. And wrote the word *killer* on the walls."

I relent. "I was in a bad place. I wanted to get drunk and get away from people and forget every shitty thing I'd ever done."

"What pulled you out of it?"

I get out of the car. Here, standing up to Madsen, I discover he's about an inch taller than me. Which is annoying. I hold his eyes. "Anders," I tell him bluntly. "He saved my life. He gave me a job. A purpose. And now we're at each other's throats, all because of you."

Madsen's mouth twists in a grimace. Could that be remorse on his smug, annoying face? "Trust me, I don't like this any more than you do."

Trust me. Trust me, trust me.

I'm so fucking tired of those words.

I pick up the roll of tape and toss it at him. Madsen catches it.

"Make yourself useful and take a side."

9

KENNEDY

Look, I'm fine with minimalist living.

I went through a period with my upper-middle-class parents where my friends and I dumpster-dived for food every Friday. It's exactly what it sounds like—a bunch of white kids with cushy college funds sticking their hands in trash, pulling out entire loaves of perfectly good bread that have been tossed because they're a day past their expiration date. I brought my "prizes" home to my parents like a cat with a fattened field mouse in its mouth. My mom, graciously, accepted anything that was wrapped and inserted it in some fashion into dinner that night. Although, to be fair, I never actually saw her unpack the food *directly* to the table, so it's entirely possible she threw it back in the dump and swapped it out for a loaf of bread bought that day.

The point is—I can live *without* creature comforts. But I can't live without creature necessities. Food, clothing, and water are pretty nonnegotiable.

So we leave the house and go scavenging. I take Gabe with me. I leave Jack.

This is a peacekeeping mission, and Jack will, undoubtedly, bring the nukes if he tags along.

Besides. I want to get to know our "prisoner."

So far, all I know about him is: he's a former SEAL (as if there's such a thing as "former"—once a SEAL, always a SEAL, so Jack claims), he has a bunch of guys who want to kill him, and he gets under Jack's skin. He seems alright to me, though. So far, his only crime is that he rolls his window all the way down when we're driving so he can let his arm hang out, like he's a wild tree that's outgrown his container. The cloth that he and Jack taped to the rear window billows like a parachute as we drive. The wind laps at Gabe's dark hair, making it flutter around his ears.

There's a mini-mall about a twenty-minute drive from the property. It's shaped like a horseshoe and comes complete with—among other things—a liquor store, a dollar store, and a Chinese fast-food joint.

You know, the essentials.

Jack has provided us with an allowance. Cash money. We raid the liquor store, stockpile groceries, and then reward ourselves with a tour of their department store.

The clothes are slim pickings, but I like the challenge. Finding the diamonds in the rough is my expertise.

Gabe and I chat as we work. I find him easy to talk to, and he likes talking. As the two of us pick through a table of mismatched button-ups, the conversation slips to Jack.

"Is he always this much of a hard-ass?" Gabe asks.

I have to think about that for a second. "No? I mean— he's mostly just quiet. Keeps to himself. Not always this..."

"Asshole-ish?"

"Grumpy."

"Right."

He holds a black button-up to his chest, considers it, and

then refolds it and sets it back down. "Relationships are a bitch."

I arch my eyebrows. "Do you have someone waiting for you back at home?"

"Oh, God, no," he says, as though I asked him if he owned a rabid raccoon. "When you did what Jack and I do... it was too complicated. I don't like lying to people."

"Jack told me what he did. On our third date. I thought it was some sick joke. And then we started living together, and he'd go away for days at a time with nothing but a duffle bag and come back with an insane amount of money. I tried not to ask too many questions. In my mind...I guess there was part of me that just didn't want to believe it was real."

Suddenly, my face goes hot, and my throat goes tight.

Oh, God. Where is this flood of emotion coming from?

"Hey." Instantly, Gabe is beside me. His hand rests gently on my arm. "Are you okay?"

My eyes connect with his. They're so blue, so earnest, and...God. It feels *so good* to be seen. The small, tender touch is enough to make me unravel completely, right here in the department store.

But I don't. I button it up and take in a sharp, shaky inhale.

Get it together, Kennedy.

I look back at the shirts because if I stare into Gabe's honest eyes one more time, I'm definitely going to start crying. So instead, I shrug and flick my fingers through shirt tags.

"Yeah. My boyfriend's a government-sanctioned hit man, and I have to drop out of law school because a secret agency is after us. It's every little girl's dream, right?"

"He's a lucky man to have you."

I hold up the simple black shirt. "What do you think?"

"It'll be a little big on you."

"It's for Jack."

"Mm. No. Try this." He pulls out a floral-patterned, Hawaiian button-up, and I laugh.

"I don't think I've ever seen Jack in more than two colors at a time. He'll never go for it."

"When I met your Jack, believe it or not, he was wearing a shirt not unlike this. It was a good look on him." He frowns. "Of course, he tried to kill me soon after, but... nothing to fault a shirt for."

He refolds it into his arms and hands it over. I take it and circle my finger around one of the buttons.

"I guess there's a lot I don't know about him."

"Clothes can subconsciously dictate your attitude. So. Let's put our Jack in a sunny state of mind."

Our Jack. I don't know why, but I like that.

I can't help the smile that crosses my lips.

"I like the way you think," I tell him.

We walk out with three new wardrobes. On our way back to the parking garage, Gabe suddenly nudges into me with his shoulder.

"Let's pop in here for a tick," he says.

He scoots the both of us into a corner by the water fountain. Suddenly, I'm up against the wall, Gabe's body covering mine.

"Uh...what are you doing?"

His breath tickles my ear.

"Three o'clock. Two guys in dark blazers. You see them?"

I look over his shoulder. In the thin crowd of people, I find the two he's talking about.

"Yeah. What about them?"

"They're military."

"How can you tell?"

"The haircuts. The Submariner watches. The Ray-Bans. Check his neck ink."

My gaze scans over the two men. One of them has a tattoo of a wolf, right underneath his ear.

Wolfpack.

My heart hiccups in my chest. "Did they see us?"

"You're the eyes," he says. "You tell me."

Purpose sizzles through my blood.

I'm the eyes.

Here we are, cornered in a mini-mall, and Gabe is letting me take the lead. His tone is patient, and his clear, sea-blue eyes don't leave mine.

He trusts me implicitly to take care of us. I'm determined not to fuck this up.

I hook my arm around him and nestle my face into the crook of his neck. To anyone else, it will look like we're hugging. The scruff from his jaw is rough against my cheek. He's warm here, and I sink against him as my eyes scan for the men.

He's right: they do look like they're hunting. They stalk up and down the hall like a pair of bloodhounds. One of them begins to turn, and I realize he's heading *right for us.*

"Kiss me," I tell Gabe suddenly.

His eyebrows furrow. "Are you sure?"

"Yes."

He doesn't argue with me after that.

He just does it.

His lips press against mine. They're soft and warm. I inhale his scent. He smells like a bonfire. Like the earth.

I want to dig my hands into him.

The mall and the men fade away. I don't have control of my body. My limbs work of their own accord. I open my mouth, and Gabe invites himself in. His tongue sweeps against mine, sending a lick of pleasure through the core of me. My hands drop from his shoulders and touch his sides. The slim trim of his waist.

I tell myself I am *not* enjoying this. But my nipples go hard against his strong chest.

My fingers notice things my brain refuses. Like: his body is lean. Svelte. Comfortable. This is a body that makes love.

Jack and I have done nearly every position in the Kama Sutra. Doggy-style. Cowgirl. Kink. Bondage. We've had a threesome. We've eaten food off each other. We've dripped candlewax over each other. We've done it all. Except one thing.

We've never made love.

It's not a conscious thing. Not something we've talked about or avoided. I just don't think his body is *built* for it. The same way his body isn't built for Pringles.

His hand is always going to get stuck in the can.

His hips are always going to pound me into oblivion.

It's not something I've missed—not something I *think about*, even. Except that, suddenly, with Gabe's body flush against mine, like a pregnant woman, I'm stuck with an inescapable craving:

I want to make love.

When his lips break apart from mine, we're both breathless.

"Status?" Gabe says.

It takes my mind a second to realize what he's asking. It's the same disorienting sensation of waking up in a strange bed.

I look over his shoulder. "They're gone. Getting Chinese food, I think."

We both share a laugh. His breath patters against my lips.

I want to kiss him again. And the way his blue eyes are shining...

I think he wants it, too.

"Party's over," Gabe says, and his voice is quiet, his breath light. "Let's scram."

Gabe winds his arm around my back, takes my bags, and whisks me away. We walk together, heads down, and rapidly make our way unseen out of the mall and into the parking lot.

10

JACK

The entire "town" of Kepchaw, Georgia, consists of a single Main Street, which features a hodgepodge of Monopoly-style houses: an antique shop, a bookstore, a law firm, a diner. An old set of out-of-commission train tracks runs through the town, like someone once had a grand plan for this place, then promptly forgot about it.

In another life, I could get used to a place like this. I could make Kennedy happy here. We'd get coffee at the Stump every morning. Build a fire to keep warm at night. Raise chickens.

It's a dream, but it's a nice dream.

It's 7.5 miles from the cabin to Main Street. I know because while Kennedy and Madsen are out shopping, I put on sweatpants and a hoodie and run the road, clocking my time on my watch.

I like the Stump for two reasons:

One, it has Wi-Fi, which we don't have at home. I can hook up and scroll through news articles to see if there is any mention of me, Kennedy, or Madsen.

Two, I can get a lay of the land and the people in it.

Dale is the burly woodsman who runs the coffee shop. His dad is Henry, who works at the law firm. Margo is the old lady who runs the antique shop, with her flock of old-lady friends, Not-Margo and Not-Not-Margo. Susan is a frail, anxious woman who owns the bookstore and shivers like a terrier anytime someone talks to her.

It's important to know who lives here. Strangers stand out.

Like this motherfucker.

I catch his license plate. *Florida*. Same as Madsen.

If the Wolfpack has sniffed us out, I want to see it coming before I wake up to a gun in my face.

And this guy is suspicious.

I'm sipping my black coffee and scrolling through when I see the small yellow car glide down the street. It comes to a stop outside the coffee shop and parks but stalls in place.

I feel like I'm up against a bull. I can't see through the tinted windows, but the car exhales smoke as it watches me through the coffee shop window.

Waiting.

Alright, bull. Let's dance.

I kill my coffee, thank Dale, and drop the cup in the trash on my way out.

As I pull up my hoodie, the driver's window rolls down.

"Hey, pal," the driver says. "You live here?"

His eyes are hiding behind round Warby Parker glasses. His age is hard to guess; he's got a young face but a shock of gray hair. He's wearing a sweater that's too big for his frame.

I step in beside the car. "You lost?"

He flashes me a Cheshire cat grin, and I don't trust it. "Aren't we all?"

"Maybe I can help."

"I'm actually looking for a recommendation. How's the coffee here?"

"Coffee?" I ask incredulously.

"Yeah. Coffee. Cup of joe. Java. Bean juice. You can give it to me on a scale of one to Starbucks."

"It's strong."

"How strong are we talking? Superman or Clark Kent?"

I grunt. "It'll make you Mocha Frappe Shit Your Pants."

If possible, his smile widens. "That's what I like to hear. Thanks for your service."

For a minute, I think my dog tags have fallen out. Then I realize he's just thanking me for the coffee review.

I nod. "Have a good one." I tap the back of his seat.

And drop my phone in his back seat in the process.

I've turned on location services. I leave him and book it back home. When I get to the house, my hoodie is sweat-stuck to my body.

I'm greeted with an unexpected sound.

Giggling. Kennedy's giggling. Coming from Madsen's bedroom.

I throw the door open.

The two of them turn to look at me. They've got newspapers lying on the ground underneath them, and they're covered in paint, too-small brushes in hand. The word "killer" is half blotched out on the wall.

"Jack!" Kennedy squeals and gets to her feet. But then her eyes drop to my empty hands, and her smile falls. "No coffee?"

I could kill myself. I don't.

"What's going on here?" I ask.

"Redecorating," Madsen says and points to the word. "Since the war, I've been trying to access my Zen Buddha side. So, you know. Waking up to this every morning was a little jarring."

Okay. Fine. I turn to Kennedy. "I need to borrow your phone."

She bounces over and holds out her phone. She has a spot of paint on her cheek. "What for?"

I unlock her phone and go to my contact information. She's tracking my phone and—now—tracking the suspicious Honda.

I watch the blue location dot cruise through the neighborhood.

"I'm tracking a car," I explain. "I think it's one of theirs."

Kennedy looks over my shoulder. Her hair brushes my cheek. "How are you doing that?"

"I dropped my phone in his car."

"Oooh. Smart. What do you do when you catch him?"

"Then we get answers."

The three of us sit on the floor, with Madsen occasionally swiping his brush on the wall. We watch the dot bounce around the town until it finally comes to a stop. The location sets the dot about fifteen minutes out in a quiet, residential area.

"You think that's his house?" Kennedy asks.

"Only one way to find out." I pocket the phone and get to my feet. "Madsen. You're coming with me."

Kennedy pops up. "I want to come, too."

I shake my head. "Stay."

"Fuck you. I'm not a dog."

Madsen scratches her under the chin and coos, "Who's a good girl? *You're* a good girl."

Kennedy giggles like a little schoolgirl.

I scowl. "Why is it okay when he does it?"

"Because I'm not an asshole." Madsen throws his arm over my shoulder. "We'll be back! Don't wait up, love."

11

GABE

The trees sound different here.

In the Keys, when palm leaves blow together, the sound is sharp and heavy, like a porcupine shaking its quills. *Hssht-hssht-hssht!*

Here, the wind moves through palm trees like water with a low, smooth *shuuuush.*

As though the woods are saying *quiet, quiet.*

They know they have bodies buried here, and they protect their secrets.

The phone tracker led us here—across the street from a small, single-story brick house nestled in beside much larger, more imposing houses. There's a yellow Honda Fit in the parking lot and a welcome mat that says, "Home is Where the Heart is."

I take a swallow from my thermos. I left tea to steep overnight, iced it, and now it tastes like an herbal cocktail.

I kick my boots up on the dash. Jack says nothing, but I can feel his entire body go tense beside me. It's not that I like being a jack-off...it's just that it's kinda fun to rile up the Hulk sometimes.

"How many people are inside?"

"Don't know," Jack replies.

"Do we even know if our guy is in there?"

"No."

As I drink, Jack hunches over the steering wheel. He's loading his Glock in his lap, and I watch him attach the clip.

"So what's the plan? Go in, guns blazing?"

Jack cuts me a sharp look. "Have you got a better one?"

I stash the iced tea in the console, and my feet find the floor again. "Nope. Let's blaze."

Jack pulls out a second gun and hands it over to me. When I touch it, however, he doesn't release.

"Don't make me regret this," he says.

"Your trust is overwhelming, tough guy."

He holds an extra second before finally letting go. I check the piece, flip off the safety, and we exit the car together.

We're doing this home invasion-style. Jack and I flank either side of the door. Those dark eyes of his meet mine, and it's nice, in this way, working side by side with a fellow SEAL. We can communicate using no words at all.

There's a shadow moving behind the curtain. Jack rings the doorbell, and the shadow retreats.

I listen and wait. Three seconds. Five.

Locks grind, and the door clicks open.

"Who the fuck—?"

But the guy behind the door doesn't get the rest of his words out. Jack grabs him by the shirt and shoves him back into the house.

I back him up from behind. We enter the cottage-core-style house, and Jack throws the guy to the ground. His back hits the sofa, and he groans.

"What the *hell*?"

"Who are you?" Jack growls. "Who sent you?"

He's vicious like this, his voice an animal's.

The man on the floor squeals, "Goddammit, Gabe, call off the dog!"

And that's when I get a good look at him.

Shock of gray hair on a young face. Obnoxious flamingo shirt. That constant look of annoyance stamped on his expression.

I lower my gun. "Kip?"

Jack tears his eyes away from Kip just long enough to shoot me a glare. "You know him?"

"Well, yeah…"

"Who the fuck is this guy?" both Kip and Jack ask simultaneously, and suddenly, I feel like I'm stuck in a Spanish soap opera love triangle.

"Kip, meet Jack. Jack, meet Chris 'Kip' Kidd. Jack is Wolf-pack, but he's on our side."

Kip grunts. "That explains the shoot-first-ask-questions-never introduction."

"Kip is my friend and confidant. You can take your gun off him now."

Jack reluctantly lowers his gun. Kip lifts his hand for help up, but Jack just glares at it, so Kip pushes himself to his feet and dusts off his pants.

"You forgot *smartest man alive*," Kip adds.

"That, too. He's like…a tech genius."

"He's the one that's been keeping you off the grid," Jack says, putting two and two together.

"Correct."

"I got your SOS and came running," Kip explains.

Jack narrows his eyes. "SOS?"

I shrug. "Right, well. Back when I thought there was still

a good chance you'd flip on me and sell me out to the Wolf-pack, I sent out an SOS."

"And I answered." Kip beams.

"You were two seconds from eating my lead," Jack growls. "Not much of a rescue."

"Technicalities." Kip waves it off.

"Can anyone else track this SOS?"

"Show him," I tell Kip. Kip takes out his phone and scrolls to a text chain between the two of us. The last thing I sent him was an audio file, and he plays it.

A song plays. "S-O-S."

Jack gives me a sidelong look. "Your failsafe is a Rihanna song?"

"Hey, the girl is fierce."

"*Fierce*." Kip nods emphatically.

Jack looks about at the end of his rope.

"Do you have anything to drink?" I ask hopefully.

IT'S NOT EVEN NOON YET, so Kip fixes a couple of screwdrivers.

You know, breakfast drinks.

I sip mine because my adrenaline is still kicking through my bloodstream. We get comfortable in the living room. Now that I'm seeing it without the tunnel vision of attack mode, I can appreciate the woodsy aesthetic of Kip's rental. I put my screwdriver down on a coaster that resembles a slice of a tree trunk circled with rings.

Our guns sit like lethal paperweights on the glass table.

Jack doesn't sit. Jack doesn't drink. He stands with his back to the imitation fireplace, arms crossed.

Kip jerks his chin in Jack's direction. "I take it he's up to speed?"

"Yes. Well. Mostly."

"What's *mostly?*"

"He got the details, but—"

"It's a lot to take in," Jack interrupts, his voice like black ice.

Kip motions so vehemently with his glass that the orange juice sloshes and nearly spills over the rim. "What's so hard to understand? Anders found an artifact worth millions. Saw an opportunity. And decided he could make more money being one of the bad guys than one of the good guys."

Jack's mouth screws into a frown. "I've known Anders for a long time. It just doesn't sound like him."

Kip lifts a finger. "I'm curious. How well do you *really* know the guy?"

"Well."

"Oh, really? Do you know what his religion is? How about where he spends his summers? How many children he has?"

Jack's eyes widen at that.

Kip laughs. "Trick question! He has no kids. He spends his summers in Big Bend, though. Camping."

"How do you—?"

"I hunt people. We all have our talents. That's mine. I also tell it like it is, so here's the facts: you didn't know the guy. Not really. You were just happy to get assigned a new case every month."

"It wasn't my job to know. I didn't have to know."

"No, you didn't *want* to know. There's a difference. It's easy to absolve responsibility when you're nothing more than a dumb grunt with a gun—"

"That's enough, Kip," I cut him off.

I love the guy, but he's got an uncanny ability to shove his foot in his mouth. And the truth is, he doesn't get it.

Jack got stabbed in the back. The same way I did. Did the guy try to kill me? Sure. But he also saved my ass, and I'm not about to let Kip rip him a new one over it.

Jack pushes himself off the fireplace. He makes his way to the door, and as he passes me, his hand clasps my shoulder. "We need to talk. Outside."

I take a healthy swallow of my drink, set it down, and follow Jack outside. I close the front door behind me so we can talk in private.

He's gripping the thin railing in his big hands, staring out onto the highway. He looks like he could bend the rail like a paperclip in his hands.

"You trust this guy?" he asks.

"With my life."

Jack is quiet. Too quiet. Something's going on in that tank's head.

"Penny for your thoughts?" I ask.

He shakes his head. "I thought we were the good guys."

I exhale and lean back against the railing. "Every family has a bad apple. Anders is just...one of those apples."

"I trusted Anders. He was like a brother. Then he sent me after a brother. Like he thought I wouldn't know. Like I'm some idiot. Like I'm just a—"

"Killing machine."

"Yeah."

I need a cigarette for this conversation. A tall glass of whiskey. A hand job. Something to quell the ache in my chest. I know what he's going through. I know what it is to feel ugly inside. I know that sick, dark voice that tells you that your hands are only good when they're covered in blood.

I've spent the last couple of months retraining my brain. Love instead of bullets. Peace instead of fists. Jack is like a ghost of my past self beside me, choking on the hairball of his own self-hatred.

I rake my fingers through my hair and shift my body so our shoulders brush. *I'm here*, the gesture says. From what I've learned about Jack, he's not the kind of guy to accept hugs or heartfelt condolences. But maybe a quiet show of solidarity will do the trick.

He doesn't pull away from me, which is a good sign.

"What do you want to do about it?" I ask.

His lips are a thin, thoughtful line.

"If he wants a killing machine, I'll give him one." His eyes meet mine, and there's nothing but cold, hard determination in those irises. "Let's burn these motherfuckers to the ground."

I can't help the grin that ghosts my lips. "Spoken like a good guy."

He continues. "We finish your mission. Together. Find Anders. Return the necklace. And end this once and for all."

I've been on the run nonstop since my return, and the concept of *not running* tastes like sand in my mouth. My palms tingle at the word *together*. I don't have to do this alone. Not anymore. But my hope is a cautious, careful thing. A scared rabbit creeping from shadow to shadow. I suck in my lips and choose my words carefully before responding. "I mean...yeah. That would...obviously be ideal. But I can't ask you and Kennedy to do this. Who knows what kind of team Anders has amassed for himself? Going up against him could be...well..."

"Suicide. Unless we're smart about it."

Jack is a mountain—arms crossed, face set, eyes dark. And *I get it.* He's the bullet that, once released, won't stop until it hits its target. Easy to see why the Wolfpack clung to a guy like Jack. He's going to get the job done, no matter what. Jump first, ask questions later.

On my own, I'm a sitting duck. But with Jack's blood-thirst, Kennedy's brilliant mind, and Kip's tech savvy...

For the first time in a very, very long time, I feel a candle light up inside of me. A flicker of hope.

"Yeah." I nod. "Okay. I'm in."

Jack clasps me on the shoulder and squeezes before letting his hand fall away. "Let's do this."

I know what this is. It's a *pact.* The look in Jack's eyes is different. I'm not the enemy anymore.

I'm his partner. Brother in arms.

We go back inside. This time, Jack takes the seat across from Kip. He leans forward in his chair and announces, "We need you to find someone."

Kip's smile is crooked. "You know who you're talking to, don't you? Inspector fucking Gadget."

"Go-go," I reply.

"So who's the lucky fella?"

"I want to find Anders. And I want to find who he's working with. If he's trying to sell the artifact, he's not doing this alone."

Kip's laugh is a wheeze. "You're joking. He's joking, right?" He swivels to me, and I shrug. Kip lets out an exaggerated sigh and throws up his hands. "If we *could* do that, we would've. But the Wolfpack is a dead end. No one knows who runs the company—the whole *point* of it is that it's off the map. Nonexistent. No paper trails, no witnesses, zip, nada, zilch—"

Jack reaches into his pocket, opens up his wallet, and

pulls out a folded-up piece of paper. "Will this help?" he asks as he hands it over to Kip.

Kip squints at it and adjusts his glasses over his face. "What is this?"

"My down payment for Madsen's hit."

"Let me see that." I rip it out of Kip's hands and twist it over. The check is—sure enough—made out to Jack. From the so-called *Semper Fi Foundation*. But it's the number that makes me balk. "Forty *grand*?" I snap. "That's it? I'm worth *way* more than forty grand. That's not even a fucking Maserati. That's like...uh..."

"A Volvo?" Jack looks amused.

I hold up a warning finger. "Fuck you."

Jack chuckles, a low, purring sound. *Dick.*

Pride wounded, I hand the check back to Kip. He looks at it and furrows his eyebrows, mouth pinching to the side. "Okay—yeah. I can work with this. A money trail isn't nothing. Give me a couple days, and I'll see how far I can follow it."

Jack plucks a pen from Kip's desk, turns the check over, and scribbles out his number. "Call this number when you find something."

"Speaking of. You might want this back." Kip gets up and goes to a table by the foyer. He picks up a cell phone and tosses it toward Jack, who catches it. "Don't try to hack a hacker," he warns.

Jack and I leave Kip's place. It's startlingly bright outside —that disorienting feeling you get when you leave a movie theatre and it's still daytime. We crunch through the overgrown lawn and get into his car.

I flop into the passenger side and drape my arm over the back of the chair. "Can I ask you a question?"

"Go ahead."

"That forty grand. That was just the first payment, right? So, what—you were going to get double that when you finished the job? Triple?"

Jack shakes his head. "That's for me to know and for you to never find out."

He starts up the car, and we peel out of there.

12

JACK

Twenty-four hours later, I haven't heard from Kip.

I go on a run. I build an outdoor enclosure for Clucky with a length of chicken wire. I do push-ups in the living room while Kennedy sits on my back, reading.

Forty-eight hours tick by. Now I'm going through the options in my head.

1) He reported us to the Wolfpack, and they're building their army as we speak.

2) He reported us to the FBI in exchange for immunity.

3) He's lying dead in a ditch, bullet through the brain.

4) He's working on it. And these things take time.

But I'm not good at waiting. Never have been.

Waiting makes my blood itch. Makes my teeth hurt. Makes me think too much and drink too much, makes me do dumb things like paint the word *killer* on the wall so I don't blow my brains out.

"Jack. Earth to Jack."

I blink at Kennedy. Her legs are tucked against her body, wearing nothing but a long shirt that doubles as a dress and knee socks to keep her legs warm. Her lips and teeth are stained red-wine purple, the bottle shared between us on the table.

"Sorry." I take a sip from my glass. "I was elsewhere."

"I noticed." Her fingers rake through my hair, nails tickling my scalp. "Want to take me with you?"

I shake my head. "It's nothing."

I don't want to think about Kip. I just want to focus on the scrape of her nails dislodging all the bad thoughts from my head.

Her nails draw down and play on the nape of my neck. "What'd Nothing do to you?" she asks. "I'll wreck him."

I can't help the grin that sneaks up my lips. "That's a terrible pun."

"You're a terrible pun."

She draws me closer, and I kiss her. Her lips are sweet and soft, and her tongue melts in my mouth.

Kennedy is the only thing in this world that can quiet the storm inside of me. She straddles me, her small weight fitting into my lap, and drapes her arms around my shoulders. I draw my hands up her sides, under her shirt, and pet the bare skin above her hips. I lick the inside of her mouth, and she moans softly. The sound vibrates through me, deep in my bones, and my cock seeks her like a fucking divining rod.

"Don't mind me, kittens."

That voice—like a mosquito buzzing in my ear—zaps through me like lightning.

Madsen stands in the kitchen in a velvet robe, sash slung around his waist, potato chip bag in hand.

"Fuck—Madsen," I growl.

"Don't let me interrupt." He digs into his bag, pops a chip in his mouth, and crunches.

Kennedy shifts in my lap and draws a strand of hair behind her ear. "Shouldn't you be in bed?"

"Well, that's a bit forward, but sure, I'll join you."

Kennedy laughs. My lap feels empty when she leaves it, sitting beside me and draping her legs across mine instead. I'm throbbingly frustrated and need him to leave.

"Good night, Madsen," I tell him pointedly.

He salutes us, chip in hand. "Sleep tight."

Then he shuffles off. Clucky follows him like a dog, picking up the crumbs of potato chips he leaves in his wake. I glance over the couch to make sure he's gone into his room.

"Is he wearing rabbits on his feet?"

"Mmhm," Kennedy says. Her toes flex and curl against my thigh. "Slippers. They're super cozy."

I give her a questioning look. "You two are peas in a pod, huh?"

"I like him. He's like you. But a version of you that actually talks. Has a sense of humor. Is fun."

"I have a sense of humor."

"Oh?"

"What do you get when you cross a rabbit and a Rottweiler?"

"What?"

"Just the Rottweiler."

She throws her head back when she groans. "Thank God you're pretty."

Her feet squirm, and it's making me uncomfortably hard, so I take one in my hand. I push my thumbs into the bend of her arch, up the balls of her feet, and spread her toes. She groans again, but this time, it's a nice sound.

"Hey," she says, "you remember Candy?"

"From your club?"

"Uh-huh." She flexes her foot in my hand. "Remember *that night* with her?"

That night. When Kennedy invited her fellow stripper back home after a long work night. The three of us drank too much. The girls showered together, and when they came out, they were naked, all warm skin and giggles and running makeup. We spent the night rolling around in bed, fucking and sucking and licking until we lost track of how many times we'd come.

The next morning, we woke up late and got a brunch down the street. Candy left, I got the check, and then I sat down while Kennedy finished her coffee.

"Guess what?" she'd said, her fingers playing with mine.

"What?"

"Chicken butt. Guess what else?"

"What else?"

"I love you."

It'd been the first time she'd said it, too. That's when I knew—

I was never going to find anyone as weird, or depraved, or fun as Kennedy fucking Furhman.

It wasn't something we made a habit out of—we hadn't invited anyone, or Candy for that matter, to our bed since. I hadn't thought twice about it.

Why would I? Kennedy is all I need—and all I will ever need.

But now that she's brought it up, memories are stirring. Like warm smoke tickling across my skin.

I nod. "Mmhm. I remember."

"It was fun, right?"

"Yeah. It was."

"Something you'd be interested in doing again?"

She asks it so casually—her knees curled up, her elbow

propped on the sofa, heart-shaped face resting in her hand. Like we're teens exchanging midnight secrets.

She's got *that look* on her face. That Mona Lisa smile twitching at the edge of her mouth.

I narrow my eyes at her. "What are you saying?"

She cocks her head toward Madsen's room. "What do you *think* I'm saying?"

I know what she's saying.

When I get bored, I get violent.

When Kennedy gets bored, she gets horny.

And she's angling for a threesome.

We're combustible right now, and with a wildfire like Madsen...

Well. We might explode.

I pull away and reach for the bottle of red. "I think I need more wine."

Her toes knead into my thigh. "Okay, stuffy."

But then she drops it.

We talk a little longer. We finish the bottle. I tuck her in my arms and carry her upstairs. We shower together. We kiss under the water, and she runs her nails up my back and my shoulders. We dry each other off. She's still damp when I take her to bed. I touch her cunt. She's wet here. Wetter. Slick as oil.

"Jack?"

"Yeah?"

Kennedy catches my face in her hands and pulls me on top of her. "Make love to me."

She asks for it in a whisper, like a prayer.

"What?" I ask, not sure I heard her correctly.

"Make love to me," she asks again.

It's so sweet, so sincere, that I have to try.

I corrupt her mouth with my kiss. I line my body up with hers and ease myself inside of her. Slowly. Inch by inch.

She gasps. She holds my shoulders as I rock my body, seesawing over her.

Our gazes connect. My body is used to railing her, and it takes effort to hold myself back. But I hold her eyes all the same as I concentrate hard on giving her what she wants.

Her eyebrows furrow. "What're you doing with your face?"

"Being intense."

"Stop it."

"Okay. How's this?"

I draw a thin line with my mouth. I tell my eyes to look *in love*. I think they squint.

She squints back at me. "You look like you're in pain."

Clearly, she has a script she made up in her head, and I'm not following it. Frustration builds. In my balls. In my blood. "How should I look?"

She slips a hand over her face. "You know—forget it. Pound me."

I frown. "You sure?"

She nods. "Yep. Pound me." Her fingers clutch my shoulders again, but this time, her nails dig in. The pain is familiar, and I draw in a quick breath. "Make me see all fifty stars of the American flag, hero."

She punctuates her point by taking my dog tag in her hand and playing her tongue over the ridged letters. We're back to being filthy, dirty animals. My cock gives a grateful throb at being let off the leash. I plunge inside her and fuck her hard. The baseboard slams the wall. She screams when she comes.

I don't think about Madsen downstairs. I don't think

about him listening in on us. I don't think: *See what I do to her?*

See how much she loves my cock?

See how loud she screams for me?

I don't see stars when I come.

I roll off Kennedy and catch my breath. Kennedy nuzzles against my chest. Her fingertips trace the lines on my abdomen. Old scars and birthmarks.

The monster is sated. For now.

"Tell me your weirdest fantasy," she muses. "One you've never told anyone."

So I close my eyes and let the words come out.

"I have this dream. The entire world is underwater. Like Noah and the flood. I'm swimming, and you ride my back like a dolphin. It's just us. We're the last people in the world."

She kisses my chest. Her lips are gentle and soft.

Her sweetness breaks my fucking heart.

"You have a strange brain, Jack Crossed," she says. "I like it."

What I don't tell her: my dream has updated.

Now, there's a spit of land in the distance. Nothing but sand and a palm tree. On that piece of land, Madsen waves to us.

The last good man alive.

13

GABE

They rut like animals upstairs.

The sounds vibrate through the entire house. Old floors groan. The headboard slaps rapidly against the wall that connects our rooms.

If I touch it, I can feel the vibrations.

Clucky sleeps on the pillow beside my own. She gets up, perturbed by the sex noises, putters around for a minute, and then settles down at the foot of the bed inside, feathers officially ruffled.

I'm not a man that's good at being alone. Never have been.

It's been too long since I've felt someone run their hands down the sides of my body.

It's been too long since I felt a tongue on my neck.

Jack and Kennedy are stunning creatures. The chemistry between them makes me ache in the worst ways possible.

I can't help it. I close my eyes and picture the scene upstairs.

Jack diving into Kennedy's sweet cunt. Pounding her.

My hand reaches under my briefs. I'm wound so tight,

just the feeling of wrapping my fingers around my rigid cock makes me groan, my tongue pushing against my teeth.

I want to be touched by fingers that aren't my own.

I want Jack's rough hands in my hair.

I want Kennedy's soft lips on my mouth.

I want, *I want*, greedy, starving fucking *want*.

I choke on muffled, tortured pleasure when I release. But my orgasm is empty and nowhere near scratches my itch. I'm getting too close to them, and it shows in the white mess dripping down my stomach.

There's a trill from the foot of the bed.

"Stop judging me," I tell the chicken. "Haven't you ever had the empty nest blues?"

Clucky tuts and flutters her wings briefly.

I sigh. "Yeah. I know. *I know.*"

14

JACK

When I make my way downstairs in the morning, the smell of coffee rises to greet me.

Madsen is already in the kitchen. Already dressed. His dark hair hangs wetly on the back of his neck, remnants of his morning shower.

He drinks coffee while sitting perched on the kitchen counter, even though there are two perfectly respectable seats at the table.

The coffeepot gurgles next to him, so I reach for a mug and fill it.

"Good morning," he says, chipper.

"Morning."

"Sleep well?" He's grinning, and there's that annoyingly cheeky implication that he's fully aware we did not *sleep* much at all last night.

His taunting makes me prickle.

"Do you ever sit in a chair?" I complain.

"No, because then I can't do this."

Quick as a viper, Madsen wraps his legs around my hips and uses the strength of his thighs to yank me in close.

I let out a grunt of surprise, and our eyes meet.

We're close like this. Too close.

Our heights match up. Hip to hip. Cock to cock.

I'm gripped with the sudden thought—

I could grab his leg. Crush him against the counter with my body. I could hump him, our erections rubbing together, heat-seeking missiles seeking heat until we both blew. Right here. Right on the counter.

Right before Kennedy's cup of coffee gets cold.

As soon as the thought comes, I send it scattering. Like scaring off a deer with a buckshot. But my blood is slower to cool. My heart knocks wildly against my chest.

I pray he can't feel me thickening.

As if he can read my mind, Madsen winks at me.

"What, never been in an *ashi garami* hold before?"

My frown deepens. "I hate you."

My pocket buzzes. Madsen releases me from his thigh grip so I can reach my phone.

The caller ID is blocked. I answer it anyway. The voice on the other end sends a thrill through me that's better than a kitchen quickie.

"Who was that?" Madsen asks when I hang up.

"Kip. He's ready. He wants us to come over. Now."

15

GABE

This time, when we get to Kip's place, he doesn't offer refreshments. It's down to business.

Jack and I sit on either side of Kip on the couch, crowding him as he taps away at the laptop in front of him.

"You, Jack, sent me down a rabbit hole."

Jack is, quite literally, on the edge of his seat. "Tell us what you found."

Kip pulls up an image grab of the check. "Well, the money transaction you gave me was secure. Deposited through a ghost account—every time I reach for it, it vanishes into thin air. However, our friend Troy Anders runs a very successful nonprofit."

"Semper Fi Foundation," Jack fills in. "They provide housing and jobs for displaced vets."

"Correctamundo," Kip continues. "Anyway, the great thing about nonprofits is that they have to declare the money that goes in. A benefactor recently made a rather large donation which matches the number on your check to the penny."

Kip clicks away.

"And the winner is...Fletcher Waters."

He pulls up the image of a guy who could be a Bible salesman. Crisp suit. Glasses. White-bread smile.

"This is our big, bad guy?" I ask. "He looks like a banker."

"Financial advisor, technically," Kip corrects. "My guess? Fletcher is your middleman, moving funds from one source to another to keep the Big Cheese's hands clean. If you're doing black-market deals like, say, purchasing stolen artifacts, you want as many layers of insulation between you and the transaction as possible."

"So how do we get to the *Big Cheese*?"

"We make a rat squeak," Jack responds. His voice is calm but intense. "We find Fletcher. Then we get him to tell us who hired him."

I have the sneaky feeling that the interrogation tactics running through Jack's head are less than delightful. But I keep my mouth shut.

We'll bleed that bridge when we get to it.

"Pretty much," Kip says. "Big long game of telephone, isn't it?"

"Where is he now?" Jack asks.

"Well, that's the best part." Kip leans back in his chair, resting his hands behind his head in a *job well done* posture. His chair rolls backward only an inch before Jack stoppers it with his boot. "I've been tracking his credit card statements. Fletcher isn't far. He escapes the missus and children right before the holidays for a, quote, *spiritual retreat*, end quote, in Augusta. It's about a thirty-minute drive from here."

I look at Jack. He hasn't torn his eyes away from Fletcher's image. Not once.

Hound dog on the scent of blood.

"Print out what you have on Fletcher," he says. "Everything."

"A *thank you, Kip* would be helpful."

"*Thank you,* Kip." I emphasize my gratitude because I know it's going to have to count for the both of us. I squeeze his shoulder affectionately.

Kip looks pleased by the acknowledgment. "Well, that's all I got for you. Good luck hunting."

"Do you have a safe place to hole up for a bit?"

"Aw. Is that concern? Don't worry, the only people who have tried to kill me so far this week are you two—if there's one thing I'm good at navigating, it's grids."

Jack has already disengaged from the conversation. He takes the printout of Fletcher and paces to the other side of the room with it.

Jack is thinking.

Bad sign.

JACK IS quiet on the drive back.

When we get to the house, I ask, "So what's the plan, Jack?"

He cranes his head upward, listening like a dog.

There's the sound of running water upstairs. Kennedy is in the shower.

Aka: Kennedy is occupied.

It's clear Jack doesn't want her involved in this any more than she has to be.

"There's a road map in the kitchen cabinet," he says. "Go get it."

I do as he asks and fetch the road map. I come into the living room, and he spreads it out over the dining room table.

Jack picks up a pen. He tucks it between his teeth and stands beside me. He plants his palms flat out on the map, hunting.

It's hard not to notice the thickness of his biceps. The wingspan of his hands when he splays them out like that. Those veins that cord around his forearms and up the backs of his hands like ivy.

Focus, Gabe. Now is not a time to salivate over the asshole beside you.

Pretty asshole though he might be.

Jack uncaps the pen and jots an X on the map. "This is us. And this—" Another X upward, to the right. "—is where we find Waters. It's about a forty-mile drive. We head out tomorrow. Keep an eye on him. For a day. Maybe two. Follow his routine. Get him alone."

"And then?" I pry.

Jack lifts his eyes to meet mine. Those eyes are dark. He's irritated I'm making him say it.

"Then we make him speak. Any means possible. You have a problem with that?"

"No problem here. As much as I love guns blazing...this guy is a banker. On a spiritual retreat. We're going to—what? Go in and sucker punch a bunch of yoga moms and monks?"

Jack's eyes flash. "I don't care if he's sucking Gandhi's dick. He wrote checks for the wrong people. He made his bed. Now he has to lie in it."

"Yeah, what about *our* beds?"

Jack just frowns at me.

"All I'm saying is...for all we know, he could be an innocent in this."

"No one is innocent," Jack says. "It's time you get that out of your head."

Before I can respond, we hear—

"What's going on in here?"

Kennedy scales the last couple of steps and walks into the living room. She's wearing a thin cotton shirt that rides up her soft frame and hugs her small breasts. She reaches up to tie her hair back into a loose ponytail.

"Go back upstairs," Jack orders. "I'll be right there."

She lowers herself on the couch beside Jack and stabs the picture with her finger, sliding it around on the table. "Who's the sleazebag?"

"Fletcher Waters," I tell her. "He's the one who financed the hit on me."

Jack cuts me a glare. I shrug. It's a half-hearted apology.

Maybe she's not my girl, but she deserves to know. And she's not quite the helpless kitten Jack seems to think she is.

She's strong. And smart. And part of the team. Hiding this from her is just going to cause trouble down the line.

"And you guys are going after him?" Kennedy asks.

"We're going to get answers," Jack says.

"Great! I'm coming with you."

"No. You're not." Jack's voice is even, hard. Daddy's in charge. "It could be dangerous."

"It's *all* dangerous." Her ponytail whips back and forth as she looks between us. "We're in this together."

"No," Jack says. I hold my tongue.

"I'm not a wilting flower," she snaps.

"When was the last time you killed a guy?"

"Oh, *fuck you*—"

"It's just a ride along," I say, interrupting the discord in paradise. They stop and look at me. I shrug. "We could use a driver. What's the worst that could happen?"

If looks could kill, Jack's eyes would have me disemboweled right now.

16

KENNEDY

You know what I learned about stakeouts?

They suck. So boring.

We drive to "the Sanctuary." Turns out, it's not an overgrown oasis for people who enjoy yoga with goats or whatever. The Sanctuary is a pit that makes the Pink Pony look like a classy joint. It's off the side of the highway. The walls are all black, the whole place sealed up like it's been wrapped in bondage tape. The "Sanctuary" sign is in small gold letters at the front. So small that Jack passed by the place the first time we navigated here.

I can practically smell the Axe body spray from here. I imagine this is what the billionaires call "discreet." I call it: the last place I want to be after the sun goes down. And yet, here we are. Sitting in the parking lot. Waiting.

Gabe and Jack sit in the front; I'm tucked away in the back seat. I stretch out like a cat with my extra legroom. Jack has the radio playing, a low compilation of rock music.

"Do we know when he's coming out?" I ask.

"No," Jack replies.

"Are we even sure he's in there?"

"Nope." Gabe sounds as equally bored as I do.

"There should be an easy way to find out, right? Call up and ask for him or something?"

Jack tilts his head in my direction without actually turning around to look at me. "You could have stayed home if you wanted to."

I huff and sink back into the back seat. "What's the point in coming all this way if we're just going to stare at the door?"

"It's called surveillance," Jack says.

He's talking to me like I'm a child.

Screw this. I'm tired of being the runt of the litter.

I unlock the door and push it open.

"What are you doing?" Jack snaps.

"I have to pee."

Jack calls my name, but I'm already walking down the parking lot to the door. I hear their twin doors open and shut behind me and Jack swear.

There's a bouncer sitting on the stool outside the black outline of a door. He's scrolling on his phone, bored.

I speak the language of strip clubs. I tug my tight T-shirt down so my cleavage pops through.

His eyes lift, but they don't make it above my neckline.

"Hey." I smile. "The greaseballs behind are with me."

His eyes flicker over my body, then at the two men ambling behind me. I must pass the sniff test because he nods me in.

It's so cold inside, and my nipples pinch and harden the second I step in. And maybe that's the point. The place is nicer on the inside than I anticipated. Absinthe-green lights illuminate the edges of the stage, which rolls like a runaway down the center of the space. There's a bar in the corner— also under-lit by the same toxic-green-colored lights—and I find a spot there. It's a good place to look out at the swarm of people. For 9:00 p.m. on a Thursday, it's packed. Guys in dark blazers and fancy watches. Not a High Life in sight. Here, they drink scotch on the rocks or have a bottle of champagne on the table.

The music dies down and then picks up again, an electro-punk thrumming beat. When the dancer steps through the emerald curtains, a low mist curls around her kitten heels. She's wearing a silk nightie, and she hooks her leg around the pole and twists with the precision of a Cirque du Soleil performer.

What in the slutty Alice-in-Wonderland is this place?

At least in the Pink Pony, the wolves looked like *wolves.* Hairy and hungry and drooling.

Here, the wolves look like sheep. Fluffy and pampered with a wickedness that lives underneath the zipper.

Jack orders two beers and an old-fashioned. He hands me my drink and scoops his arm around my middle. He's protective in here.

"I don't see him," I say, my eyes flickering over the crowd.

"I don't see anyone," Jack replies.

He isn't wrong. It's dim as hell here. Even when my eyes adjust, I have a hard time making out the faces of anyone in the crowd. Mostly just dark shapes.

That, I'm sure, is by design, too.

Gabe's hair tickles my cheek as he leans in on my left. I have a boy on every shoulder. "Check your one-a-clock," he says, just loud enough for us to hear. "By the stage. *Slowly.*"

I try to see what he's seeing. Then I make it out—there's a booth next to the stage. The booth has a long, curved velvet back, and it's large enough to fit a few people, but right now, it only houses one man.

It's hard to make out too many details in the darkness,

but I can see that good-boy haircut and thick glasses. Is he the man in the photo? Could be.

If only I could get closer.

An idea hits me.

"Do you guys hear that?" I say.

"Hear what?" Gabe asks.

"God. Saying *time to rise and shine, Liberty.*" I knock down a third of my drink and then set it on the bar.

17

JACK

Kennedy has lost her fucking mind.

All this time, I've been keeping her away from my work to keep her safe.

As it turns out, Kennedy isn't the one who needs to be protected.

It's the world that needs to be protected from Kennedy.

She goes off like a fucking bomb in every room she walks into, and now I find myself playing catch-up and trying to keep my tenuous self-control from slipping through my fingers.

"*Kennedy*," I snap at her as she slips through the crowd.

She turns around, only once, to press her hands together in faux prayer, a gesture that says *trust me*, before she vanishes through a black curtain in the back like she owns the place.

"So." Madsen stands beside me. "I take it Kennedy is our team captain now?"

I choke the neck of my beer.

"Keep an eye out," I tell him.

"For what?"

"I'm not sure Waters came alone."

"He's an accountant. Looks pretty alone to me. I don't think most accountants come with an attaché of bodyguards."

"He's not *most*," I remind Madsen.

"Copy that."

I scan the room. You can usually spot a bodyguard on duty. They look...well. Like us. Alert. Body shifted toward the door. Positioned in a spot in the room where they can keep an eye on everyone and everything.

So far, I'm not seeing a lot of people that fit that description. Everyone in here looks rich, and soft, and drunk.

Waters is no exception. He's hammered in his booth, two empty martini glasses sitting at his table. He waves a fistful of bills at one of the off-stage strippers until she finally relents and sits beside him. They don't have the same hands-off rules here as they did at the Pink Pony, and he's got his fingers all over her, squeezing her bare thighs, his grin extra-wide.

The whole goddamn human race should be exterminated, if you ask me.

The girl onstage finishes her set, and the track changes. When the next song comes on, my heart slams against my rib cage.

You've got to be shitting me.

Beyoncé belts over the speakers. The upbeat, high-energy tempo of the song seems to wake up everyone in the crowd, who've been lulled into a daze of lust and one too many shots.

On the center stage, Lady Liberty extends her long leg through the curtain.

She shakes. Teases. There are hoots and shouts when she finally pulls herself all the way through. Kennedy has done a quick Lady Liberty job—she's found a green robe backstage and is wearing someone else's crown. No green makeup this time, but that doesn't stop her from killing it onstage. She wraps her fingers around the length of a pole, hooks her ankle, and spins, and the crowd really lights up.

I get it. She's electric. I've seen her naked. I've had her bent backward over the arm of her couch and pounded her cunt until she screamed. But my blood still goes hot every time I see her onstage.

It's her energy. Her smile. She's the only one up there who isn't dead-eyed and hollowed out. She's life and heat. Like the sun. It's blinding.

"Holy shit," Madsen says. "You didn't tell me your girl could dance."

I inform him, "If you get a boner, I'm cutting the thing off."

Madsen kisses his beer and swallows deeply.

He's not the only one gawking. Waters has completely lost interest in the woman in his booth. His four eyes are fixed on Kennedy like a hawk.

He doesn't even have the decency to close his mouth, gaping at her like a frog.

Kennedy kills it onstage. She works up a sweat and works the crowd into a frenzy. When she's finished, she salutes and steps backstage.

Madsen claps and shouts, "America!"

I let it slide.

There are shouts for more, and I think everyone's disappointed when the next song kicks up and a new woman walks onstage.

It only takes her thirty seconds before Kennedy walks out from behind the curtain, entering the floor. As soon as he spots her, Waters unceremoniously kicks the other stripper out of his booth. I hear him shout for Liberty, and he waves his money in the air.

Fucking shameless.

Kennedy pretends not to hear him at first. Then she turns his way, smiles, and goes over. Smoothly, she puts her hands on the table and leans over to speak with him. I can only see the back of her, but I'm sure he's taking in her cleavage from that angle.

My nerves are scraping against each other like flint.

Waters is probably harmless.

But it's hard for me to hang Kennedy's safety on a soft *probably*.

Waters motions to the booth. He lifts his glass out for her. He's trying to coax her into his booth like a humming-bird. I watch her shake her head. She tosses her hair over her shoulder and nods toward the adjacent wall. It's a row of four private rooms, sequestered off with black curtains.

Waters stands and takes Kennedy by the arm. I tighten my grip on my bottle. I make a decision. I'm going to break the hand that touched her.

But she doesn't look like she's in trouble. Instead, I watch as she lets him limply lead her over to the private rooms. He pushes the curtain back and motions her in.

She casts a single glance my way before she vanishes inside.

That's my cue.

"We're up," I tell Madsen.

He straightens up, and quiet as shadows, the two of us weave through the crowd and go toward the back rooms.

No one stops us as we move, one after the other, into Waters's room.

Kennedy's moans hit my ears. A loud, fluttery, fake sound.

The room is small, closet-sized. The walls and floors are painted black, with long mirrors hanging on either side. The only illumination comes from mood-setting beads of light that line the box of the floor like emergency exit stripes.

Waters is sitting in the single chair in the center of the room. The top of his shirt is unbuttoned, falling like flaps on either side of him. His necktie is wrapped around his eyes in a makeshift blindfold, so he doesn't notice when Gabe and I intrude into his space.

It's hard to hear much of anything over the pound of music outside, anyway.

"C'mon, baby," Waters whines, "let me see you."

Kennedy has squashed herself in the corner, flat against the wall. She's still wearing her robe, but every now and then, she lets out a small moan.

"Almost…" she teases. Her voice is breathy and sultry, but her eyes are wild when they meet mine. She's high on adrenaline, pupils tight, exhilarated and panicked at the same time.

I give her a nod. *We'll take it from here.*

Madsen swings his leg around Waters and straddles the other man's lap. I fall into place behind Waters's chair.

"Alright, peekaboo," Madsen says. He pulls the tie from Waters's face, letting it drop around his neck.

In the mirror behind Madsen, I see Waters's wolfish grin quickly fall into a wide-open gape.

"What…the fuck…?"

Waters starts to lift his hands, but I grab him by the arms, locking them against the chair behind him.

"Don't worry, the girl is still here," Madsen says. "We'll let you get back to your regularly programmed debauchery soon."

"Is this a prank?" Waters's head swivels between Madsen, Kennedy, and me. "Did Frank put you up to this?"

"No, we're here of our own volition."

Madsen still straddles his lap, and Waters's face is starting to go red.

"If this is some...*gay thing*..."

"Not that either. Sorry." Madsen is unnervingly calm and collected. He smiles like a salesman. "Look, the good news is we're not even interested in you. We're interested in who you know."

Now, all the color goes out from Waters's face completely. "I don't know what you're talking about," he says, his voice rising in pitch.

I squeeze my grip on his wrists.

"Scream," I warn him, "and I'll break your fingers."

"He will." Madsen nods. "I wouldn't test him on that."

Waters's breath goes ragged and shallow. A bead of sweat rolls down the side of his neck. "Listen," he says, his voice thin, "you have the wrong guy. I don't *know* anyone—"

Madsen shifts to reach into Waters's pants. Waters makes a whimper of a sound, but Madsen gives him a wink. "Relax. Just going for this." He pulls out Waters's wallet and flips it open. It's stuffed with cash. Madsen splays the wallet open to display his ID—*Fletcher Waters*, sure enough—and holds it up next to Waters's face.

"This is you, right? Fletcher Waters? If not, you have an evil twin out there—the resemblance is uncanny."

"Please..."

Madsen digs through his wallet. "Is this your family?" He pulls out a folded-up picture. "Real cute. Does your wife know what you get up to on your fun little meditation trips?"

Waters is shaking. I can feel his wrists trembling.

Madsen was right about one thing. He's an accountant. Not a soldier. You apply even the slightest pressure to him, and he breaks.

"What do you want?" he whispers. His voice is quieter now. He's ready to talk.

Madsen can sense it. He smiles. "You arranged a transaction of a large quantity of money to the Semper Fi Foundation. Do you remember that?"

Waters swallows. He mumbles something.

Madsen cocks his head. "What?"

"*Yes*," Waters articulates through his teeth.

"Great. We need to know who initiated the transaction. A name, ideally."

Waters goes quiet. Bad sign. He's thinking.

"This was a setup," Waters says, a flash of recognition lighting in his dumb eyes. He narrows his gaze at Kennedy. Kennedy is still flat against the wall, keeping her distance, but her eyes go wide when he snarls at her, "You fucking bitch."

Okay, so we're playing this game.

I move my hand down to his, entwine my fingers in his, and twist his middle finger until I feel the bone snap.

He howls. Or starts to. Madsen covers his mouth quickly, his eyes briefly flickering to mine with an anxious smile that says *warn me next time*. "I wouldn't say things like that," Madsen says. "The odds are against you on this one, and the big guy here really doesn't need a reason to hurt you."

When Madsen pulls his hand away, Waters is blubbering. "I'm an accountant," he whimpers. "Just an accountant. I don't know anything about this—"

Madsen sighs. He nods to me. "Okay, his other finger."

I start to apply pressure when Waters whines. "Caine!"

he says. "Aldous Caine! He hired me for the transaction. I swear, I have no idea what it's for…"

"Aldous Caine?" Kennedy, who has been silent up until now, pipes up from her corner with surprise. "Mayoral candidate Aldous Caine?"

"You know this guy?" Madsen asks.

Kennedy just shrugs. "North Carolina stuff."

"That's him, please," Waters whimpers. "I didn't know what the money was for. I don't know what he wants. Please let me go, I've given you everything."

I make eye contact with Madsen. He nods lightly. He believes the guy.

"Okay," Madsen says. "We appreciate your cooperation. I think we can all agree that this never happened."

Madsen stands up. Waters is silent now, exhausted and shaken. But I'm not finished.

I glance up. Kennedy is staring at us. She has that deer-in-headlights look.

"Hey," I say, in that soft tone meant only for her. She snaps out of it, her eyes on me now. "Turn around."

She hesitates. Her eyes flicker from me, to Waters, and back to me again.

I repeat slowly, "Turn. *Around.*"

Finally, she does, turning her back to me.

I give Madsen a look, and he understands. He puts his hand over Waters's mouth.

"Wait," I hear Waters mumble into Madsen's palm. "Wait, wait, *wait*—"

No waiting. "This is for putting your hands on her," I whisper into his ear.

Then I take his forearm and snap it. His scream gets swallowed in Madsen's palm and drowned out by the thumping beat of the music outside.

18

JACK

My mood has dramatically improved.

We barely make it out of the Sanctuary in one piece.

The second we exit the private room, I spot three body-guards dressed in black making a beeline toward us. They part the sea of people, leaving ripples in their wake.

I grab Kennedy by the arm and tug her out the door.

The three of us pile into the car. Kennedy is shouting at me to go, go, *go*, and I get the wheels spinning just as the first bullet pings off the car door. I floor it, and we fly out of the parking lot. One of the guys jumps in his car to follow us, but I swerve down side roads at top speed until we lose him.

When we get back to the house, the three of us are buzzing.

"Am I a genius?" Kennedy asks, dramatically throwing down her robe. "Or am I a genius?"

"A MacArthur Award winner, baby," Madsen goads her on.

"Drinks!" Kennedy says. "Wine!"

"Shots," Madsen corrects.

Kennedy shoots him with finger guns. "Bingo."

I drop my jacket over the back of the kitchen chair. "Who the hell is Aldous Caine?"

Kennedy waves her hand as though batting away a fly. "Big, rich family. The Caines pretty much owned Cobblersville—that's where I grew up. Everyone knew them. Loved them. Aldous was like the Godfather, I guess. If you needed a loan, or a job, or advice on how to get even with your cheating husband, you went to Mr. Caine." She breaks out a bottle of whiskey and three mismatched shot glasses. The glasses go on the table (on top of the all-important map, in case anyone gives a shit), and Kennedy fills them.

"You think he's involved in all this?"

She shrugs. "Their family was huge collectors. Like... priceless pieces of art everywhere. I wouldn't be shocked."

She's not looking at me. Her eyes are focused on the glasses.

I press, "And how do you know him, exactly?"

Kennedy's eyes meet mine. "Our families were friends."

But her eyes are vibrating. There's something she's not telling me.

"Questions later—first." Madsen lifts his glass. He has that cocky, tilted smile. "Cheers. To Kennedy. For being a goddamn badass."

"I'll drink to that," I say and lift my glass.

By which I mean: *Fuck you. I can be a supportive boyfriend, too.*

"You are morons." Kennedy cackles, and the three of us knock back our shots.

The whiskey is cheap. It burns. I keep my expression stoic and lock my gaze onto Madsen.

He, too, downs it like water.

"I'd like to make a second toast," Kennedy announces.

"Here we go," I mutter, and Kennedy elbows me to death as Madsen refills.

"To the three of us," she says, lifting her glass. "We may have started out a little rough...but if today taught us anything, it's the importance of *this*. The three of us can do anything as long as we work together."

"And trust each other," Madsen adds.

They're both looking at me like they expect me to say something smart.

I don't.

"Hooyah" is all I say.

We drink. Kennedy refills this time.

"Your turn," Kennedy tells me.

"My turn for what?"

"Say something you're grateful for. Anything."

"Instant coffee."

Kennedy rolls her eyes.

Her cheeks are rosy red. She looks like Sleeping Beauty, the way they drew her in old cartoons, with porcelain skin and blushing cheeks.

This means something to her. I revise my toast.

"To our brothers," I say suddenly. "Those fallen, and those fighting to stay upright."

Madsen's blue eyes lock on me from across the table.

"To brothers," he says, voice low, and the three of us clink before knocking them back.

Kennedy lets out a "whoop!" when she finishes her whiskey.

The third shot hurts him. Madsen winces as it goes down. Inwardly, I rejoice.

I won this round.

Madsen, 0. Me, 1.

Kennedy leans against me, her arm pressing to mine. Her skin is warm, and her hair is undone and messy. I want to bite her neck. Kennedy turns to look up at me. Her eyes are moons, and I know she's thinking what I'm thinking. *She wants me.* Just the same as I want her.

We're buzzing with it. The adrenaline from our trip to the Sanctuary. The flush of victory. The booze.

Danger has always excited Kennedy, for better or worse. She tilts her mouth up to mine, and I don't need any other permission. For one glorious moment, Madsen disappears. The world narrows to only Kennedy and her gentle, needy lips. She seals the kiss before I want it to end. When she does, she's smiling. There's something devious in her smile.

I'm in trouble.

Kennedy twists to face Madsen.

"Question," Kennedy says.

"Shoot," Madsen replies.

"Do you like girls or boys?"

She's so blunt about it I almost choke.

He's a good sport, though. His mouth breaks into a crooked grin. "You're asking the wrong question."

"Oh?"

"The question should be: *do I like you, or do I like Jack?*" His eyes flicker up at me. "And the answer is, I think you're both beautiful."

Beautiful. The man looked me in the eyes and called me beautiful.

There's that strange clench in my stomach again.

"I think *you're* beautiful," Kennedy murmurs, and she's trapped in his trance, too, half in a swoon when she presses her body against his.

The moment she kisses him, I exhale into it. Like stepping into a hot bath.

It hurts at first, but then it feels good.

A rush of warmth. A tingling through my veins. A tightening in my balls.

I want to hit him. I want to fuck her.

I want to fuck him. I want to choke her.

Wires cross in my brain. Sex and violence. Violence and sex.

I should've been a fucking caveman.

My hands are fists, and I don't realize it until Kennedy's eyes sweep over me. She breaks away from Madsen (who is flushed, lips wet) and flocks to me instead. Her nails tickle the hair on my forearm.

"Hey," she says, her voice soft and heavy like a blanket, "is this okay?"

"Kiss me again and I'll tell you."

Kennedy gets up on her tiptoes to press her lips to mine.

This time, I'm not gentle.

I cup the back of her head and plunge my tongue into her mouth. I taste every tooth. I kiss her so deeply she sighs and sinks into me, her knees buckling.

I open my eyes and look past Kennedy. I make sure those blue eyes are watching me.

I want to show off.

I want to show him:

This is how I fuck her.

See what a good girl she is? See how much she loves my cock?

See how I make her legs shake?

See how she moans my name?

But when my gaze connects to his, his eyes are like blue flames. The hottest tip of the fire.

It sends a shiver through me.

Kennedy and I break our kiss. We're both light of breath.

She looks at me, question in her eyes.

"I'm yours," I tell her suddenly.

That makes her smile. "I'm yours, too."

"Then that's all that matters."

That makes her smile wider. She bites her lip.

I squeeze her arm, then kiss the side of her face. Then I unwind from Kennedy, slip around the circular table, and get between Kennedy and Madsen.

I leave Kennedy's shot glass abandoned, but I pinch my glass and Madsen's and drag them over. I pick up the bottle of whiskey and pour the two of us each a shot.

"A gentleman's agreement," I tell him. "Eyes on me. I'm going to ask you questions. You're going to answer honestly. Then we're going to drink on it."

"*Jack*," Kennedy complains with a whine of my name, but Madsen holds up a hand and shakes his head. There's a grin.

"It's alright." His blue eyes meet mine. "I'm ready."

"Do you want to fuck my girlfriend?"

This isn't a game—my questions and my tone are serious.

To his credit, he doesn't bat an eye. He matches my intensity. "Yes. Who wouldn't? She's a fox."

I can't argue there. We take our shots. I refill.

"If I let you fuck her..." His eyes trail to Kennedy. Probably fantasizing already. I cut and remind him, "Eyes on me." Those blues snap to attention. "Good boy. Now—*if* I let you touch her, you understand you're putting your hands on an angel. That means you treat that woman like the divine creature she is. From now until morning, your sole purpose on Earth—the only reason God created you—is to give that woman pleasure. You understand?"

Madsen wets his lips with the tip of his tongue. Seems like he likes the idea. "I understand."

We knock back our shots. I refill again. We're making a real dent in this bottle now.

"If she tells you to slow down. If she tells you to stop. Her word is God, and you listen. You obey. No questions asked."

"Yes. I promise."

The whiskey is going down way too smoothly now. Bad sign. I ignore it and press on.

Kennedy's hands hug my hips. Her breasts press to my back. Her chin rests on my shoulder. "How long is this interrogation going to last?"

"Last round," I inform her. Eyes still on Madsen, I tell him, "When you fall in love with her—and you will—it's impossible to fuck her and not fall in love with her. *When* you fall for her, I want you to remember that Kennedy and I, we're unbreakable."

Now, that crooked smile climbs up his mouth. "I don't want to break you two," Madsen states. "I just want to be in the middle."

The image that conjures makes my blood hot. "Just say you understand."

He rakes his fingers through his thick hair. "I understand."

"Drink on it."

We both take our glasses, clink them together, and then tip them to our lips, eye contact still intact.

Madsen swallows.

I don't.

I grab the front of his shirt, pull him in, and push my tongue into his mouth. Whiskey tumbles past my lips and into his. He lets out a muffled moan.

His kiss is warm. The scruff on his face is rough. He tastes like cinnamon whiskey and ash.

I crush him against the table. He opens his legs for me, accepting me between them. When we collide, I feel his chest, hard and thick and flat like mine. I feel the erection between his legs swelling on my hip.

I want my spit to be his spit. My air to be his air. I want him to need me to breathe. I want him to need me to live. I want him to need me.

I want him to submit.

But he doesn't.

I'm rough. I claim his mouth. I grip his shirt. I dominate him.

And he stops me.

Madsen closes his hand over my wrist, forcing me to release my death grip, slowing my pace.

He exhales a breathy laugh against my lips. "Easy, tough guy." His voice is a low, velvet purr.

And it's the strangest fucking thing—

His touch slows me down. Because I can feel the strength of it.

This is what it feels like when an immovable force meets a...

No. An unstoppable force.

Immovable object?

Fucking...

Math.

Madsen. When an unstoppable force meets Madsen.

I've never fucked anyone as strong as I am. Never been met pound-for-pound. Didn't even know that was something I *wanted* until right this second, with Madsen's hand like a vice on my wrist.

Suddenly, I swell so hard it pulls a whimper from my throat. I can't help it.

Madsen, I. Me, I.

Madsen slides his other hand up my chest. He settles his palm on my heart.

The effect is unfamiliar.

Calming. The effect is calming.

"Your heart is pounding," he informs me. "Inhale. We have all night."

It's then I remember that Kennedy is in the room.

Guiltily, I turn to her.

She's never seen me kiss another man. I don't know if I've crossed a line.

But the look in her eyes isn't revulsion or disinterest. Instead, those brown eyes are sparkling with curiosity.

"We're going to need lube," she announces. "A lot of it."

"I have some in my room," Madsen says. Then he adds, almost sheepishly, "Never go anywhere without it. Be right back."

Madsen releases me. I take a step back, releasing him. I'm cold without the heat of his body as he brushes passed me and vanishes into his room.

Kennedy fills his spot. She slips her hands over my chest.

"How're you feeling?" she asks.

I grunt.

I'm devolving. Caveman.

She picks up my empty shot glass and wiggles it in front of me. "A little tipsy?"

"I'm fine." My inhibitions are 80 percent loosened, and my ability to stay alert is down to 60 percent.

"I'm going to need to catch up with you boys." She puts the shot glass to her lips and pushes her tongue inside of it, swirling around the small space, sucking up any residue.

Watching her tongue maneuver the curves of the shot glass is almost too much to bear. My cock goes steel hard to diamond. "*Fuck*," I hiss.

She puts her hand on my chest and guides me backward. "Sit, sir."

I don't exactly "sit." I stumble into the seat behind me. It's a miracle the legs hold.

Kennedy braces herself on my thighs. Her forehead touches mine. "You take care of me all the time, Jack," she says. Her warm breath beats against my lips. "My turn."

She sinks to her knees. She pulls at my belt, fights through my pants, and uncages me, releasing me from the confines of cotton and zipper.

She wraps her fingers around my swollen organ, and I melt. Then there's the softness of her plump lips. The wet warmth of her tongue.

I drop my head back and moan.

She is toe-curlingly good with her tongue.

My eyes fall shut, and I'm so lost in her that I don't notice when Madsen walks back into the room. Not until he steps behind my chair and runs his hand down the front of my body.

Instinctively, my brain thinks, *Invader*, and I snap my hand around his wrist.

"Just me, tough guy," he murmurs. Then he kisses my ear. Nibbles the lobe. Kennedy's tongue swirls around the tip of me. Madsen's hand is doing that chest-rub thing.

I'm about to embarrass myself and come before I've even had a chance to sink my cock into Kennedy's tight cunt.

I grip her hair. "That's enough, baby."

She pops me out from between her lips. It's cold outside of her mouth, and it takes everything in me not to shove her back down.

Her eyes are glittering when she rises.

"I want you inside of me," she says. Then her eyes flicker between me and Madsen. "*Both* of you."

19

KENNEDY

I've entered a dream.

No, a *wet* dream.

A twisted, perverted fantasy that has me soaking my panties.

I was scared at the Sanctuary. Frightened. Excited. Exhilarated. All of it. And now all of that emotion is channeling into one feeling...

I want to rip Jack's and Gabe's clothes off.

It doesn't help that watching them paw at each other is one of the most erotic things I've ever seen.

I've only ever known Jack the giant. Jack the tin man. But the way he melts under Gabe's touch...

This is something different. Something new. And I want so badly to explore it. Peel away the edges. Find this gentler, more compliant Jack underneath.

It's his eyes. Gabe leans over the back of Jack's chair. He's holding a bottle of lube in his hand. With his free hand, he rubs a palm down the front of Jack's shirt and creases the stiff material on his way back up.

"What do you say, Jack?" Gabe asks. "Should we give the lady what she wants?"

"Mmmhm" is Jack's response.

Gabe may not know this, but Jack letting you touch him is Jack's *enthusiastic consent*.

I've seen the man go feral anytime someone so much as accidentally brushes against him.

That he's letting Gabe manhandle him, kiss him...

That's *huge*, in Jack-speak.

I don't know if he's doing it for him, or for me, but it makes my heart double-skip in my chest.

Gabe steps around the chair and comes to me. He takes my face in his hands and tilts his forehead to mine. "Hi," he says.

"Hi." My voice pitches. I giggle.

Giggling? Squeaking? Who is this woman?

Gabe apparently turns Jack into an obedient soldier and me into a blushing schoolgirl.

"Have you ever had two men inside of you at once?" Gabe asks.

"No."

"Have you ever been fisted?"

"No."

Gabe makes a fist out of his hand and holds it up to show me.

"If you can take my fist, you can take our cocks. Let's start there, yes?"

He has large hands with big knuckles, and suddenly, I'm wondering what I just got myself into.

Wondering, and throbbing.

Gabe sets a bottle of lube on the kitchen table. Then he slips his hand to the hem of my shirt. "Can I take off your clothes?"

"Please."

Between the two of us, we make quick work of my clothes until I'm completely naked. Gabe guides me to sit in Jack's lap.

Jack's fingers grip my hips tightly. I hear what his touch is saying. *Mine.*

I tilt my head back and kiss the rough stubble underneath his jaw. I swivel my hips, grinding my bare ass against his cock. *Yes, yours.*

He growls pleasantly in my ear.

"Fuck, you two are beautiful." Gabe's voice drops low and rough, and the heat in his tone sends a shiver through me.

Gabe's lips are soft when they graze my breast. His mouth ghosts over my hardened nipple, making me arch upward. But as my body hunts for friction, he pulls away. This is on *his* time. He nuzzles at my belly, placing a soft trail of kisses downward. I'm quivering by the time he reaches the nest of hair between my thighs.

"You smell like heaven, Kennedy," he purrs. Then he presses his face to my sex, and his tongue slides between my nether lips.

I moan and grind against his face.

Jack reaches around me and grabs my breast. Unlike Gabe, he's not gentle or featherlight. He gives me the hard pinch I need, and I whimper, my thighs tightening around Gabe's head.

When Gabe lifts his head, his plump lips are glistening with me. He licks them clean. "I'm going to start inserting fingers inside of you," he tells me. "When I can fit my whole hand in you, then you get rewarded with our cocks. You think you can handle that?"

"Yes."

Gabe grabs the lube, rubs it around his hand, and then moves between my legs. "Alright. First finger..."

When he slides inside of me, I whimper with relief. He crooks his finger, stroking my inner walls, and it makes my toes curl.

"Oh God..."

"Good. Two."

I'm so wet it takes almost nothing for him to slip a second finger inside of me. I bite my lip and arch back against Jack's chest.

"You like the way he fingers you?" Jack asks.

"Yeah," I whine, "it feels so good, baby..."

"Give her another."

Gabe slips a third finger into me, and now I'm mewling.

"You're doing so good," Gabe tells me.

It's painful, but a warm pain. He coaxes my pleasure from me, his three fingers curling and thrusting. His thumb slips upward against my pussy and expertly finds my sensitive clit. He begins to rub it, slick, slow circles, and now I'm gyrating into his hand, moaning.

"Four," Gabe says.

When he presses this one inside, I nearly come.

"*Fuck*," I hiss. I'm stuck somewhere between unbearable pleasure and aching pain. I squirm, unable to decide if I want to escape Gabe's fingers or press deeper down on them.

"Do you want me to pull out?" Gabe asks.

"No," I gasp. "Please, no. Just...slow...give me a...a second..."

"Stop moving," Jack growls. His hands go tight on my hips.

His erection throbs and leaks against my ass. *Whoops.* In my thrashing, I must have pushed him straight to the edge.

"Sorry," I whimper. "I'm trying…"

But Gabe adjusts his fingers, and I can't stop myself from wiggling. Jack lets out a pained groan in my ear. His fingers go tight.

"*Breathe*," he chokes out, his breath hot on my neck.

I follow his command. I close my eyes. I take in a deep, long inhale.

My body relaxes. My muscles stop twitching. And just as I exhale, Gabe slips his final finger inside of me.

"Five."

"*Oh*," I moan.

I'm stretched deliciously wide.

"Is that good, baby?" Gabe asks.

"Uh-huh…"

I can't form words. My entire body clenches around Gabe's hand as he works it inside of me. He slowly wiggles his fingers, petting deep. When he twists his wrist, the ridges of his knuckles make my legs quiver.

Did I come? It's hard to tell. It feels as though every motion of his hand sends another wave of orgasmic pleasure through me.

"That's good," he murmurs after what might be minutes or years. "I think you're ready for us, angel. I'm going to pull out."

"No," I whine, "please."

Jack gives me a love bite underneath my ear. "You want me inside of you, don't you?"

My throat nearly closes with want. "Yes…"

Slowly, Gabe pries his entire hand out from between my legs. Once the ridges of his knuckles pop out of me, his fingers slide out easily. I whimper from the emptiness.

But I don't have to wait long. "Lift your hips," Jack says.

I almost can't—my legs are jelly—but I'm able to wiggle

myself up Jack's body enough for him to position his cock at my entrance. He pushes inside of me, and we both let out the same moan of relief.

He belongs here. He always has. He always will. My cunt responds to him, knows him, loves him.

Gabe gets naked. He has a swimmer's build, fit and lean. He squeezes lube into his palm and slathers his cock. When I see the length of him peek in and out from the circle of his hand, my mouth falls open. I see why he wanted to prepare me first.

Both of these men are well-endowed. And it's going to take a lot of lube and a quiet prayer to make this work.

As if he can sense my thoughts, Gabe asks, "Are you sure you want this?"

"Yes. More than anything. Please."

Gabe fits himself between my legs. He holds my thigh around his hip and guides himself in and—

I gasp.

I'm unbearably full. Gabe pushes slowly inside of me, letting me adjust, but I'm so tight around *both* of them.

"That's it," Gabe murmurs, his voice low and hazy, "Oh God...that's good...you're taking our cocks like such a good girl..."

"Don't stop," I whine. "More. All of you."

The stretch is wonderful. The stretch is bliss. I'm smothered in them. Sandwiched between these two strong, powerful men. Lube and my own arousal drips down my thighs and onto the chair. Jack's breath is hot on my throat, and Gabe's cinnamon-and-smoke scent lingers in my nose, and I want to drown in them. The pull-and-push sensation of the both of them fucking me simultaneously sends a rush of heat through me. I cling to Gabe's bare chest, and I'm clinging so tightly I think I draw blood, but *I don't care.*

Nothing matters once they start moving inside of me, Gabe's low, slow thrusts, and the pleasure is so intense it blinds me.

"Please," I beg, "please, please, *please*."

I don't even know what I'm asking for at this point. Please stop? Please don't stop? Harder? Faster? All I know is that I'm greedy for it, and I want everything they have to give me.

Jack's fingers wrap around my throat. He growls in my ear, "You're so close."

I gasp. "Yes, sir."

"Come for us, Kennedy."

I hit it—the pinnacle of pleasure—and I cry out as my body throbs and pulses around them. Gabe groans, and Jack's breath shudders in my ear, and I'm clinging to them. I wrap my arms around Gabe's neck and hug him close. Jack winds his arms tightly around my middle. My heart hammers in my chest. I can feel Jack's, too, his heartbeat pounding against my back. My head is spinning. I'm sore and drenched in pleasure. But it's more than that.

I feel *safe*.

Maybe for the first time since we left Atlanta, I feel completely protected and safe. I'm safe in their arms.

Which is why I break.

"Hey." Gabe takes my face in his hand and swipes his thumb over my cheek. "Are you okay? Do you hurt?"

That's when I realize I'm crying.

"No...I mean, yes...I don't..."

"I'm going to pull out of you."

They shift together to empty me.

I feel like I've been cleaved in two by these giant, protective men.

And now everything comes spilling out.

"I'm supposed to be in law school," I sniff. "I'm supposed to be studying for exams."

Jack draws my hair behind my ear. Quietly, he kisses my throat.

"Instead, I'm getting chased by gunmen and hiding out in some safe house and...and uncovering some government fucking conspiracy in an overpriced strip club..."

"Are you okay?" Gabe asks again. But this time, the question makes me choke on a sob.

"I'm scared," I admit, "I'm so fucking scared..."

Jack holds me from behind, and Gabe covers me from the front, and I cry in the middle, cradled in their arms.

20

GABE

It's like a switch flips in Kennedy.

One minute, I'm having the hottest threesome of my life, buried inside Kennedy's sweet warmth with Jack's steel heat rubbing up against mine.

Then next, Kennedy is crying—a soft, kitten-like thing in our arms.

Sex—especially intense sex like that—can really break a person open. It's as though the reality of our situation suddenly caught up with her.

Good news? I love aftercare.

It heals something inside of me to heal other people.

Besides, I made a promise to Jack:

From now until dawn, it's my duty to take care of Kennedy.

I catch Jack's eyes from over Kennedy's shoulder, and those browns that were smoldering with heat are now glazed with concern. With a single look, we make some silent, telepathic agreement.

I help Kennedy into Jack's arms. I follow them as he carries her upstairs and into the bathroom. We strip off any clothes that managed to hang on, and I get the shower hot before the three of us step in.

Kennedy has stopped sobbing now, but she sniffles as we take care of her. We lather her in soap. Rinse her off. Jack massages her scalp with shampoo. I clean off the lube and come that sticks to her thighs and between her legs. Kennedy compliantly lifts her arms so I can wash her armpits. I don't miss a spot. I place small worship-kisses over her clean skin. Kennedy's eyes fall closed, and she sighs deeply, slipping into some beautiful sub-space as we cherish her.

The shower steams, and the walls are thick with condensation by the time we're finished. I do a quick and dirty rinse-off of myself before killing the water. I grab a towel, and Jack and I pat Kennedy dry before we cocoon her in it. There are only two towels up here, so we swap the second towel between us before carrying her off to bed.

The bed is narrow, and the three of us still have to cuddle up to fit in it. Kennedy lies with her head on Jack's chest. I get diagonal and use Kennedy's hip as a pillow, twisting my legs up with Jack's. We make a sexy, naked triangle.

I'm dully aware that, downstairs, Clucky has the whole bed to herself while the three of us are stuffing into a single mattress. Spoiled bird.

"What's the 411 on smoking in bed?" I ask. I badly need a post-fuck cigarette.

"Knock yourself out," Kennedy responds.

I have to remove myself to get my cigarettes, but I light one and quickly snuggle back in. The first drag burns so good. I'm lazy and warm; I came so hard, my muscles are tight and sore and spent. Kennedy's fingers rake through my wet mane of hair, and the scratch of her long nails on my scalp nearly makes my toes curl.

"Do you want to talk about it?" I ask.

"About what?" Kennedy replies.

"Any of it. Your first double penetration. Jack's first gay moment."

Jack grunts. "Who says it's my first?"

Well. Color me surprised. Here I was, thinking he was straighter than a ruler. I should know better than to judge books by their covers.

Apparently, I'm not the only one who is surprised because Kennedy asks, "Have something you want to share with the class?"

Jack closes his eyes. "You two talk everything to death."

"Talking is the highest form of intimacy," I argue.

"So is silence."

For once, I shut my mouth and let us live in the quiet for a minute. Jack isn't wrong. It does feel nice just to exist with these two. I savor their warm bodies. Their effortless intimacy.

This feels so *easy*. Natural. As though we've been doing this forever.

I smoke and glance up at them. Jack has his eyes closed, but I don't think he's asleep. I didn't get a good look at his body before. I admire it now. He has a classic soldier's physique; he's all muscle and scars. Crisscrossed ridges from blades and shrapnel tattooed over his body. A light smattering of dark chest hair that trickles down his middle. A monster cock asleep on his thigh.

Kennedy looks like an angel with her head on his heart. Her eyes are red from crying, but she looks relaxed now, her skin blushed from the shower's heat. As if she can sense me staring at her, her brown eyes meet mine. She gives my hair a light tug before untangling her grip from it.

"What's this?" She dances her fingers down my chest and catches my necklace under her nail.

I lift my hand to slip it off and hand it over to her so she can examine it. It's a thin, gold necklace. A pendant hangs from it, a curling piece of metal.

I inhale smoke. "It's Arabic. It means *love.*"

"It's beautiful."

My cigarette has a long tail. "Anyone have an ashtray?"

Jack cups his palm and holds it out for me. He lets me shake it out into his hand.

And they say gentlemen are a dying breed.

"I take it back," I say. "*This* is the gayest thing that's happened tonight."

Kennedy sucks in her lips. "I had a thought."

"I love thoughts."

"My parents have a place. In North Carolina. We could stay with them and check out Aldous Caine."

Even after sex and a cry-fest, Kennedy's brain is still working. She is, truly, the smartest person in this room. *That's my girl,* I almost say, but she's not my girl, and Jack might choke me if I try to claim her.

Then again, I might like that, too.

"That'd be nice." I move my hand to her thigh, rubbing. "Old people love me."

"We'll make a plan in the morning," Jack mumbles. His eyes are closed again. He's fading fast. Come-and-done.

I squeeze Kennedy's leg. "You two get cozy. I'll be right back."

"Don't be long." Kennedy yawns. "I need warmth."

The sex was mind-blowing. But the thought of cuddling

up with the two of them all night makes my heart double-beat in my chest.

I slip into the bathroom and close the door behind me.

I didn't grow up religious—my parents were agnostic intellectuals from the hippie peace-and-love generation. Even now, I can't say I exactly ascribe to *one* religion. I see beauty in God, Yahweh, and Allah. But somewhere around my first tour in Iraq, I picked up the habit of praying every night.

It's a private experience and something I'm not ready to share with the two lovebugs in bed just yet.

I stub my cigarette out against the sink bowl and flick on the water to drown the embers. Then I get on my knees on the worn-out bath rug, rest my elbows on the edge of the tub, and clasp my hands together, bowing my head.

I touch the necklace that hangs from my throat.

The last person who wore it was Omar.

We were lying in bed the morning after. Smoking together. I touched the piece along his throat.

"What does it mean?"

"*Love*," he said.

"Pretty."

He sat up and took it off his neck. Then he held it out to me. "You wear it."

I balked. "I'm not taking it from you."

"Why not?"

"I'm a soldier. Love isn't in the cards for me. You got one that says *death*?"

"We aren't a compilation of our worst sins. Our hearts our measured by our intentions." He looked at me, those dark eyes endless. "I've seen you. You kill, but you don't enjoy killing. You do it because you love. You love your country. You love your fellow man. You're a lover, not a killer."

He held the necklace out again to me. "Take it. Don't make me beg." A smile quirked the edge of his mouth. "Again."

This time, I took it. I snapped the gold chain around my throat.

A lover. His words hit deep.

I've tried to be a lover ever since.

I rub my thumb over the metal, close my eyes, and exhale.

"Are you there, God? It's me again, your idiot son. I don't know what I did to deserve this, but thank you for the amazing sex. And these two beautiful humans. Like, seriously, they might be your hottest creations, so. Well done, you. Please take care of them. And, if the three of us bang again, well. I might just actually go to church. Okay. That's it. Forever and ever, amen."

Yeah. Dope prayer.

I squeeze my palms together, then unlace my fingers. With that, I go back to bed and climb under the covers with Kennedy and Jack.

21

KENNEDY

I went to sleep blissfully squished between two strong, loving men.

But when I wake up, I'm alone in the middle of the bed.

There's no sign of Gabe. I can hear Jack brushing his teeth in the bathroom.

I laze around in bed. I'm completely naked. I slip my hand down my body and between my thighs. I'm still in one piece, but my cunt feels wonderfully sore and stretched from taking both of them last night.

It was a rush, and I want to feel that way again.

I hear Jack spit, and I pull my hand back over the covers before he steps back into the bedroom. Grey sweatpants hang low on his hips. He's trimmed up his beard to a clean, sharp line along his jaw.

"You're nice to wake up to," I tell him.

"Good morning," he says. But there's something off in his voice. I can hear it.

I sit up immediately, holding the blanket over my chest for the warmth. "What's wrong?"

Immediately, my brain goes: *Last night was too much for him. Too weird. Too kinky. You've finally scared him away with your crazy.*

Jack sits down beside me on the edge of the bed.

"Last night. You cried. A lot."

"You say it like it's a bad thing."

His lips thin.

To Jack, emotions are a hole in a boat. They need to be plugged, or we'll all drown.

I feel the reflexive, knee-jerk kick of anger, but then I realize—

I don't let Jack see me cry. Not really.

He protects me from guns, violent men, and secret mercenary groups.

I protect him from my tears.

Jack is the kind of guy who, if an onion made me cry, would make it his life's mission to salt and burn every onion crop. Last time, I let myself be vulnerable around him. It has to be a shock.

"I wanted it," I reassure him. "I wanted Gabe. I like who we are with him."

Jack's expression softens a little.

I take his hand and give it a squeeze. He can be so damn stubborn—but I *need* him to hear me.

"Last night was real." My voice is firm when I say it. "It was real to me."

The color in his eyes shifts.

"Take a knee," he says. We go into our position, our safe space. Both of us shift to the floor, each on a knee across from the other. The energy shifts between us. Jack cups my face, and I feel small in his large hand suddenly, and safe. Those dark eyes look directly into mine. His voice is quieter, like two kids whispering under the blankets on a sleepover.

I take his hand. I squeeze it. "How do you feel about last night? Really."

I can see him rolling his words around on his tongue. "I enjoyed it."

"It didn't feel like it did with Candy."

"No," he admits. "It didn't."

"With Gabe, there's...*more*."

Silence.

"I want more. And I think you do, too."

More silence.

"*Jack*."

"I'm listening."

"Well, stop listening and start *talking*. I feel like I'm going crazy here."

He swallows, and his Adam's apple bobs like he's unplugged something in his throat. His eyes dart away from me, then back again.

Pulling emotion out of Jack isn't like pulling teeth.

It's like disconnecting his fucking *jawbone*.

"What do you want me to say?" he asks, and that question—*I hate that fucking question.*

Frustration pricks the backs of my eyes, and my vision blurs and burns.

"Tell me it's okay to want more. Or tell me it's not okay, and I'll stop. I mean, I don't know how I'll stop because, to be honest, all my emotions just feel so big right now, but if that's what you want...goddammit, Jack, I want to do this together or not at all—"

He takes the back of my head, pulls me in, and kisses my forehead. His kiss is like putting my feet on solid ground after being at sea for a year. I choke on a whimper and can't hold back tears now.

"It's okay," he says. His breath is warm and brushes against my bangs.

But my anxiety still batters inside my chest as though someone is smashing a beehive with a hammer.

Please, Jack! Please say the thing that'll set me free—

"It's okay," he repeats. "I want more, too."

I nearly sob with relief.

"Thank you," I whisper. I let my head tumble against his chest. I ball my fingers into his shirt and feel the hard, muscled chest underneath.

Jack is impenetrable. Jack is a tank.

But today, Jack cracked open. Just a little bit.

Just for me.

And I've never, ever felt closer to him.

22

GABE

It's time to clear out.

That's the intel I'm given when I return to the bedroom with three cups of coffee, feeling like a hero.

But, nope. No time to snuggle in bed, sip our coffee, and maybe go for round two or three.

Instead, Jack is pulling down bags and shoving what little we own into them. He instructs me to do the same.

Gone is sweet, puppy-eyed Jack from last night. Now, we're back to all-business-no-play Jack.

I shoot Kip a quick message to let him know we're ghosting. I don't want him thinking that we've been found and buried. I don't really think anything of it until I leave to pack the car and see Kip standing outside.

"To what do I owe this pleasure?" I ask as I step off the porch.

Kip pats the hood of a purple Dodge Charger. "A parting gift."

"Jesus, Kip. Don't make me get on my knees and blow you."

"Couldn't have you guys riding around with the window blown out."

I wrap my arms tight around him. He squeezes back.

I don't have a lot of friends.

I can't tell him how much it means to have this one.

"Do you like chickens?" I ask him.

"For eating? Or...?"

"*Or.*" As if on cue, Clucky exits the house, starts down the porch, and falls down all three steps. She rights herself, flutters her feathers, and stabs at the ground with her beak.

I pat Kip on the shoulder. "I wouldn't trust her with anyone else."

"Gee," he says dryly. "Thanks. Any other annoying requests?"

"Yeah. Stay safe."

"I'd say *you too*, but I know it'll fall on deaf ears." We break apart. As he hands over the keys, he adds, "Gabe?"

"Yeah, buddy?"

"Give them hell."

23

JACK

North Carolina is a seven-hour drive.

It feels like twenty hours when you take into account the show tunes that Madsen and Kennedy sing karaoke-style nearly the whole way there.

She's Mimi, he's Roger.

She's Maria, he's Tony.

She's Eliza Schuyler, I want to die.

The Charger drives like a dream down the interstate, at least.

God bless Kip.

Somewhere between *The Sound of Music* and *Jacques Brel Is Alive and Well and Living in Paris*, Madsen actually decides to do some homework.

"Aldous Caine," he reads as he scrolls through his phone. "From North Carolina. Squeaky-clean record. Ex-wife. No kids. Owns a boat. What's the W.S. Historical Society?"

"So...Winston-Salem is sort of *steeped* in tradition," Kennedy explains. "We have a lot of recreations of the pilgrim times. It's like stepping into another world. The

Historical Society leans on that...they believe the old ways are better. That sort of thing."

"Yeah, you're not about to catch me churning butter," Madsen says.

I snort a laugh at the image.

Then Madsen shouts, and I nearly jerk the car off the road.

"Holy *shit!*" Madsen exclaims. "He's wearing a *bonnet!*"

He's climbed in the back seat with Kennedy, but he leans over the divide to shove his phone in my face. I glance away from the road just to see what he's talking about.

There's Aldous Caine. An older man with red cheeks, like a little boy. Sure enough, he's in a group photo with everyone dressed up in old-world garb, looking like they just got off the *Mayflower*.

"The man who wants me dead wears a bonnet," Madsen says.

"You sound disappointed."

"I *am*. He should at least try to be terrifying." Madsen flops back into his seat with a huff. "How am I going to kill a man who is wearing a bonnet?"

"We're not trying to kill him," Kennedy says, swiveling her head between me and Madsen. "Right?"

"Right," Madsen and I reply in unison. Maybe too quickly.

We're also not, *not* trying to kill him.

I flex my fingers around the steering wheel at the thought.

Madsen smartly changes the conversation. "What do I need to know about your parents?"

"What do you mean?"

"I mean, what are they like? I've never *met the parents*, so to speak."

"*Never*?" Kennedy gawks.

"To be fair, I've also never dated anyone longer than a month..."

"But you have met *people*," I say.

"Sure. But parents are a different breed."

"Okay, well..." Kennedy drags out her words. "Um..."

I glance in the rearview mirror. Kennedy has buttoned her bottom lip between her teeth. She stares vacantly out the window.

"Well," she says, "they're mostly your typical, rich suburban parents, I guess. Daddy's a history professor. Mom is a psychologist. They're judgmental and unforgiving, but they'll be friendly to your face."

"That's...actually a great overview. I can work with that."

Kennedy keeps looking out the window, though.

She has a complicated relationship with her parents. She always has. She doesn't talk about it often, and I don't push her, but I can tell it's weighing on her as we inch closer to the state line.

"We can always book a hotel," I tell her.

Kennedy's eyes catch mine in the mirror. The worry in her eyes vanishes as she softens with a smile.

"Don't be silly," she says.

She reaches over the seat and rubs my shoulder.

I can handle it, she's saying.

I squeeze her hand.

I'm here for you, I reply.

She leans back and snuggles up next to Madsen again. She rests her head on his shoulder and closes her eyes.

They look good together.

Really good.

Unbidden memories of last night trickle through my brain.

Madsen's head between Kennedy's legs.

Kennedy whimpering in my lap.

Kennedy's hair tickling my bare chest.

The dark heat in Madsen's eyes when his gaze connected with mine.

I'm gripping the wheel. Tight.

I unlock my knuckles. I reach for the energy drink in the center console instead and knock back a swig.

I need to distract myself before I pop a boner on the road.

"We should establish ground rules," I say.

"Ground rules?" Kennedy echoes.

"For the three of us."

I've opened a can of worms, and for a second, there's a moment of silence in the car.

"I think that's a great idea," Madsen says finally. He puts a little space between him and Kennedy, as if he can feel my stare. "I, for one, very much enjoyed last night. I wouldn't mind if it happened again."

"I loved it." Kennedy grins.

"But I know the two of you have your own relationship," Madsen continues. "So...am I allowed alone time with each of you as well?"

His eyes connect with mine in the rearview mirror when he asks the question.

I catch the low sweep of those eyelashes. The promise in the slight upward turn of his mouth.

I grip the steering wheel tighter.

Kennedy looks between the two of us. "I'm fine if the two of you fool around without me," she says. "That's kind of hot, actually. Jack?"

I chew on my words.

I'm picturing it. Madsen and Kennedy.

"I don't know," I say.

"Okay," Madsen says. "We'll take it slow."

"While we're...saying stuff." Kennedy cringes. "We kissed once before."

"What?"

"It was...while we were shopping. When we saw the two men following us. It was just to avoid attention. It wasn't... like that."

"If it wasn't *like that*, why wait until now to tell me?"

"You would've lost your shit."

"I'd never hurt you."

"No, but you would've hurt *him*. And don't you think it's fucked-up that I have to factor that in?"

I grind my teeth. I'm close to hurting him now.

"Jack." She leans forward. I'm surprised to see her eyes are wet. "Please," she begs. "Don't make this weird. Not after...everything."

She's just had sex with two men. She's vulnerable, and I'm making her feel like shit for no reason. No. For *a* reason. Because I want to kiss him in a mall. I want to shove him against a wall and press my tongue into his mouth. And I'm taking it out on her.

Whatever is going on inside of me—this weird, confusing *newness*—I can't punish Kennedy for it. I soften. "I'm not mad at you. I promise. It doesn't matter. You can kiss him."

Kennedy knits her eyebrows. She doesn't look convinced. "Really?"

"Really."

"So it doesn't bother you if I...do this...?"

My gaze flickers from the road to the mirror. Kennedy pushes Madsen's hair back. I watch as she brushes her lips lightly against his. His hand finds that lovely dip above her hip. The pink of her tongue slips against his in a way that I know is fucking divine.

When they play together, it's not jealousy whipping through my veins.

It's something else.

I like watching him enjoy it. I like watching her enjoy him. It makes my blood rush south so fast I get light-headed.

God fucking dammit. She loves to play with fire.

He moans, and my cock rages against my zipper.

"Stop," I say. My voice comes out in a rasp.

Kennedy pulls away. She looks at me. "Why? Does it make you jealous?"

"No. Because if you keep going, I'm going to pull this car over and fuck you both."

The words come tumbling out before I can stop them.

Kennedy smiles.

Madsen, for once, is quiet. He adjusts himself.

The tension in this car is suddenly way too thick.

"Someone DJ." Kennedy's phone is hooked up to the dashboard and resting on the centerboard. I toss it back into Madsen's lap, and he catches it before it nails him between the legs. "No more show tunes."

24

KENNEDY

As the Dodge Charger growls like a modern monster through the streets of sleepy Old Salem, I think to myself, *Why did I hate it here?*

There's beauty in everything. The North Carolina maples boast bursts of orange, red, and yellow leaves. Gurgling rivers and streams. The tall, classical stone houses reminiscent of the 1700s. This is a state steeped in history, and they hold on to every nugget of it.

"Am I sleep deprived, or did we just step through a time machine?" Gabe asks.

We've been sleeping on and off on each other. He's warm, and I feel impossibly safe with my head on his shoulder.

I lift up to look out the window. The Charger bounces down the cobblestone streets. We pass an alehouse with a smoking chimney, a quaint restaurant, and a paper goods store called *Ink & Quill*. A woman walks down the street in an ankle-length frock, her hood pulled over her head to keep her warm.

"This is Old Salem," I tell him. "It's sort of a...museum

town. It's supposed to look like the old Moravian communities that settled here."

Something in my chest lifts at the sight. I used to walk through these streets as a little girl, thrilled by the old-world magic of it all.

But then I remember:

Old-world magic comes with an old-world price.

My hometown, Cobblersville, is only twenty minutes out. They didn't only honor the traditional ways. They also *practiced* them. I never had to churn my own butter, exactly, but I had certain expectations. There was a pattern. My twin sister followed it. She married her high school boyfriend, bought a house on the same street as our parents, and popped out two babies before she hit thirty.

So did everyone I went to high school with. You were born in Cobblersville, you died in Cobblersville. That was the Cobblersville Curse.

If I didn't get out, I'd be cursed, too. So I burned down my life, hopped on my broomstick, and flew to Atlanta.

I have to steel myself to meet with my parents. They're nice people—really. Polite. Reserved. But they're terrible liars. Every time their eyes meet mine, I see the same thing:

Welcome home, family disappointment.

I love them. And they love me. I just don't think they *like* me very much. They don't approve of my life choices, and that's limited my interactions with them over the years.

I unbuckle my seat belt so I can curl myself around the back of Jack's seat. I wrap my arms around his seat, settling my palms on his chest, and rest my chin on his headrest.

"Want me to drive?" I ask.

"No. We're almost there."

He's wearing a red button-up with floral pops of white flowers and green tropical plants. I like this new look on him. I slip my hand through the open buttons at the top and run my fingers over his curly chest hair. My thumb rolls over his nipple, playing with the nub.

"Stop that," Jack grunts.

"Stop what?" I ask innocently.

"Don't fuck with the driver."

"Am I distracting you?"

I play with him, teasing my nail over the tight skin.

Jack takes my wrist and pulls my hand out of his shirt. He kisses my palm, then gently bites the soft flesh underneath my thumb before kissing that, too.

It's a warning bite, but his wet tongue and sharp teeth trigger a tight pulse in my core.

It gets me out of my head, at least, which was the goal.

I unwind from Jack to let him drive the last leg of the journey. I relax my bones against Gabe instead. He pulls me into his lap. I reach behind and cup his jaw. He mirrors Jack's action, using his thumb to splay out my hand, and then sweetly kisses the inside of my palm.

Who knew my hand would be such an erogenous zone? I'm buzzing all over.

"We should probably get our story straight," Gabe murmurs. His breath is hot on my fingers.

"What story?"

"I mean...how do you want to introduce me to your parents? A friend? Coworker? Co-lover?"

Co-lover. That one makes me smile.

My parents would blow a *gasket.*

"How about...you and Jack know each other from your military days." I glance at Jack in the rearview mirror. "Does that work?"

Jack nods. "Works for me."

The Charger chugs at the stoplight, ruining the antiquated aesthetic.

While it stalls, reality settles into my bones.

I'm taking my boyfriends to meet my parents. This is a *big deal*.

But there's A Thing. The Something I'm Not Telling Them that's currently itching away at my skin. The closer we get to my old childhood home, the harder it claws at the inside of my throat, begging to be let out.

"Oh," I say casually, scratching at my inner arm. "By the way. I used to be engaged to Aldous Caine's son."

Jack hits the brakes so hard the seat belt clotheslines my tits.

25

KENNEDY

Okay, so.

The story.

Before I was a stripper, and a law student, and Jack's girlfriend, I was a Southern beauty queen Barbie Doll. A pageant princess. The princess of Cobblersville.

So it only made sense that I hooked up with Langston Caine, the prince of Cobblersville. With his Irish skin, thick black eyebrows, and old-school Clark Gable mustache, it felt like a fairy tale in the flesh.

And it sort of was. Except it was more of a Grimm's Fairy Tale.

I moved into their mansion, and after that, my entire job was to be Langston's arm candy. We went to fundraisers and political events, and I was dolled up to high heaven.

Except Langston—surprise, surprise—turned out to be a controlling asshole. We looked like the perfect couple on the outside, but inside, I was falling apart.

It changed the night of the Gustav Klimt reveal.

Langston's father had purchased a priceless Klimt painting (which, all things considered, now I'm wondering about the legitimacy of that transaction, too). He'd decided to immortalize his fresh catch by hosting a party at his estate that featured the most respectable families in North Carolina, a full live orchestra to accompany the painting's reveal, and a trained monkey.

To this day, I'm not sure what the monkey was about.

The party was about to start, and I was in the dressing room, poured into a swooping, white dress and fitting on a pair of gold earrings.

I saw Langston's approach in my vanity mirror. He didn't announce himself. He just did that door-lean thing that guys do when they're trying to seduce you or they're drunk.

He was definitely drunk.

The glass hanging from his fingertips had barely a swallow left, and Langston couldn't hold his whiskey. It made him sharp, stubborn, and mean.

"You're pulling out all the stops," he said, his drooping gaze trained on my earrings.

I fixed him a smile in the mirror. "Is it a Klimt night if you're not head to toe in gold? Anyway. I have to. It'll be my last appearance of the summer."

The air tightened. I looked away from him, hunting through my jewelry chest to pick out a matching bracelet.

Langston invaded my space. He stepped beside me and leaned his weight against the vanity, upending a perfume bottle.

"You're not *really* still thinking about going to law school in the fall."

"Correct. I'm not thinking about it. I'm *doing* it."

I kept my voice light but sharp. I did *not* want to get into this right before the party. But Langston wouldn't let up. He put his glass on my table and scooped my face in his hand. His thumb pushed roughly against my cheek.

"Poor Kennedy. You'll work yourself to death. You don't want to damage that pretty face with wrinkles."

I gasped with faux shock. "If you think wrinkles are bad, you're going to have a heart attack when I get grey hairs."

I was aiming for coy, but I missed my target. His mouth twisted into a sour frown. "Don't be cute with me."

He used his body to wedge me against the vanity. I shrank backward, trying to get away, but he grabbed my wrist and held it like a cuff.

"Langston. You're hurting me."

"If you leave, do you understand what you're giving up? These earrings aren't yours." His fingers snapped off my earring so fast that, for a second, my heart leapt into my throat, thinking he'd torn the lobe.

He *did* tear the dress, though. He ripped the sleeve off my shoulder, adding, "This dress isn't yours."

The pounding of my heart punched the air out of my lungs. "Langston. *Stop.*"

His final warning. But he didn't stop.

Instead, he grabbed me by the hair—and I hated myself, right in that moment, because even as he snarled at me, smelling like whiskey, all I could think about was the *literal hours* it'd taken to twist my hair into perfect, Caine-approved ringlets.

I'd turned into a ghost of myself, and I didn't recognize this woman.

He pressed himself against me, and I could feel the hardness of him on my hip, informing me of what he wanted (sex) and when he wanted it (now).

What I wanted didn't matter. Not in Caine's world.

"You're my prize," Langston growled, the heat of his breath tattooing his words on my cheek. "And you'll bend to me."

So I bit his precious, pretty-boy face. I bit until I tasted metal. He shouted and released me. The second his fingers unlocked, I ran. Half-naked. Blood on my lips. Screaming. I ran like a madwoman through a crowd of rich, bored socialites.

You know—and I bet you'll *never* believe this—but the funny thing about a woman who cries sexual assault on her ridiculously wealthy fiancé?

He always walks away scot-free.

Meanwhile, everyone paints her as some spoiled woman who had to be absolutely insane to leave such a handsome, well-spoken, well-dressed man.

I escaped to Atlanta, cut all ties with Cobblersville, and never looked back.

Until now, I guess.

And, well.

Now you know everything.

26

KENNEDY

The car glugs in the resounding silence.

Jack says nothing. We're parked on the side of the road. I let my legs hang out the side door, and Jack sits on the ground in front of me.

He stares at nothing. His silence sends my nerves on end.

I dig my fingers through his hair and tug at the roots. "Hey. What are you thinking?"

He doesn't look at me, and my heart wrenches. "Why didn't you tell me?"

"Because I'm not my past," I tell him pointedly. "Just like you're not yours. I was an outcast. Everyone was ashamed of me. I wanted to shed all of it. And I did, with you. You saved me."

Gabe stands a polite couple of feet from us as he smokes. He gestures toward me with the burning tip. "The way I see it, we're all orphans."

I hug my arms around Jack's shoulders. "This is the only fucked-up little family I need. You're my home."

Jack's hand slips up my arm. He squeezes my wrist. "You're mine."

His eyes are dark. Predatory. Possessive.

Want pulls at me, heat whipping through the center of my body, all the way to the soles of my feet. I kiss the back of his head and plead, "Say it again."

This time, he climbs to a half hunch. He positions himself so his hands brace on the seat on either side of my hips. He looks directly into my eyes now as he says firmly, "You. Are. Mine."

Then, before I can respond, he grabs my hips and lifts me. The air leaves my lungs as I'm suddenly hoisted in the air. Jack throws me over his shoulder, his arm wrapped around my ass.

"Madsen," he orders, "get the rope from the trunk and follow me."

"Copy that."

The...*rope*?

My body bounces helplessly as he carries me away from the car and into the woods. Dry leaves crunch under his boots. I'm not sure how far he carries me before he comes to a stop. He shifts and gently lowers me back to the ground.

I blink. We're in the middle of the woods.

Jack puts his fingertips to my chest. He presses in, and I step back, hitting the thick trunk of a tree behind me.

"Up against the tree," Jack says. "Take off your underwear."

"Here?"

Jack cups my face in his big hand. He pushes his thumb against my mouth, damaging my bottom lip. "You need a reminder of who you belong to."

I shiver. "Yes, sir," I say as I reach down and pull my panties down from my legs, kicking them from my ankles.

Jack takes my panties from me. He shoves them into his back pocket, and they hang out like a flag.

"Now your dress," he says.

I swallow. Hard. My sensible brain is telling me it's insane to get naked in the middle of the woods, in the middle of the day, beside the highway where anyone could walk up on us.

But my body...*wants to lean into the insanity.*

I take off my dress and let it drop. My nipples are hard pebbles on my chest, tight with excitement and the fall chill.

But it's hard to feel the cold when all I can feel is this intense, hungry heat burning in my core.

The predatory look in Jack's eyes makes me throb.

Gabe has patiently recoiled a thin rope into loops.

"Madsen," he says, and that's apparently all he needs to say.

"I'm on it."

Gabe steps closer to me. He takes one end of the rope and quickly ties a knot in it, making a loop.

"Give me your hands," he says.

I obey, lifting my arms.

He traps my wrist in the loop and then tightens it, securing it. Then he pulls the rope around the trunk of the tree. He ties off my other arm with the opposite end of the rope, making it taut. My arms strain backward, successfully pinning me in place.

Gabe steps in front of me. His eyes sparkle as he admires his work, that mischievous smirk I've grown to love playing on his lips.

"Do you two have a safe word?" he asks.

Jack and I exchange a look. "Not really," I say.

"You do now. If you want us to stop, say *Chicken*. Got it?"

I can't help but grin. "Yeah, got it."

"Good." He takes a drag of his cigarette, thinking. Then he says, "Almost perfect. Needs one more thing."

Then he takes my panties from Jack. He steps over to me, cigarette between his gritted teeth.

"See you later," he tells me. The last thing I see is Gabe shooting me a wink before he covers my eyes with my own panties. He attaches the fabric to my ears, securing the humiliating blindfold in place.

Holy shit. What've I gotten myself into?

I'm naked. Blind. Tried to a tree. And completely at their mercy.

It makes me ache.

"Well, well, well." Gabe blows smoke in my face. It tickles my ears. "Looks like we've caught a wild Furhman girl. What should we do with her first? Fuck her? Make her beg? Brand her?"

There's a new heat at my thigh. I recognize it as the tip of his cigarette. He drags it so close to my skin that, if I hadn't just shaved, I'm certain the hair there would be singed. I choke as the little tip of heat climbs a slow trail up my inner thigh. It glows near my bare, vulnerable pussy. I force my muscles so, so still to avoid getting burned.

He flicks his cigarette. Ash tickles as it tumbles down my leg.

I'm shaking. My cunt is weeping.

They're claiming me with cruelty, and I'm getting off on it.

"Eat her," Jack says. "Tell me how she tastes."

"You heard him. Spread your legs, baby."

I do. I spread them wide. Gabe doesn't tease me anymore. His fingers push roughly against my slit. I'm so wet they slide.

"Fuck, she's soaking." His voice is a hoarse growl. "Our little captive is getting off on this."

Our little captive. I shiver and mewl, pushing my hips forward into his hand. Wanting more friction.

But Gabe pulls his hand away. "See that?" he says to Jack. "She's dripping down my fingers. Naughty girl."

He slaps me suddenly between the thighs. I choke on my breath. The sting sends such a whip of pleasure through me I wonder if I've come already.

My face goes hot, and I know I must be bright red. *Oh God.*

I hear Gabe drop to his knees. When his mouth finds me, I almost weep with relief. His tongue works me, licking at my arousal.

"Fuck," he mumbles, and I feel a hot puff of breath against my sensitive skin. "She tastes like honey."

When he pushes his tongue deep inside me, I shout. I raise up to my tippy-toes as my orgasm crashes around his tongue. He sucks and licks, fucking me with his tongue, and I'm helpless to do anything but ride his face.

When Gabe pulls back, I'm panting.

"All yours, brother." I hear the slap of palm on chest. "Warmed her up good for you."

I don't get a second to rest. Jack is between my thighs next, his rough tongue sucking and licking at my clit.

It takes him no time at all to pull a second orgasm from me. I'm dizzy with it.

When I hear the claws of his zipper hissing, I almost moan.

"Yes," I whimper. "Please. I need you inside of me."

Jack fucks me with abandon. When Jack rails me, I lose all sense of time and place. I can't remember who I am. I can't remember my name. All I know is that I'm *his*. My cunt is so wonderfully sore as he slams his hips over and over, and I hear myself shouting.

The third orgasm hurts, but I can't stop myself from going over the edge.

He groans and curses in my ear, and I get the feeling he didn't want to finish, but he can't help it, not now, now that I'm pulsing so hard around him. His hardness bursts inside of me, filling me. I whimper as his thick heat pulses, and he pants heavily in my ear.

"You're mine," he says again, and when he says it in that low-throated growl, crushing my body between his and the trunk, his hot need dripping between my thighs, I swoon.

He pulls out of me, but I'm not empty for long. Gabe fills the space, pressing his length against my body.

His fingers pull through my hair, and I'm so blissed-out it feels like he's muddling my brain. "Come on, baby," he coos, amping me up like I'm about to hit the final lap in a marathon. "One more for us."

My whole body is tight and raw and aching. The thought of orgasming again sends a ripple of actual fear through me. "I can't," I whine.

"*Chicken*?" Gabe asks.

Is it? Have I had enough?

No.

Because the truth is—*I need Gabe inside of me.*

Even against two of the hardest, strongest, toughest military men alive...I won't break.

I shake my head. Gabe purrs, "Good girl."

When he enters me, I shout, and tears of pleasure burn my eyes, wetting my panties. Gabe is smooth, graceful, and each thrust sends a sweet wave of pleasure through me.

His fingers fit between us. He drums against my clit, little taps that send me reeling. I can't stop my legs from shaking now, can barely keep myself up, and when I feel my body clench his, he hisses, "That's it. Come for me, Kennedy."

I cry out. This orgasm pulls everything from me. Bursting, blinding pleasure that feels so good I nearly pass out.

My legs give, and the rope goes tight on my wrists. If it wasn't for the restraints, I'd be on the floor right now.

Gabe moves his arms around me. He holds me to him.

"Anytime you feel out of place," he says, his voice dark and velvet, "I want you to feel our come sticking to your thighs, and I want you to know that you belong."

Belong. What a good word.

I belong to them. I belong with them. I belong.

These men will take me. Whenever they want. However they want.

Because *I'm theirs.*

After years of people abandoning me, distancing themselves from me, it feels *so fucking good* to be claimed by these two men in broad daylight.

My heart settles.

"What do you think?" Gabe asks. "Has our girl had enough?"

"For now" is Jack's reply.

I wet my lips. They feel dry. "Kiss me first," I beg. "Please."

One pair of lips claims mine. His kiss is warm and smoky and makes my toes curl.

And then he breaks, and a second pair of lips follows. Hard, rough, his tongue pushes into my mouth, invading me. Owning me.

My heart beats in my throat.

They've fucked me stupid. Now, they take care of me.

They remove my makeshift blindfold from my eyes and untangle my wrists from the tree. Then they redress me like a child. I balance on Jack's sturdy form while Gabe helps me step into my panties, pulling them up my legs, and then they both work my dress back over me.

I'm shivering now. The cold is finally sinking in. Jack pulls me up against him.

"Need a ride back to the car?" he asks.

"Please."

I wrap my arms around his neck, and he carries me. I rest my head against his chest. He smells like autumn and earth. I never want to leave his arms.

As if Gabe can read my mind, he says, "I'll drive for a bit."

Jack doesn't argue. He gets into the back seat and pulls me in with him.

"How do you feel?" he asks. Those dark eyes are looking so intently at mine. The predatory fire has left, and now, there's nothing but my caring, protective Jack.

"Loved," I tell him.

"You are."

Gabe gets in the front, closing the door behind him. "We need to hit up a gas station," Gabe says. "Kennedy needs to clean her thighs, and I need some...*things*."

"Probably a good idea," Jack says. He pets my legs, and I shiver.

We drive to a gas station. I'm cozy and full of cuddles and don't want to get up, but I force myself to head to the bathroom. When I see myself in the mirror, I realize Gabe was right. My hair is sex-mussed, my cheeks are flushed, and my thighs are sticky. I look...well. Like I just got railed in the woods. I wash my face, comb my fingers through my hair, and clean the mess between my legs. My pussy aches wonderfully, and I can't help but smile.

God, I'm giddy.

I pull myself together and head back to the car. Jack has fixed himself back into the driver's seat. Gabe comes out a couple of minutes later with a bottle of wine, an armful of half-wilted flowers, and a box of chocolates.

"Rule number one of meeting the parents," Gabe announces. "Never go empty-handed. Flowers or chocolates, Jack?"

"Flowers," Jack says.

Gabe rests the flowers on the seat next to Jack.

My heart flutters. I'm quietly touched.

These are insane, impossible circumstances. I'm returning to the hometown that chewed me up and spit me out. We're chasing a dangerous, villainous operation. But right now, it's nice to pretend that it's just...my two guys, meeting my parents for the first time.

I'm so exhausted by the trip and the countless orgasms I just enjoyed at the hands of my two favorite men that I fall asleep in the back seat, tangled up in Gabe.

It's early evening by the time we make it to my parents' house. They live at the top of a jarring hill, flanked by a horse stable and about ten acres of wild forest behind them.

Jack kills the engine. In the new silence, I can hear a horse bray in the distance.

Welcome to the country.

The three of us climb out of the car. It's brisk, a sharp contrast from Gabe's warmth, and I tug my sweater around myself.

There are two cars already in the parking lot. Jack nods to the cars. "Looks like they have company."

He's trying to keep the paranoia out of his tone, but it's not working.

"That's my sister's," I say.

I wasn't expecting to see her, but, well, *into the fire* we go.

I stand outside the big red door to their cottage-style home. Gabe files in behind me. Jack steps beside me, flowers in his arm.

I shiver. Jack takes my hand in his.

"Ready?" he asks.

"Yup." I put on a wide, unconvincing smile.

He laces his fingers between mine and squeezes.

I knock loudly.

It takes a couple of minutes, but then the door opens up. Both my parents are standing behind it.

Mom is a willowy woman with shortly cropped hair and a stern jawline. Her hair was salt-and-peppered last time I saw it, but now it's gone completely grey.

My father's hair sticks out in white puffs around his head like clouds.

They both look shocked when they see us.

"Kennedy?" Mom asks.

"Hey, Mom," I reply.

"You're...here," she says.

Ah, yes. There's that disappointed frown I know so well.

"Chestnut!" My father throws up his hand in celebration. "We had no idea you were coming!"

"Surprise!"

"Well, come in, come in."

We step inside, and I cling to Jack's arm. "This is Jack and his friend Gabe."

"Good to meet you in the flesh," my father says.

"Sir." Jack shakes my father's hand stiffly.

Gabe goes for my mom. "Are you a hugger? I'm a hugger. Come here, Mrs. Furhman." He scoops my mom into a tight squeeze. "What's that scent—vanilla? It's fantastic."

"Oh! Yes...well. You're too kind."

My mom, who is more frigid than an ice sculpture, blushes.

That's the power of Gabe.

"I'm Evelyn," Mom says, "and this is my husband, Arthur."

Suddenly, Gabe breaks out into a huge, lightbulb-going-off moment smile. "*Arthur*." He stretches out the name as he looks pointedly at Jack. "I knew an Arthur once. Tried to kill me. But I won't hold that against you, Mr. Furhman."

Jack's jaw goes rigid with annoyance, but he swallows it back.

When I pull off my jacket, I realize suddenly that we've walked into something.

The long dining room table is already occupied. My sister, Rebecca, and her husband, Donnie, sit beside each other. And—

"Granny?" I blink. "What's everyone doing here?"

Rebecca sniffs. "Just like you to show up *late*, Kennedy."

"Late?" I echo.

Uh...

Wait a second.

The table is set. With the fine silverware. A brown runner. Gold napkins. Butter in the shape of a lamb. A large turkey square in the middle.

My brain slowly puts together all the pieces.

Hold on...is today—?

"Happy Thanksgiving, honey!" Granny croaks from her seat.

GABE

 law student.

An assassin.

An elite soldier.

And not one of us thought to *check the calendar*.

To be fair, it's easy to forget national holidays when you're hunkered down in a remote safe house, trying to stay alive.

But, truly. One would think that *one of us* would've had the foresight to remember Thanksgiving.

Not that I'm complaining. This is the most traditional Thanksgiving I've had in a very, very long time.

Since my parents' divorce at the tender age of six, Thanksgiving was less of an event and more of a marathon. Half a slice of turkey and a few bites of stuffing at Mom's before heading out to have the exact same meal at Dad's. And then getting the same complaint at both houses: *Why don't you stay and eat more?*

At least here, we have the whole family.

Let me introduce you to the cast:

Mr. Furhman at the head of the table. A tall, lanky

fellow with a mad-scientist vibe. Always smiling, though you get the impression he can't hear a word of what anyone is saying.

Mrs. Furhman. Poised, composed. A woman drawn in charcoal. So thin, she's almost hollow, and every now and then, the edge of her mouth twitches disapprovingly.

Kennedy Furhman, who keeps picking at her napkin.

Jack. Dearest Jack.

At the other side of the table, the grand "Granny." A truly fantastic woman, with weathered skin and thick, bulbous pearls strewn around her throat. Many men have loved this woman hard throughout her life, and it shows with her gemstone earrings and her chunky rings.

Then there's moi, beside her.

Flanked by Rebecca, Kennedy's twin sister. Rebecca's brown hair is pulled back in a ponytail that looks far too tight to be comfortable. The women are identical, and it's bizarre to see Kennedy's warm, sweet face turned cold and stoic when worn by her twin. Rebecca's eyes flit over frequently to her sister, as though she's waiting like a hawk to pounce the second the other Furhman makes a mistake.

Beside her is Donnie, Rebecca's husband. He's a thick man with an over-the-sink haircut. He, apparently, works in IT, and he fills the empty lulls in conversation by droning on about tech facts that no one else understands.

They apparently have two kids, who have already had pizza and are upstairs playing video games.

What a life. My father would've slapped me upside the head if I'd tried to sneak away from the dinner table.

"Gabe," Mrs. Furhman starts, "how is it that you know Kennedy?"

I feel Jack's and Kennedy's eyes on me from across the table.

I've got this, children.

"Jack and I were in the military together," I announce as I lift my glass of wine to my lips. "Hooyah."

"Oh. You must know each other quite well, then."

"Very." I wink at Jack. He doesn't return the favor.

"Donnie, the turkey is dry," Rebecca complains. "I told you, you left it in the oven too long."

"Better too cooked than too pink," Donnie says.

"He's always overcooking food," Rebecca announces. "I made the stuffing."

She takes in a deep breath and then goes still. I imagine she's holding her breath until someone compliments her on the stuffing.

"It's just wonderful," I tell her. "The turkey, too."

Rebecca frowns at that, but Donnie beams.

"I've started cooking," Rebecca says. "Macrobiotic food. I lost twenty pounds!"

"It's great," Donnie agrees with his wife, then pats his gut. "I'd be in the same place if I could just stay away from red meat."

"Those burgers!" Rebecca squeals. "Killers!"

They both laugh, but it has no humor in it.

"I can't eat her food," Granny grumbles beside me, her eyes slits. "Gives me the toots."

I love Granny.

"Kennedy," Rebecca says suddenly, "you should look into it."

"Oh?" Kennedy says, but I can see her defenses go up.

"It's all clean, healthy eating." Her eyes do a quick once-over on Kennedy's form. "It'd be good for you."

Kennedy's mouth twists. The barb doesn't go unnoticed.

I have two older brothers—I'm intimately familiar with this game of *one-upping*. In a house of three boys, our challenges were usually physical. Who could do the most push-ups? Who could carry his girlfriend on his shoulders? Who could take the most shots of Fireball before puking in the backyard?

Toxic masculinity is a snakeskin I have worked hard to shed.

But if *boys will be boys*, girls will be nuclear warheads. Both Kennedy and Rebecca look like they've got their fingers on the button.

Sensing a catfight coming on, I attempt to steer the conversation with, "Speaking of food—these beets. *Divine.* Granny, is that your doing?"

She leans forward and pats my arm. "The secret is in the apricot preserves."

Which answers the question: *how did that flavor get in there?*

"I didn't pick up cooking in Atlanta, I'll admit that," Kennedy says, and it's clear she hasn't dropped the bait her sister left for her. "But that's only because I was busy learning about the criminal justice system."

Kennedy's father leans forward so quickly he almost upends Donnie's glass of wine. "Oh—shucks. Sorry, Donnie." *Shucks?* Do nonanimated humans still say shucks? Mr. Furhman tents his fingers and turns to his daughter. "Yes, Chestnut, tell us about your studies."

Except now that she's thrown it out there, Kennedy gets shy. She shrugs and pokes at her carrots with a fork. "It's great. I mean, law school is hell, but I'm learning a lot."

Jack leans in closer to Kennedy and half murmurs, "Did you tell them about moot court?"

Kennedy squares her shoulders. "Oh, I mean, it's not that big of a—"

Jack announces to the table, "Kennedy got into moot

court. A very competitive program. Only a few of her class-mates got in."

"Oh, Kennedy!" her mother's voice pitches. "Isn't that wonderful?"

"Stellar, Chestnut." Her dad's mustache puffs proudly.

Rebecca looks like she just bit into a lemon.

"I always said this one would be a good lawyer." Granny stabs her fork in Kennedy's direction. "Girl could never lose an argument."

Kennedy's face colors. She bumps her shoulder against Jack's. "It's not that big of a deal," Kennedy murmurs.

"Yes. It is."

Jack puts his hand on her leg.

He's a good boyfriend. Seeing the two of them like this—domestic, not surrounded by gunfire—makes my heart unexpectedly warm.

"Oh, that reminds me, honey," Kennedy's mom says, "we got a strange call from your school. Something about your attendance falling off?"

"Yes," Mr. Furhman says, concern edging into his voice, "the dean said you've been noticeably absent the past couple months. To the point where you may not have enough credits this semester. I told him it must be a mistake, but—"

"Oh, yeah," Kennedy quickly jumps in, "it's nothing. I'll talk to them when I get back."

Rebecca makes a noise that almost sounds like a whimper of glee.

"That's typical, isn't it?" she says. "I said this would happen—Daddy, didn't I say it? You can never pick one thing and stick to it. Always changing direction halfway through."

"That has nothing to do with this!" Kennedy snaps.

"Oh? Really? I *knew* you'd drop out of law school. You can't finish anything you start!"

"Says the woman who's never accomplished *anything* except pushing two babies out."

Rebecca's face goes crimson. "Don't tell *me* about accomplishments. I was valedictorian. I won first place in all of my barrel-racing competitions. I was the prom queen *and* the class president. I married my high school boyfriend. *Happily.*"

"Yeah, well, I've taken two dicks at once," Kennedy snarls, "ever do *that*?"

The table goes silent.

"Fuck this," Kennedy says. "I'm not hungry anyway."

"Kennedy," Mr. Furhman chastises, "*language.*"

"Oh, *shuck off*, Dad!" Kennedy gets up from the table, slaps her napkin down, and rushes into the kitchen.

There's a vacuum of silence when Kennedy leaves. I clear my throat. "To be clear. She was talking about our dicks. It's not like...getting gangbanged by two strangers. It was very loving, actually—"

Jack narrows his eyes at me. "Stop talking."

I shut up.

"I'm going to check on her," Jack says.

He starts to stand, but Mrs. Furhman gets up first.

"You better not. I'll go." Mrs. Furhman gives Jack a disapproving frown. "I think you've done enough here."

Jack-two-dicks (or, at least, that's how I assume the Furhmans will refer to him once we leave) sits back down. Mrs. Furhman vanishes into the kitchen.

The silverware beside me rattles. Granny leans forward, her wiry hands clasped together.

"So," she says, "two at once. How does that *work*, exactly?"

28

KENNEDY

This was a terrible idea.

I'd rather get cold called in Professor Jefferson's class. I'd rather get in a gunfight with Anders. I'd rather be fending off grabbing hands at the seediest strip club in the world.

I'd rather do *anything* than sit at the dinner table and get judged by every member of my family.

My emotions are burning. Boiling. Too hot. I pace back and forth in the kitchen, trying to kill the adrenaline, but I can't. I crouch down instead, elbows on my knees, and put my head in my hands.

My dark hair frames my face, blocking everything else out. I need to be alone. I need to breathe.

My anger got so bad in there all I could see was red. I need to get it out, or I'm going to lash out again.

Unfortunately, I don't get my space. I hear the familiar shuffle of my mother's feet.

"Kennedy," she says sternly, "what's going on?"

I shake my head. "I can't. Leave me alone. Please."

The tops of her tennis shoes come into my view. She's standing over me now.

"You can't cut me out. You may not like me very much, but I'm still your mother."

I push my hair back and tilt my head up. "I like you, Mom."

She huffs. "How am I supposed to know that? You never come around. You never call. And when you do finally show up—unannounced, I might add—it's with two boys I've never even met before—"

"Can you blame me?" I stand up now so we're face-to-face. "Why would I come home when I have to deal with *that*? It's been like this my whole life. If I didn't make the bed as soon as I woke up, you'd all act like I was some hardened criminal."

She crosses her arms. "So now we're not supposed to correct your bad behavior?"

"I'm not saying that! I'm just saying...maybe don't act like you're waiting for me to do something wrong."

"Have you? Done something wrong?"

Yes. I've dropped out of law school. I'm on the run from mercenaries. I've been shot at, I've been in a car chase, and I watched my boyfriends violently interrogate a man at a strip club.

When I can't answer her right away, I see the life fall out of my mother's eyes.

She's disappointed in me. This is nothing new, but it doesn't make it sting any less.

"Kennedy," Mom says, her voice low and serious, "who are those two men?"

I bite my lip. What comes flying out of my mouth is "I love them."

Her eyebrows scrunch together, confused. "*Them*?"

I exhale. I've said too much.

The edge of her mouth pinches. "We know, darling."

"Know what?"

"About the..." Her voice lowers to a hush. "*Stripping*."

Well. You ripped off the I'm-dating-two-men Band-Aid, Kennedy. What's one more? "How do you know?"

"We hired someone. An investigator. And he found... well. Are you in trouble?" My mother puts her hands on my shoulders. Her irises bat wildly between my two eyes. "Blink twice if you're in trouble."

"What are you even talking about right now—?"

But I don't get to interrogate my mom anymore.

Because the dining room breaks out into sudden commotion.

29

JACK

At the dining table, the clock has become unbearably loud.

Donnie is sweating. Physically. Sweating. I can see it bead up on his hairline and on his upper lip.

Meanwhile, Granny stares at Madsen through scrunched eyes.

"How do you do it?" she asks. "Two men...together?"

Madsen clears his throat and picks up two carrots. "Well, Granny, when two men love each other very much—"

"Put down the carrot," I snap.

Madsen puts up his palms and drops the food.

I'm on edge. Something doesn't feel right. I can't put my thumb on it.

"Donnie," Rebecca says suddenly, her voice an octave too loud, "cut more turkey."

Her husband, flustered, adjusts his napkin in his lap. "Oh, I don't think anyone is—"

"*Now*, Donnie," she snarls.

I'm starting to wonder if Rebecca moonlights as a dominatrix. It would fit the bill.

The turkey is tucked between me and Granny. I take the carving fork. "I'll get it."

"Don't," Rebecca says, and her eyes turn into slits. "We were having a *perfectly* good Thanksgiving until the three of you showed up."

Alright. Bitch. I release the fork.

Donnie rises like a chastised dog and goes to carve more slices into the bird.

Madsen leans back in his chair, clasping his hands behind his head. He smiles. "Well, as far as I'm concerned, if I don't ruin every event I walk into, I haven't done my job."

Why does he always look so fucking relaxed?

My skin is buzzing. Something is off. *Really off.* It's a tingling sensation. Like holding on to a grenade after the pin has been removed. Something is about to blow, and no one seems to notice but me.

I glance out the window. At the door. Nothing. No one. It's just us and Kennedy's family.

Donnie walks around the table and stands beside me. He picks up the carving fork and hovers over the turkey.

That's when I notice it. There's a sharpness in Rebecca's eyes as she watches Donnie.

He's panting. Lightly. But I can hear his breath.

Why are they so unnerved?

My hands tense into a fist.

"Do it, Donnie," Rebecca says. There's an urgency in her voice.

"I can't—" he whines.

"Now!" she snaps.

Then I feel it. A sharp, piercing ache in my back.

I suck in a breath. I don't move. I can't. Everyone is suddenly staring at me. Madsen's eyes get wide.

"Holy shit..." he says.

"I'm sorry," Donnie splutters. "I had to. I'm...oh God, I'm so sorry."

I look to the side. I see Donnie, ghostly white. The turkey. No carving knife.

I reach over my shoulder, and my fingertips touch metal, confirming my theory.

The carving knife is in my back.

I've been stabbed.

Donnie fucking stabbed me with a fucking carving knife.

I've got eyes on the back of my head. I can see trouble coming out from any corner. But Jesus fucking Christ, I wasn't expecting Donnie to stab me in the back over Thanksgiving dinner.

Which is when Rebecca smashes her wineglass, lets out an Amazonian-warrior-style shout, and charges at Madsen with the broken stem.

She's quick. But not quick enough. Madsen is on his feet, too. He's already removed the switchblade from his jacket, which makes her stop short.

"Hold on," Madsen says. "I had a line for this. Oh, I know!" Then he brandishes his switchblade and starts to sing, "*When you're a Je—*"

"I've been fucking stabbed!" I roar. "Now is not the time for a fucking musical number!"

Out of the corner of my eye, I see Mr. Fuhrman twitch. His hands are on the table. His eyes are on the large, lethal-looking knife in the ham.

His gaze snaps to me. I know what he's thinking. He *knows* I know.

"Don't," I tell him, but he charges anyway.

We both lunge across the table for it. He grips the handle first, but I grab his arms, pinning him down to the table.

"This is all a...terrible...misunderstanding..." he huffs, his face beet red and his mustache quivering.

Madsen disarms Rebecca when he grabs her and yanks her toward him. She yelps, immediately dropping her wine stem, and he puts his blade to her throat. She thrashes like a wild animal. Meanwhile, Granny double-teams Madsen, whacking him in the back with her cane.

"Ow! Et tu, Granny!"

Donnie just stands there, whimpering.

Rebecca was right. He is useless.

"What the *fuck* is going on?" Kennedy shouts, and we all freeze.

She's standing in the entranceway, her mouth open in shock.

I watch as her eyes travel from:

The carving knife sticking out of my back...

Her sister in Madsen's grip...

Granny going apeshit...

"I'm sorry!" her mother sobs. "He told us to do it!"

Kennedy turns to her mother. "Who is *he*?"

But I don't get an answer. Because a serving plate hits the back of my head, and everything goes black.

"Earth to Jack...talk to me, Jackie boy."

I grunt. It's all I can do.

My mouth feels like the inside of a sock.

I blink blearily. The world spins around me.

I'm stuck in a hard chair. I try to move, but my arms are bound behind me. So are my legs.

Something is hitting me. Repeatedly. In the face.

My gaze refocuses.

There's a child standing in front of me. One of Rebecca's snot-nosed kids. He pauses his onslaught. Reloads his Nerf gun. Then points it back at me. Another dull *ping* as the foam bullet bounces off my cheek.

I can hear voices in the background. I try to twist my head to look around. Kennedy is arguing heatedly with her parents. Rebecca and Donnie are arguing among themselves. I can only catch snippets of conversation.

Do we take the knife out?

No, he'll bleed to death, you idiot!

Not crazy!

"Jack...you with me, buddy?"

That's Madsen's voice. A soft, lulling growl in my ear. He's right behind me, and it takes a second to register that we're tied together, back to back.

"I'm here."

"Oh, good. Thought you might've gone the way of the turkey for a minute. Some pickle we've got ourselves in, isn't it?"

I can't bring myself to agree. I sneer at the child and jerk my body an inch forward—as far as the rope will let me go. His eyes go wide, and he stumbles backward. Then, when he realizes I can't escape, a bratty smile crosses his mouth. He aims the gun at my face, closes one eye for precision, and cocks his head.

"Bad guys die," he says.

Another foam sting between the eyes.

This is more irritating than the blade still sticking two inches into my shoulder.

"So let me catch you up," Madsen says conversationally. "Apparently, the Furhmans are convinced we're thugs who are trafficking their daughter and forcing her to be a stripper and a prostitute. So. That's fun."

I groan. "Great."

"How're you feeling?" Madsen asks.

"Stabbed."

I struggle, but it's useless. Whoever tied this mess of knots did it with gusto. We're stuck.

Madsen fills the empty air. "Is Jack short for anything? Jackleson? Jackamo?"

"Stop talking."

I need to think. I need to get us out of this.

I don't know what's worse. That I've been stabbed, the child shooting pellets at me, or the fact that two military-trained, elite soldiers let four civilians and an elderly grandmother get the drop on them.

Note to self: never, *ever* let your guard down. Not even among family.

Especially not among family.

The voices get louder. Kennedy storms out of the kitchen and stands over us. She blinks when she sees me, and then she drops to a crouch, putting her hands on either side of my face.

"Oh, thank God you're awake."

"Mm."

"My family has lost their fucking mind. I'm so sorry. I'm getting you out of here—"

But the second she tugs on my ropes, Donnie materializes beside us. He has a shotgun in his hand, and he raises it.

"Step away from the prisoners," he says in his best impression of a tough guy.

"Or what?" Kennedy snaps, rising to her feet. "Are you going to shoot me?"

He goes white.

God, she's beautiful when she's mad. Like an angel. Halo around her head.

Huh. I might be concussed.

"Mom!" Kennedy leaves me to rush to her mom. "Tell them that they've lost it!"

Her mother, however, has gone cold. She folds her arms over her chest. "We know, Kennedy."

"You know *what*?"

"Everything! You've been working at a strip club. You left school. Then these are your...what...*your pimps*?"

"Mom! It's not like that!"

Rebecca scoffs. "This is worse than that time you were convinced your boyfriend was a lizard."

"That was different!"

"How?"

"He had a cold tongue!"

"Girls!" Mrs. Furhman chides.

"I mean, I get it, actually," Madsen says. "It's easier to believe that your daughter is caught up in some sex trafficking ring than the alternative. Government conspiracies, secret military assassination organizations, Helen's lost gold rediscovered—"

Kennedy's father turns to Madsen then. His mustache twitches. "What did you say?"

"Which part?"

"Helen's...lost gold?"

"Oh, yeah. That's what all this is about."

Mr. Furhman adjusts his glasses on the bridge of his nose. His hand shakes.

"Arthur," Mrs. Furhman says. Her voice quakes. "Do you know what they're talking about?"

"I do," he says. His voice is quiet, pensive. "And I'm afraid they might be telling the truth."

30

GABE

They let us out of our restraints. Apparently, I uttered the magic words.

Just when things were getting fun.

The first action item is to get the knife out of Jack's back.

My rule has always been: The only thing worse than getting stabbed?

Getting *un-stabbed*.

The moment the knife goes in, it sucks. It hurts. Every instinct tells you to tear the foreign objects out.

But the second it comes *out*, that's when the real danger starts. Right now, the knife in Jack's back is holding everything intact. Once I yank it out, he's going to start bleeding like a pig.

And in the Furhmans' bathtub, equipped with an old lady's sewing kit and some towels, the situation isn't exactly ideal.

But today, I'm a doctor, and we're doing the best with what we've got. I have Jack out of his shirt, his large body perched on the rim of the bathtub so I can get behind him.

Kennedy—my on-hand nurse—watches with worried eyes from her seat on the closed toilet.

Her family is downstairs, giving us space. Rightly so.

"How bad does it look?" Kennedy asks. Her voice is tight, and her knee rapidly bops up and down.

The knife is maybe an inch into his back, underneath the shoulder blade. The good news: it didn't pierce his heart. The bad news: his arm looks pretty limp.

"Could be worse," I say, trying to be chipper. "You know, when I said I wanted to be *inside of you*, I didn't mean, like, a *gaping wound*."

"Focus, please."

"Copy that."

I take the handle of the blade and hold Jack's opposite shoulder for leverage. "I'm going to pull it out on three. Ready?"

"Just do it," Jack growls. His fingers are clenched around the porcelain of the tub.

He's tense. This must be how a veterinarian feels giving medicine to a tiger. I'm not convinced he won't bite my arm off the second I pull this out.

"Nurse Kennedy, come distract our boy, will you?"

Kennedy—the saint—crouches in front of Jack. She slips her hands to either side of his face and strokes tenderly.

"You're doing so good," she tells him in a sweet, cooing voice. "My big, brave man."

Damn, I suddenly wish I was the one who got stabbed.

"Three," I tell him. "Two."

I yank before *one*.

Jack doubles forward with a vicious growl. Immediately, the wound starts to bleed.

Kennedy is holding Jack, comforting him. Which is

good, because I'm busy. I put pressure on the wound, using the towel to hold it back. The blood is coming steadily but not so heavy that it seems like any major vessels have burst. In other words? Our boy isn't hemorrhaging to death today.

A Thanksgiving miracle.

I'm used to quick, shoddy life-saving work. I've patched wounds on the front lines while bullets were whizzing all around us. I can do this in a fancy bathroom.

I hold the pressure until the bleeding slows. Then I get to cleaning the wound. The Furhmans have a decent first aid kit, so I wash it off, clean it, and then stitch him up.

"You're doing good, baby," I tell him. "How're you holding up?"

"Peachy," Jack mumbles. He's short of breath. But he's conscious.

There's a noise in the door, and all three of us look up.

It's Mr. Furhman, clearing his throat. He stands in the hallway with Mrs. Furhman behind him. Mr. Furhman is holding a stack of books and wearing an uncomfortable smile.

"When you have a moment," he says politely, "I'd like to show you something."

As JACK and I rub the rope burn out of our wrists, Mr. Furhman explains the situation in the way only a high school professor can.

He escorts everyone to his study except Granny, who has had enough excitement for the day and decided to shut her eyes in front of the fireplace. Mr. Furhman's study is a shrine to beautiful oak wood and dusty, clothbound texts. He breaks out an old projector, the likes of which I haven't seen since sixth grade, and dims the lights.

The projector brings up a soft square of light on the wall. Mr. Furhman slides on a luminated page that throws up the image of an ancient Roman city.

"Legend has it," Mr. Furhman begins, "Helen was the most beautiful woman in the ancient world. The story goes that Eris, the goddess of strife, offered a golden apple to the most beautiful goddess. Zeus, the king of Gods, invited the Trojan prince Paris to judge. He was to choose between Athena, Hera, or Aphrodite. Aphrodite promised Paris the most beautiful woman in the world if he chose her. He picked Aphrodite."

A new slide comes up, depicting a stone image of Paris.

In the chair beside me, Jack's head droops forward. He's quietly snoring.

"Paris claimed his prize when he went to visit the home of Sparta king Menelaus. Menelaus was married to Helen. When Paris saw Helen, he was immediately entranced by her. They eloped and ran away from Sparta.

"There are some accounts that state that, on their way back to Troy, Paris stole not only Helen but also Spartan gold. One item was a golden necklace, which he adorned on his kidnapped bride. And Helen...hmmph."

His next slide has been marked. Beautiful Helen has a blue-marker mustache scribbled over her upper lip.

Rebecca's little brats snicker in the back. Rebecca shoots her kids a dagger glare, and they immediately shut it.

Mr. Furhman coughs and recovers. "You can see the necklace depicted here. It's pure gold, with the iconic Hercules knot in the center—you can see the two half-knots bound together. It's a symbol of everlasting love, meant to bind the two together.

"Their love was, naturally, doomed. Helen's kidnapping sparked a decade-long war that lost countless lives, all for two stubborn men fighting over the love of one woman."

Mr. Furhman takes a minute to adjust his glasses. I can see how he might command a classroom; there's a unique fire that lights up in the eyes of intellectuals once they've been set off.

I steal a glance at Kennedy from across the table. She's watching her dad with a fixed gaze, hardly blinking, simply absorbing. I can imagine a child Kennedy snuggled up in bed, eyes wide, poring over the textbooks her dad has pulled off the shelves for a bedtime story.

The thought makes me smile.

"Of course, this is all mythology. There was no Helen of Troy. No Trojan War. Except...some scholars believe that Homer's story is a retelling of an event that did take place many years ago. No one has been able to find physical evidence of it, however. Hence why the story has been cataloged as pure myth. If this were, in fact, the gold Paris used to seduce Helen, an artifact of a previously believed nonexistent time, well, it would be bigger than...than..."

"The Beatles?" I guess.

"The Holy Grail," Mr. Furhman finishes. "I never thought a discovery like this would be made in my lifetime. Until I saw it for myself."

Jack sits straight up. "You did *what*?"

"Oh, good morning, sunshine," I tell him.

Jack narrows his gaze.

Politely, Mr. Furhman adjusts his glasses. "Well, Langston Caine invited me to his estate to confirm the authenticity of an ancient Greek necklace. He claimed he had purchased it from a museum. He said he had the papers."

My heartbeat has taken residence in my throat.

The necklace. *Here.*

After all this time, we're reunited. Almost.

"Did you *see* those papers?" Kennedy counters.

Now, Mr. Furhman's thin lips tighten in a wince. "No. I had no reason to doubt him. If artifacts like that had been obtained illegally, it would be...well..."

"A war crime," I fill in.

He nods quietly.

"Why did Langston call you?" I ask.

"Because of my credentials," Mr. Furhman says as though it's obvious. "I'm one of the leading experts in Ancient Greek history in the United States. Besides, I believe we owed the boy, after...well..."

His eyes flit to Kennedy. Even in the dark, a shame blush bruises her beautiful cheeks.

Her father is good to swallow his tongue.

He clears his throat and changes the topic. "There is something else," he continues. "It's said to be cursed. That it wasn't Helen's beauty but the spell of the necklace that drew people to madness. Love is a crazy thing. It can drive peaceful people to violence."

"And violent people to peace," I add. My eyes connect with Kennedy's, and she smiles, the warmth returning to her expression.

That's my girl.

"This necklace," Jack cuts in. "Do you know where Langston was storing it?"

"Well, not exactly. But I informed them it needed to be sealed in a temperature-controlled space, cold, at least sixty-eight degrees—"

"*Them?*" Jack asks.

"Yes. There was another man with us—strong build, arm in a sling."

"*Anders*," Jack mutters darkly under his breath.

The bad blood between these two former brothers is impressive. Not that I'm complaining. Jack is hot when he gets all murder-y.

The slideshow ends. Mrs. Furhman flicks on the lights too quickly. We all let out a single, collective groan.

"We've set up the guest house," Mrs. Furhman announces. "If you'd like to stay, that is."

Mr. Furhman's mustache twitches. "Yes. We're very sorry about all the, well. Miscommunication."

"Yes," she parrots. "Very sorry."

I've experienced enough of the South to know what's going on here. The only thing these people hate more than being attempted murderers is being *rude*.

They'll stab you in the back, but they'll apologize about it.

Mr. Furman continues. "It's a small town, you know, and we just don't trust people around here."

Jack spits out, "No, you don't trust your daughter. There's a difference."

Their eyes bat to Kennedy, then to Jack, then back to Kennedy.

"Well," Mrs. Furhman begins, her voice a panicked pitch, "we understand if you'd prefer somewhere else. But the bed is set up, and—"

"We'll stay," Kennedy says. She settles back against Jack like a sated cat, but it's hard to tell whether she's claiming him or he's claiming her. Maybe both.

"Good." Mr. Furhman offers a weak smile. "Perhaps in the morning, we can chat. Sort this all out. But tonight, I think it'd be best if we all...well."

"Yeah," I agree. "Think that'd be best."

"Well. Good night, then." Another trying smile from Mr. Furhman.

He's a nice guy. But he's caught the three of us in a bad mood.

The Furhmans leave to set up our lodgings. The old wooden floors creak as they go down the hall.

I roll my shoulders back. They crack. "And they seemed like such nice people."

Kennedy tilts back against Jack. "I'm sorry my brother-in-law stabbed you."

I reach over and take her hand. She squeezes my fingers. "Thank God you're the black sheep," I tell her.

She smiles at that, and for a minute, the world rights itself again.

31

JACK

The Furhmans have a guest house on the property.

It's a small, two-bedroom space behind the main house. It comes with a common area, a kitchen, and a bathroom. The walls are a cheery, sunflower yellow, and I feel a headache coming on.

I claim one of the bedrooms, tossing down the two duffle bags we stuffed with clothes (mostly Kennedy's) and guns (mostly mine) before joining the duo in the living room.

Madsen collapses into the lounge chair. Because he can't sit like a normal human, he sits in the thing sideways, with his legs slung over the arm of the chair.

"Okay," Madsen says. "New plan of action. Tomorrow, we wake up, figure out our options. But tonight..."

He pulls a bottle of whiskey out from his leather jacket and shakes it.

Kennedy barks on a laugh. "Did you get that from my parents' stash?"

"I'll replenish it," Madsen says. "This felt like an emergency."

"Sharing is caring."

Kennedy flops down in Madsen's lap. He takes a swig and then passes it to her. She sips, then holds it out for me.

What the hell. I earned it.

I lower my body onto the floor, leaning against the chair, and take the bottle from Kennedy. It's good whiskey and goes down way too smoothly. I only take a swallow before handing it back.

Kennedy's legs hang over my shoulder. That, too, feels good. I'm adrenaline-high, and pampering Kennedy calms me down. I help her out of her shoes, then her socks, and then press my thumb into the arch of her foot, where the tight muscles crunch. She wiggles her toes and lets out a small, pleased sound.

"Is it weird that I actually like your family?" Madsen says. "I mean, besides the stabbing, they're charming in their own way."

Kennedy heaves a sigh. "Family is...complicated."

Madsen agrees, "I've always preferred chosen family myself."

"Yeah..." Kennedy slips her fingers through my hair. Her nails rake over my skull, and I tilt my head back into her touch, closing my eyes.

I rub her foot. She pets my hair. I'm in heaven.

"I don't know what I'd do without the two of you," Kennedy says suddenly. Her voice is soft, quiet, and I have to strain to hear it. "I know everything has been...chaotic. And weird. But this part...the three of us...always feels right."

"Couldn't *shucking* agree more, love," Madsen says.

Kennedy groans out a laugh. I don't respond, exactly. But I do press a kiss to the bottom of her foot.

"I'm shucking wired," Kennedy says.

"Same."

Madsen starts, "We could..."

"Don't say it," I growl, already hearing his punch line.

He finishes anyway. "...*shuck*?"

Kennedy laughs. "Is that your answer to everything?"

"Sex. Knives. And forty-two. *That's* my answer to everything."

Their conversation makes my blood hum. But Kennedy's fingers in my hair have Zen'd me.

I close my eyes. "Or sleep. We could sleep."

THE THREE OF us pile into one bed together.

It's not a conversation. Or a decision. It's a mutual understanding. An agreement that we've all become more comfortable in a pile than apart.

We take turns in the bathroom. While Kennedy is showering, Madsen reads a book in bed beside me.

"What's your last name?" Madsen asks suddenly.

"Crossed."

"No, I mean, your real one. Your Polish one."

"Why?"

"Humor me."

"Krawczyk."

"Krawz-*chick*." Madsen practices it on his tongue, then frowns. "How did they get *Crossed* from that?"

"You want me to dig up the officer who filled out the intake form for my great-grandmother and ask him?"

"Yeah, kind of."

I sigh and close my eyes. It's too late, and I'm in too much pain for this ridiculous conversation. "It doesn't matter."

Madsen cradles my chin in his hand, forcing me to gaze into those sharp, blue eyes.

"Who you are matters. Don't forget that, Jack Krawczyk."

The sound of my family name on his lips sends a weird, buzzing sensation through me. Like a stupid lightning bug battering its stupid head against a lantern inside my stupid chest.

I hiccup. Madsen makes a face.

Kennedy comes in from the bathroom and flops down between us. "Shower is open. What'd I miss?"

"Madsen is giving me acid reflux."

Madsen trills, "Could that weird burning sensation in your chest be...*affection*?"

"Definitely reflux."

Kennedy rolls over so she's half-draped over me, her knee wedged lazily between my legs, the softness of her breasts tucked against my arm.

"Jack doesn't feel his emotions *here*," Kennedy says, looking down at me. She trickles her fingers down the middle of my body and playfully cups my groin. "He feels them *here*."

I grunt. Her palm is warm even through my briefs.

I can feel Madsen watching us. The hunger in his gaze.

My throat goes dry. I start to swell in her hand.

"Be good," I warn her.

The three of us settle into bed—Madsen and I guarding either side of Kennedy. Discreetly, I lift my gun from the bedside table and slip it underneath my pillow...

But my hand brushes something else. Madsen's warm fingers, wrapped around cold metal.

The two of us exchange a glance over Kennedy.

"Well," Madsen says, "this is awkward."

Kennedy looks between us. "What's awkward?"

"Jack and I are fighting over pillow space."

Madsen removes his hand from underneath the pillow, revealing the knife he sleeps with. I take out my gun.

Kennedy lets out a frustrated noise. "No. No weapons in bed."

I shoot Madsen a glare. *This is your fault.*

He shrugs.

"Unless..." Kennedy starts, then buttons her lips thoughtfully.

"Unless?" Madsen coaxes.

"Unless...you put them to good use."

The suggestion makes my blood rush. A grin crawls across Madsen's face. He pets the sharp edge of his blade across Kennedy's cheek, and my heart pounds in my chest at the sight.

"Feeling dangerous, baby?" Madsen asks.

"Yes," Kennedy says. Her voice is breathless.

Madsen's eyes linger on me, though. I can feel him measuring my reaction. Testing me.

I don't know how I feel about this. It feels like we're edging toward something too close to the truth. But...

I want it. Badly.

"Jack?" Madsen asks. Waiting for permission.

Kennedy turns to me. She must sense my hesitation because she sits up and looks me directly in the eyes.

"I trust you," she says. She takes my hand in hers and guides the gun over to her. Then, her eyes never leaving mine, she runs the tip of her tongue over the grooves of the cold metal, barrel to tip. "Show me the wolf."

32

KENNEDY

Jack's eyes go dark. I've unlocked something inside of him.

His gun nestles under my jaw. Like a venomous snake licking at my skin. The danger of it makes me shiver, fear and heat whipping through my blood, tangling until I can't tell the two sensations apart.

"Do you trust me?" Jack asks.

I nod. "With my life." I mean it. The words come right from my heart.

"Prove it," he says. The gun clicks, and every nerve in my body lights up. "On your back."

"Yes, sir."

Slowly, I ease to my back.

Jack draws the gun slowly down the center of my body. Between my breasts. Over my navel.

"Spread your legs," he tells me. I part them for him. His gun nestles against my slit. The cold metal kisses my entrance, sliding up and down my slick. It hits my buzzing clit, and I knot with want.

I moan. My eyes fall closed.

Are there bullets in that gun?

I don't know. The not-knowing makes me dizzy. And so fucking wet.

"Eyes open, angel." There's a new, sharp-cold at my throat. When I open my eyes, I see Gabe bowed over me. The blade of his knife is pinned against my soft, vulnerable neck. I fix my gaze on those electric-blue eyes, and he grins. "There she is."

He draws the blade down my chest. The sharpness of it reminds me to be very, very still. My nipples are hard enough to cut glass, and he toys the cold, flat part of the blade over my pebbled nipple, making it ache.

"Poor little pet," Gabe coos, his voice a singsongy taunt. "You have no idea what you got yourself into, do you?"

No. But I want it.

God, I want it so badly I could cry.

"Please," I beg. My voice is so strained I barely recognize it. I shift my hips, pushing against the gun, my body begging for it. "Please, sir, fuck me."

Jack pushes the barrel of the gun inside of me, and it steals the air from my lungs.

It's so foreign inside of me, so hard and unyielding. But when he impales me with rapid, shallow movements, it feels so good.

I gasp. My insides go tight, and my thighs begin to tremble.

"You're so good, Kennedy," Gabe tells me, his voice a hypnotizing purr. "So desperate for us." He pets me with the flat of his blade, over my breasts, my stomach, every touch of metal on skin lighting me up.

"Oh, God," I moan. I'm light-headed, every nerve standing on end. My skin is on fire. The merciless touches of their weapons draw me closer and closer to the brink of pleasure.

"Come, Kennedy," Jack growls. "Come around my gun."

I can't hold back. I cry out as I clench around the cold steel. My orgasm flutters, gripping, wanting, but it doesn't give back. It just takes, fucking me with the same rough pace that sends a second wave of pleasure crashing through me.

"Good girl," Gabe says. His breath is hot on the side of my face. He kisses my cheek and nibbles my ear. "Say, *thank you, sirs*."

He presses the flat side of the knife to my mouth. I kiss it. "Thank you, sirs."

He removes the knife and replaces it with his tongue. The cold steel gives way to hot flesh, and I swoon.

This is what I need now. I've come undone around their cold, cruel weapons.

Now I need their big, loving, beating hearts.

Jack's steel leaves me. "Flip over," he says. I shift onto my hands and knees, ass up in offering, *needing*. The blood-hot head of Jack's cock hunts my pussy, and I moan, wiggling back. The tease makes me buzz.

"Give me your mouth, angel," Gabe says. He settles in front of me, his hand cupping my throat, his thumb putting pressure under my chin. His blushing cock stands at attention, and I eagerly swallow him down.

Jack pushes inside of me. He fills me in a way his gun never could, and I moan, vibrating around Gabe. The heat of both of them makes me ache with renewed lust.

This is what I need. Filled by both my men. I'm so content, and I tell them so with whimpers and hungry sucks.

Jack fucks me so hard I can't breathe. Gabe's grip on my throat holds me down, his thumb stroking encouragingly.

I'm dripping—my eyes, my mouth, my cunt—but I can't get enough. My body is hijacked with lust, and all I can think about is getting more, more, *more.*

I burst with pain and pleasure. My lungs burn and my cunt aches and it's all I can do to mewl through their seesawing thrusts, and, *oh God*—

I'm coming again. I shake with the intensity of it. Their hands pin me in place as my legs give out, submitting completely to their desires.

33

GABE

I'm in a dream, hugged by Kennedy's sweet, eager mouth.

Jack wakes me up.

"*Madsen.*" Jack says my name, and my gaze immediately snaps to his own. His eyes are a dark, smoky heat. He's gripping her round hips, and watching him pound sends a lick of heat through me.

Jack looks me right in the eyes as he says, "Fill her mouth, and I'll fill her cunt."

In his words, there's a promise:

Everything we do, we do together.

Fucking. Fighting. Coming.

This is a brotherhood that goes deeper than blood and service. I don't need to be told twice. I choke on my pleasure as my heart explodes down Kennedy's throat. I moan, cradling Kennedy by her neck. She lets out a small, delighted whimper as she drinks me down, that devilish tongue pulling my sanity from my cock.

"Enough," I say, my voice like gravel when I can't take any more of her sucking. I push my thumb over her lips and gently guide her up my body. Kennedy is so warm, her face bright and wet. Tears of pain. Tears of joy.

"You okay, baby?" I check in.

A wide, satisfied smile stretches across her mouth. "Never better."

"That's our girl."

I kiss her deeply and taste my own salt. She purrs like a kitten against my mouth.

Jack winds an arm around her chest. He steals her from me, shoving his tongue in her mouth, and it makes my throat dry, wondering if he likes the taste.

But I don't get to wonder for long before he turns his attention on me.

He pins Kennedy tightly between our bodies and claims me with a rough kiss. Then he drops his mouth to my throat, where he sinks his teeth into my skin. The unexpected bolt of pain makes my eyes roll back. I swear between gritted teeth, and my fingers go tight around Kennedy's hips. My cock—the insatiable slut—weeps against Kennedy's stomach as Jack bites and sucks a vicious, ugly welt into my neck.

Fuck. If he keeps this up, I'm going to need a round two, three, ten—

Jack unlatches from me and pulls back. I pant as the pinpricks of pain subside. The violent thing in him is finally sated, and he settles, domesticated, nuzzling and kissing Kennedy's shoulder.

"Fuck." I pant. "I think I saw God."

"Me too," Kennedy murmurs breathlessly.

Jack and I put the weapons down, and the three of us tangle in a pile of beating, aching hearts.

34

KENNEDY

My boys sleep the day away.

Jack is a notorious early riser. Today, it's almost nine in the morning before I feel him shift in bed.

I've already been awake for hours. I'm sitting up in bed, my phone in my lap.

Gabe is draped over Jack like a coat. When I look at Jack, those dark eyes are open, and they're staring at me.

I grin and rub my hand over the top of his head, the way I might pet a dog.

"Hey, you."

He catches my hand before I can pull away. He nibbles the swell of that soft flesh under my thumb, which sends tingles through me. I curl my fingers underneath his chin and play my nails over the growing wilderness of scruff.

This is a rare Jack. A cozy, sleepy, warm Jack.

Gabe is still fast asleep, so I keep my voice at a whisper. "How did you feel about last night?"

Now his mouth curves downward. "Do we have to talk about everything?"

"No, but we have to talk about *some* things."

How it felt to fuck me with your gun.

The way you mauled Gabe like you couldn't get enough.

Any of these would be appropriate conversation starters.

Instead, Jack says, "What do you want me to say?"

"You can start with *I feel.*"

"*I feel* interrogated."

I scowl. "That's not funny."

Now would be the correct time for Jack to apologize, but he won't. Jack has never apologized for anything. Not once in his life. He's not about to start now, no matter how hard I pout.

He rubs his hand over my thigh.

I know it's his way of saying *I'm sorry*, but I'm still bitter.

"Don't do that," I say.

"What?"

"Apology touches. One day, it's not going to be enough. Someday, you're going to have to use your *words.*"

In true Jack form, his response is:

No response.

He remains dead silent. His hand drops from my thigh.

I don't want to be angry. Last night was blissful. *Beautiful.* I woke up sore, satisfied, and floating on cloud nine. But getting Jack to communicate...it's fucking near impossible.

The worst part is I want to be snuggly. I want his touch. I want to love him.

He just won't let me in.

I sigh. "You can rub my shoulders, though, if you want."

He shifts to sit up and wedges himself behind me. His strong hands work my shoulders, kneading the muscles until they're soft as dough.

Jack is bad with his words but good with his hands.

"What're you working on?" he asks. His chin rests on my shoulder. He softly kisses my neck.

He's deflecting, but this is sweet-Jack. He feels bad.

I give a little, lifting my phone so he can see it better.

"Research. I was thinking about what Dad said...about keeping it in a temperature-controlled room. The Caines own a sailboat that they keep in the Outer Banks. They ship a lot of their artwork to and from there. They store it in this airtight room at the boathouse—Langston took me there once to show off all his daddy's art. If they're storing it properly...that would be my guess."

"Good work, Sherlock."

Another kiss to my neck. I close my eyes and lean back against this strong man.

"I want to stake it out."

"Okay. We'll go together."

"No, Gabe and I will go. You stay. Rest."

"Ken—"

I move my hand over his mouth, quieting him. "That's an *order*."

If he's going to be a stubborn soldier, I'll talk to him with words he understands.

He grunts, and I feel the puff of air against my palm, but I know what it means.

Yes, sir.

Crystal View Harbor is about an hour's drive from Cobblersville.

With Gabe at the wheel, it's a smooth forty-five, plus ten minutes for a coffee break.

We park in the gravel lot and leave the heat on. In

November, it's off-season for the Outer Banks. Most of the boats are winterized and put away, ghost ships tucked under white tarps and bobbing in the chopping waves.

We can't get past the gate, but we sit in the car and watch. I warm my hand on my paper cup. Gabe sips his—iced coffee, even in late November.

"That's their boat," I say.

A huge schooner is docked at the end of a long line of pillars. Unlike the other boats that are boarded up for the winter, this one looks ready to sail. There is even the soft, yellow glow of lights inside.

It's easy to be quiet around Gabe. Even with his gaze trained on the boat ahead of us, he's relaxed in his driver's seat.

He puts his iced coffee in the center console and rests his fingertips on the lid. I can't help but notice the size of his hands. The way his fingers splay out on the cup.

The memory of those fingers around my throat sends a heat blooming low in my belly. And then there's his neck. He picked out a wool sweater with a high collar, but even that is having a hard time covering the blossoming bruise on his throat that Jack marked him with.

My heart flutters. I distract myself with another sip of coffee.

"It's so weird being back here," I say.

Gabe's attention shifts from the boat to me. "Because of Langston?"

I nod. "He used to take me out here to make out. He didn't want anyone to know we were dating at first because I was the crazy Furhman sister. So we'd come out here and..."

"Neck?"

"Fuck."

Gabe's hand leaves his coffee. He finds my thigh instead,

those fingers tightening in an affectionate squeeze. "I'd show you off."

I lean back against the headrest and admire him. Long hair tucked underneath his beanie. Cozy scarf wrapped around his head. Those endless, bright blue eyes.

"Do you feel like a third wheel with me and Jack?" I ask suddenly.

Gabe blinks at the question, then chuckles. "I could think of worse wheels to be."

"I'm serious. I like you. And Jack likes you. And when all this is said and done...however it plays out. We don't want to lose you."

His bright smile fades. My heart tightens in my chest.

"What is it?"

He shakes his head. "I've been...on my own for a very long time. The black sheep of my family. The strange kid in my town. It's why I joined the navy, honestly. I thought I might find my clan. Turned out...I just felt more alone than ever. But when I'm with you two...it feels right." His eyes meet mine. "So, to answer your question, no. I don't feel like a third wheel. I feel like I'm part of a family."

I tilt in closer. Our noses nuzzle. I touch my lips to his. His hand slips up my leg, inviting me in closer. I unbuckle my seat belt and climb into his lap.

Kissing Gabe is addictive.

When he kisses you, he gives you everything. He holds nothing back. He tastes like coffee and warmth and *Gabe*.

It makes me greedy.

When we break apart, I can see our breath crystalizing in the small space between us.

"I like kissing you," I whisper.

He grins. "However much you like it...I promise, I like kissing you more."

He ghosts his lips underneath my jaw. Over my throat. My heart patters.

"Hold up," he says. "I need your eyes. Tell me what you see."

I look over my shoulder.

"There's a man leaving the boathouse," I tell him.

"Anyone we know?"

I shake my head. "Blond hair. Kind of looks like a Backstreet Boys reject...*oh*."

Gabe's hand slips into my pants. He massages my sex over the thin cotton of my panties. The hard ridge of his knuckle kneads against my clit, and my need swells and goes tight.

"Keep talking," Gabe murmurs.

I dry swallow. "He...um...he propped open the door. He's taking a smoke break...oh, fuck—"

Gabe removes his touch. My entire body is buzzing with unspent want.

"Good work, scout. Let's go make a friend."

35

GABE

I know we're supposed to look and not touch. But I've always been a man who lived by the rule that when you see an open door, you should go in.

No matter what might be waiting on the other side.

Kennedy and I get out of the car. She links her arm in mine as we stroll down the gravel parking lot and toward the boathouse.

Blondie is so busy scrolling through videos on his phone and burning through his cigarette he doesn't notice us approaching until it's too late. When he finally spots the two of us, a grimace curls his mouth.

"You can't be here," he says. "This is private property." He's wearing a white sweater with the marina's logo stitched in blue. A lanyard hangs around his neck with the title HARBOR MASTER and a barcode underneath.

"Hiya!" Kennedy says. She waves dramatically, ignoring him. "Oh, that's no problem. We wanted to know about your boat."

She's thickened her accent to a crisp *North Carolina posh*. I love her for this.

"The...boat?" Blondie asks.

I wind my arm around Kennedy's shoulders in a tight squeeze. "It's our one-year anniversary trip. The wife and I wanted to charter one of your boats for the evening. I told her she was nuts, but you know how it is. Happy wife, happy life."

Kennedy puts her hand on my chest, and she nuzzles her nose against mine. "He's such a gem. It's why I keep him around, isn't it, honey?"

"You know it, bunny."

God, we're good at this.

He looks between the two of us like we're crazy.

"The season's over," he says. "We don't charter boats. It's a private marina."

"What about that one?" Kennedy asks, curling her finger toward the Caines' family boat. "It looks ready to go. Surely, you can just push us out for an hour or so."

Kennedy plays the role of *entitled billionaire bride* so well, even I believe it. It's not hard to see how easily she could have, once upon a time, fit in with the Caine family.

Meanwhile, our poor boat hand looks like he wants to die. "Like I said. It's a private dock."

Kennedy rubs her hands over her arms. She shivers dramatically.

"Brrr. It's freezing out here. Can't we talk someplace warmer?"

I wind my arm around Kennedy's shoulders protectively.

"My wife is cold, boy. Perhaps you have a solution?"

We both stare at him expectantly. The joy falls out of this man's face when he realizes the only way through this is to ride it out.

He kills his cigarette and crunches it underfoot.

"Come on in. Only for a minute."

He takes us inside. The harbor master's office is a small, boxy room. There's a desk piled high with notebooks and ledgers. A bookcase stuffed with binders and a locked safe. A desk covered in maps scribbled with red ink.

I do a quick scan. There's a security camera on the wall, and it's pointed to a single door in the back marked "Authorized Personnel Only."

My second rule of life: when you encounter a *locked* door, that usually means there are really, really good things inside.

This door has a particularly fancy knob with a scanner at the top. My guess? The barcode on the harbor master's lanyard activates the lock to that door.

Blondie goes to his bookshelf and pulls out a binder, nearly upsetting the balance of three more binders stacked on top of it. "There's a few other marinas you can check out," he says. "Mostly everyone is closed for the winter, but they might be able to make an exception, I've got the numbers here..."

With his back turned to us, I nudge Kennedy's shoulder. When she looks at me, I make a *Y* motion to my throat.

I'm saying, *We need the lanyard.*

She nods in understanding.

I tilt my head toward Blondie. *Distract him.*

She nods again to tell me she understands. She approaches Blondie. "Do you need a hand?"

"No." He grunts, balancing the binders, *definitely* needing a hand. "Almost got it."

Kennedy glances back at me once more, as if to ask, *Are you sure?*

I give her a thumbs-up.

There's a large fishing net leaning against the wall. I watch as Kennedy picks up the net, lets out a warrior cry

Lucy Lawless would be proud of, and then smacks Blondie in the back of the head with the pole.

He drops like a sack of potatoes, his binders collapsing over him.

Kennedy puts the pole down and brushes off her hands. "Whew. That was kind of exhilarating, to be honest."

I gape. "What...did you do?"

She blinks at me. "You motioned me to hit him."

I make a sweeping motion with my hand. "I motioned you to *distract* him!"

"Oh." She slips her hand through her hair, her mouth pinched in concern now. "Shucks. Do you think he's okay?"

I crouch down beside him and check his pulse. Knocked out cold, but otherwise, just fine.

What's the saying? There's more than one way to cook a goose?

"Help me tie him up," I tell her.

WE LEAVE Blondie snoozing in the chair behind his desk. I tug out a couple of wires on the security camera and then borrow his key card.

When I swipe the barcode over the scanner, sure enough, the light turns green and the "Authorized Personnel Only" door pops open.

Gabe, 1. Anders, 0.

Kennedy and I slip inside. The air in here immediately drops about ten degrees cooler. When the door closes, it hisses, vacuum-sealing us in.

"Jackpot," I say.

This is a very particular storage room. There are thin panes of fiberglass lined up like soldiers with large paintings trapped inside of them. Shelves stocked with goods. Large, black containers.

"How good are you at find-and-seek?" I ask her.

"Easter egg champion," Kennedy replies.

"Put on your ears, bunny."

We split up and start hunting. I take the bookshelf to the left, and Kennedy goes into the containers at the right. The shelves with small and large glass boxes, housing glittering jewels.

Is everything in here stolen?

None of my business. I'm on a mission, looking for one item in particular.

"There has to be billions of dollars of art in here," I say. "I can't believe they only have one man guarding it."

I turn over boxes. Earrings. Red stones. No necklace.

Kennedy doesn't sound surprised. "Langston is a billionaire. Not a SEAL. He doesn't believe that bad things will ever happen to him."

"Must be nice to be so rich you can afford to be deluded."

I must be spitting gunpowder because I can feel Kennedy's eyes on me. "Sounds like you grew up on the other side of the tracks?"

"Oh, my family was rich. Once a month, every time the welfare checks came in."

"Gabe."

The soft way she says my name makes me stop my search.

Kennedy is crouched down beside one of the boxes. Those wide, brown eyes are on me.

I step around the paintings and kneel beside her. There's a black bolt of fabric wrapped around an item. A glint of gold peeks out from underneath.

My heart kicks in my chest.

Carefully, I unwrap the black velvet wrap. It's swaddled like a precious baby. When the light catches it, it sparkles. Pure gold.

My breath knots in my throat.

Kennedy's voice is a whisper, as though she's trying to keep our little, expensive baby asleep. "Is that...?"

"Sure is."

Helen's Gold. It's hard to believe something so beautiful could cause so much chaos.

So much death.

In my mind's eye, I get a flash of the first time I saw it. The awe in Kennedy's eyes matches the wonder reflected in Omar's face when we found it stashed in the hideout.

A tightness curls low in my belly just being near it.

Kennedy and I allow ourselves a quiet, reverent moment. Then I roll it up again in the protective velvet. "Good work, scout," I tell her. "Time to go."

36

JACK

There is nothing on God's green earth I hate more than being told to sit still.

Kennedy and Madsen take off without me. So I putter around the guest house.

I do the dishes. I pick at breakfast. I take my gun apart piece by piece and clean *Kennedy* from it.

I'm haunted by this nagging feeling that we went too far last night. Not for Kennedy—she loved it. I know her ecstasy noises. That delighted look in her eyes. The way her body clenched over and over around my cock.

She loved every second of it.

The problem is *me*.

Parts of me came out last night. Parts I've kept hidden from her. I'm peeling away pieces of myself, and this raw, new vulnerability makes me shaky. Makes me feel as exposed as a boot camp–fresh kid tossed on the front lines.

I distance myself from the feeling. I focus on cleaning my weapon.

I'm never going to be able to look at this gun the same way again. Every time I hold it now, I'm going to be reminded of the way Kennedy looked when she moaned around it. The trust she gave me when she let me push it inside of her.

Is that the power of Kennedy? She can turn even a killing machine into something precious?

It takes longer than it should to clean out the gun. Halfway through the task, my shoulder becomes fever-sore, burning and throbbing. The muscles feel like rusted gears grinding together every time I try to lift it.

So I bundle up, sit outside, and wait for them to return. Like a fucking dog.

I don't know how long I'm out there until I spot Mr. Furhman exiting the main house. He's wearing a thick hat with ear flaps. In his hand, he carries a rifle.

Before I can grab my own gun, he lifts his mittened paw and waves me over.

"Jack!" Mr. Furhman calls out. "Do you like hunting?"

THERE'S NO SNOW, but the ground is covered with a sheen of frost. It breaks like glass as we stomp through the yellow, dead grass in the large, empty acres behind their house.

It's beautiful back here. Tall trees. Miles of nothing.

I could fall in love with the quiet.

Mr. Furhman, it turns out, likes to talk. I hold on to the rifle, he carries the ammo, and he chats as we walk down a footpath. He talks about history, about the surrounding lands, and I stay silent and listen. Until the conversation turns to his daughter.

"We love her," he says suddenly. "Probably don't tell her that enough. I know we give her a hard time, but it's only because we want the best for her. Kennedy is a special girl. Full of potential. A handful, but—"

My feet come to a halt. I cut him off. "Sir, your daughter is the best thing that's ever happened to me. No *buts*. I wouldn't change a single thing about her. I feel very strongly about that. So if you brought me out here to have a pep talk about Kennedy's supposed failings, you might want to take this gun away from me."

I hold out the gun in offering.

Mr. Furhman blinks, and then a smile flickers over his mouth.

"Sometimes," he says, "I think I spent too much time protecting her and too little time loving her. There is a fine line."

His confession hits a chord in me, but I say nothing.

He nods to the gun in my hands. "Hold on to it. I'll line up the cans."

He, rightfully, changes the topic after that. It turns out, his idea of "hunting" doesn't actually involve killing anything. Instead, he lines up hole-riddled cans on a wooden fence, and we take turns with target practice.

The hunting rifle feels different in my arms. I respect the light weight of it. The smell of wood polish and gunpowder. There's something old-school about it I can appreciate.

When I get in position to aim at the far-left can, however, my shoulder lights up like it's been injected with a syringe full of hot sauce.

I grind my teeth as I pull the trigger. It's a miss. A *far* miss. The rifle kicks, smokes, and the can mocks me, unchanged from its spot on the fence.

I take in a breath. Line up my aim. And try to ignore the trembling in my arm.

But when I pull the trigger, it's another miss. I want to fucking die.

As if he can read my mind, Mr. Furhman suddenly says, "There's a quote by Julius Caesar. *Qui se ultro morti offerant facilius reperiuntur quam qui dolorem patienter ferant.*"

"Which means?"

"*It's easier to find men to volunteer to die than those who are willing to endure pain with patience.*"

I grunt. "I'm a soldier. All we do is volunteer to die. It's in the job description."

"And when you're not a soldier...who are you then?"

I blurt out a single word: "Kennedy's."

I squeeze the trigger. This time, the bullet grazes the can. It dances on the fence post, gives a small twirl, and then falls to the ground.

I let out a slow, tight exhale.

As if summoned, she appears.

"Jack!" Like a siren, Kennedy calls my name from across the way.

Kennedy waves her hand and bounds over to me. My heart aches at the sight of her. She's shoved in a too-thick coat, and she bounces when she walks.

I hand the rifle over to Mr. Furhman. When she's in range, I take her in my arms and pull her in close.

I need her. Like a vampire, I need to drink in her warmth. Her heart. Her love.

I need her to fill up all the empty places inside of me.

I kiss her, and she melts against my lips. She tastes like strawberries and summer and carries enough heat to thaw this entire winter away.

When she pulls away, her eyes dart from me, to her dad, and back to me again. She pouts. "I thought you were supposed to be relaxing."

"I am. How'd the scouting go?"

"Good! We went to the harbor, which—you haven't been there, I should take you, I used to go all the time as a kid—but anyway, we were watching, and Anders's men were there! He didn't see us, but we saw him, and Gabe, Jack, you should've seen it—"

Her mouth is going a mile a minute. Her eyes are thrown wide, her cheeks touched with pink, and she's practically vibrating with energy.

After the strange conversation with her father, all I can think is:

Fuck. I love this woman.

I take Kennedy by the back of her head and pull her into a kiss.

She squeaks against my mouth. I pry open her mouth with mine. I slide my tongue against hers.

Like a good girl, she melts against me. I praise her with a deep, lingering kiss, and she sighs into my mouth.

I keep my grip at the back of her head. An anchor. She's calmer now, her eyes clearer when they meet mine. Kennedy tilts her head, cute as a puppy. "Let's talk. Somewhere else." She worries her lip between her teeth, and then she whispers to me intensely, "*We have it.*"

"You have *what*?"

She smiles, and that Mona Lisa smile makes my dick hard and my chest tight.

37

KENNEDY

ead End is a dive bar on the edge of town.

The three of us settle in with a pitcher of beer as Gabe and I take turns relaying the day's events to Jack.

"It was supposed to be a scouting mission," Jack says.

"It was," Gabe agrees. "But we saw an opportunity, and we took it."

His eyes connect with mine, and my face goes hot as I remember him *taking advantage* of the opportunity. His tongue deep between my thighs. Cradling me in his palms like a goblet as he drank me down.

I cross one leg over the other and try to ignore the pulsing between my thighs.

"So where is the gold now?" Jack asks.

Gabe reaches into his pocket, pulls out the lock of velvet, and drops it onto the center of the table. The gold necklace spills out the edges.

Jack quickly lifts it from the table, pulling it into his lap.

"Jesus. Don't just whip it out like that."

Gabe wraps his hands around his beer. "I already

reached out to my contact in DC. Aaron Schilling is coming to us. He'll be here in seven hours."

His words make me light-headed.

Seven hours. That's it, and then this is over.

All of it. *Over*.

We've been on the run for what feels like years. It's hard to wrap my head around the concept of a normal life anymore.

Could I even go back to normal if I wanted to?

Jack looks less convinced. "What about Anders?"

"By the time Anders figures out his precious necklace is gone, it'll already be in Aaron's hands. There will be nothing he can do about it."

Jack still has that faraway look in his eyes. He's staring at the velvet like he can't believe it. Then he tucks it into his pocket and takes a long, deep sip from his drink.

I slide my hand over his thigh. I give him a squeeze.

"Jack. What do you want to do?"

He thinks for a long, hard moment. Then he replies, "Drink."

Gabe clasps Jack on the shoulder. "That's the spirit! Let's celebrate!"

WE ORDER a pitcher for the table, and it takes no time at all to make a sizeable dent in it.

I'm happy. Deliriously happy. Prematurely happy, maybe, but the more I drink, the more the reality of the situation starts settling into my bones.

We did it. The three of us.

I'm proud. Elated. And so happy to have made it through

this bizarre, death-trap roller coaster with my two strong men.

The three of us tucked into the corner of the bar, tipsy and just *hanging out.* This feels normal. This feels right.

This feels like the start of the rest of our lives. I'm warm and cozy, and I sip the amber beer. I'm not even a beer girl, but tonight, I want to drink what they're drinking.

I want to savor this moment.

I sit in Jack's lap. The cold started to creep in, so he forced his hoodie on me. Now, he rests his chin on my shoulder, his arms snug around my middle, stuffed in the front pocket of his sweater.

"Okay," Gabe says, slumped on the far end of the booth, his voice charged with importance. "Question. What is the first thing you're going to do once this is over and done?"

"Beg for mercy," I say.

Gabe laces his fingers together, rests his chin on them, and watches me with hungry eyes. "Go on…"

I laugh. "Not like *that.* Well. Maybe. But I meant at law school. I know my semester is shot, but I want to get back in. Do you think Aaron Schilling writes *excuse my tardiness* notes?"

I bat my eyelashes dramatically and take a sip from my beer. Gabe grins. "There's a first time for everything. I can't think of a better cause."

Jack is suspiciously quiet. I nudge him with my shoulder. "What about you?"

He shrugs. "Same, I guess."

I raise my eyebrows. "You're going to law school?"

He unwinds his arms from me so he can take a sip from his drink. "No. Beg for mercy with the Wolfpack."

A prickle of anger rustles around in my chest. *No, that can't be right.* I heard wrong. I misunderstood. Take a breath,

Kennedy. I wiggle out of his lap so I can look him in the eyes. I force as much calmness into my voice to ask, "You want to go back to work...for the people who betrayed you?"

"Anders betrayed us. Not the Wolfpack."

"Yeah. *And they still tried to kill you.*"

He frowns. "What do you want me to do? Bartend at the Pink Pony forever?"

"Yes! I don't care! Be a bartender, or a bouncer—hell, you can start stripping if you want—"

"I'd pay to see that," Gabe says, lifting a finger.

"Literally *anything* is better! Anything is better than lying awake at night, wondering if you're alive or dead or covered in blood somewhere." Uh-oh. My voice is shaking now, but I can't stop it.

Jack says nothing.

"Jack. Fucking look at me."

He does. Those dark eyes meet mine, and he's so calm about this I want to scream.

"I know too much now," I tell him. "I can't go back to the way things were. So." I take in a deep breath. "Fine. I'll say it. Wolfpack or me?"

A lengthy, dark silence falls over the table. My heart is pounding in my throat.

"We're empty," Jack says. "I'm getting another."

He takes the pitcher off the table and moves to the bar.

My eyes feel tight and shrink-wrapped. I can't breathe. I force myself to stare at a spot on the table so I don't burst into furious tears.

After everything. After everything! That's his response? A whole fucking bunch of nothing?

Tension hangings in the wake of Jack's absence. Gabe takes out a switchblade. He starts flipping it back and forth like a deadly fidget spinner.

"He'll come around," Gabe says. "Give him a moment."

I turn my eyes up to Gabe. There's a storm brewing in my chest, and it's taking everything in me to keep it at bay.

"I keep thinking about the guy. The one we left at the boathouse."

Gabe's eyebrows knit. "Worried about him? He's fine. I promise. He'll have a bump on his head, and he'll have some explaining to do to his boss, but he'll be alright."

Bad thoughts are stirring around my brain. "Jack would've killed him."

Gabe, to his credit, remains a neutral party. He shrugs. "Maybe."

"But you didn't."

"I did not."

"Why not?"

Gabe flicks back switchblade back and forth, back and forth, as he thinks.

"Because," Gabe says finally, "I think everyone deserves the chance to be a good person."

"What if..." I almost choke on my words, but I have to get them out. "What if they don't *want* to be a good person?"

Gabe must see the torment on my face. He reaches across the table and touches the back of my hand. "Kennedy..."

But his tender, kind touch is too much. The second his fingers brush me, my vision goes cloudy.

I pull away and quickly stand up. "I have to...use the bathroom. One sec."

Pull it together, Kennedy.

I stumble back so quickly, however, I launch myself against a stranger.

"Whoa there, babe," he says. I don't have to see him to know the type. He holds me against his body far longer than necessary. He's practically tucked against my neck, and it makes my hair stand on end.

"Sorry," I mumble. I try to squirm away, but his hands go tight on my hips.

"Where's the fire?" he asks.

He pulls my ass against his junk. His breath is hot and rancid against my neck.

I'm not in the mood to be manhandled. But I don't get to tell him that.

Because, in the blink of an eye, three things happen:

One, Jack snatches the switchblade from Gabe's hand.

Two, he grabs the man by the wrist and flattens it on the table.

Three, Jack plunges the knife into the back of the man's hand, nailing it to the bar.

The man screams. Blood leaks out of the wound.

My stomach lurches. My breath catches in my throat at the sight.

"So much for a low profile," Gabe grumbles.

Jack still has murder in his eyes. He reaches for the knife again, but this time, I'm afraid he's going to kill the other man with it.

I launch myself forward and put both my hands on Jack's chest. I shove him back. "Stop!" I tell him. He's made of stone and barely moves, but the act is enough to snap him out of his murder haze.

"We're leaving," I say. "*Now.*"

The man is still screaming as the three of us hurdle out of the bar.

The cool winter air hits my cheeks, but it does nothing to quell the burning in my veins.

The second we're outside, I turn on Jack. "What is wrong with you?"

He narrows his eyes. "I was protecting you—"

"Protecting me? Protecting *me!*" My voice is so fucking loud, but I can't quiet it. I *need* him to hear me, and shouting like this seems to be the only way to get through to him. "I'm the one protecting *you*! All I ever do is defend you! I tell people you're more than a murder machine. Jack is sweet when you get to know him. Jack has a good heart. Jack is kind, and Jack wouldn't hurt a fly if he could help it. But none of that is true, is it?"

He looks like I've slapped him. "This is me. It's always been me. If you can't handle it—"

"I can handle you!" I shout. "Haven't I proven that? Haven't I given you all my trust?"

At that, Jack says nothing. What can he say?

He knows. We both know.

It's true.

"But when I need you to trust me...when I need you to let me handle something on my own...you can't do it."

His jaw sets. His words remain locked behind his teeth.

My vision blurs. Tears wash my vision, but I refuse to let them fall. Instead, I shake my head and take a step back from him.

"I'm tired, Jack. I'm so goddamn tired of defending you. I need space."

Jack moves to me then. He grabs my shoulders, trying to ground me.

"Kennedy," he murmurs. "Take a knee."

I look him directly in the eye.

"Jack. Take *this* knee."

And I knee him hard. Right in the balls.

I'm done with his fucking games. I'm done with his military dogma. *I'm done.*

Jack might be the toughest SEAL I know—but he's also a man. He doubles over, hand on his knee, and chokes.

Serves you right.

I pivot on my heels and start walking in the opposite direction.

Behind me, I can hear Gabe calling my name. But I don't turn back. I can't.

I push away hot, furious tears and call my sister.

"Rebecca. I'm at Dead End. I know it's late, but—"

"I'm on my way," she says. No questions asked.

We're hell to each other, but at the end of the day, we're still *sisters*. She still has my back.

When I end the call, I find a flat bolder and sit on it to wait. The gravel crunches nearby. I *feel* Gabe settle down beside me, but I can't look at him. I can't look him in the soul-searching eyes right now. I can't look at those big, strong arms without curling up in them. I can't break.

"If you're here to apologize for him, don't bother," I sniff.

"I wasn't going to."

"I'm not going home with you."

"I know." His voice is so calm. So controlled.

"Then what *are* you doing?"

"I'm making sure you get to your sister's safe."

I go quiet because I've run out of reasons to argue with him.

I've run out of fight, too. I'm completely, exhaustedly empty.

Finally, Rebecca's car pulls up from the darkness. It stalls in front of me, and I push away tears before climbing inside.

"Kennedy." I hear Gabe call my name, and I find myself turning to look at him. Those steel blue eyes meet mine. "We love you."

My heart breaks as I close the door behind me.

38

GABE

When we get back to the Furhmans' guest house, Jack closes himself in his room and doesn't come out.

I give him some space. I shower off the day. I find a robe hanging off the back of the door, so I avail myself of it. I pour myself a glass of bourbon. It's smooth with a spicy oak finish. Mr. Furhman has good taste.

Okay. Jack has put himself in time-out long enough.

I knock on the door. "Jack?"

Nothing. Quiet.

"I'm coming in."

No protest, so I twist the door handle and push the door open. He's shirtless. His broad chest is gleaming with sweat. He's trying, unsuccessfully, to pick the bandage off his back.

"Let me help you with that."

"I'm fine."

"You can't reach. *Sit.* Doctor's orders."

He reluctantly obeys. I go into the bathroom and return with a damp washcloth. I curl up my leg and sit on the mattress behind him. Here, I'm able to peel up the bandage and clean around the wound.

Jack breaks the silence with "What the fuck are you wearing?"

"It's a robe. *Monogrammed.* I can't pass up a monogrammed robe. You know, when they're not trying to kill you, I think I could really love this family."

Jack says nothing. I clean the wound and replace the bandage.

"Do you want to talk about it?" I ask.

I expect one of his bullish, stony remarks.

There's nothing to talk about.

Or,

What is this, therapy hour?

Instead, he goes still for a moment. When he speaks, his voice is low. Quiet. "She's right."

"About which part?"

"I don't know how to be anything other than a weapon."

I offer him a sympathetic smile. "Never too late to learn. I did."

He frowns. "She deserves better. She deserves someone like—"

His gaze flickers over mine.

Someone like you. That's what he meant to say.

But his tongue catches. Pride, maybe.

He's vulnerable. I've never seen him like this. It'll break your heart.

I suck in a breath between my teeth. "What about you?"

His eyebrows knit. "What about me?"

"What do *you* deserve, Jack?"

"A six-foot hole, probably."

"You don't believe that."

He stares up at the ceiling.

"Do you remember your first kill?" he says suddenly.

I can sense we're going to be delving into treacherous waters. I'm finished with the bandage, but I pick up the washcloth and continue to pat around it, slowing this down so we can talk.

"Sure," I reply. "Everyone remembers their first. Mine was from inside a tank. I was a gunner. One shot and he went down. It was so...well..."

"*Easy*," Jack finishes.

"Yeah. Scarily easy."

"Mine was from a rooftop," Jack says. "The guy had a remote bomb. He was going to set it off, so I pulled the trigger. That was it. Everyone praised me. They were cheering. Said I did a good job." He swallows. His voice is thick when he continues. "I'd never been good at anything before. Not like that. I'd do anything to feel that way again. The more I killed, the more they praised me. I couldn't stop."

"You did what you had to."

"I sold my soul for table scraps of *attaboys*. I don't know if you can come back from that."

I rest my hand on his back.

Jack's story is an all-too-familiar story. One I've heard many times in group.

Someone in his life hurt him and let him down. Maybe it was a parent, or a friend, or a lover. It doesn't matter. What matters is that when he was at his lowest, starving for a hug or an inch of affection, he instead got handed a bulletproof vest and a sniper rifle.

The military is good at rebuilding broken boys in their own image.

My heart aches for him.

"You deserve peace, too," I tell him. "You know that, don't you?"

His eyes cast downward. His jaw is tight—that set line of someone biting back their emotions. "I wouldn't know where to start looking."

I hesitate. "Can I try something?"

"Sure."

I crawl off the bed and shift to sit beside him instead.

Here, I slip my palm over his chest.

"Breathe with me," I tell him. "One deep breath."

"I hate yogi bullshit."

"Humor me."

He closes his eyes. His chest expands against my palm with a full, complete breath. He lets it out, slowly.

"Again."

We breathe together. His heartbeat is slowing. *Good.*

I tilt in closer to him. My forehead touches his. I can feel the heat of those healthy, deep breaths against my cheek.

"You're not a weapon, Jack," I murmur to him. Affirmations he needs to hear. "You're a man. Flesh, blood, and a big, beating heart. You deserve peace, and stillness, and forgiveness. You deserve *love*."

His eyes open at that. Those dark eyes stare at me.

I stare back at him.

It's the electricity before a lightning strike. The brimstone in the air before a firefight breaks out. The calm before the storm.

His heartbeat picks up again. It's thrumming swiftly on my fingertips, matching my own.

Jack makes the first move. He isn't delicate. He isn't tentative. He grabs the back of my neck and yanks me closer until our lips collide in a messy, heated kiss.

I slow Jack down. But Jack speeds me up.

This need is like a fever.

I need some clarity. I put my fingertips to his chest. "Is this—?"

"I want you," he says clearly. All blunt force, this guy.

"Yes, but...how...?"

"I want you inside of me." His eyes flash over mine. "Break me in."

It's like plucking a chord inside of me. There's a tremor, and then my entire body is vibrating with pure, greedy need.

Fuck. Why is that hot?

We get naked. Quickly. The first aid kit is splayed out on the bedside table. We don't have lube, but we do have petroleum jelly, and that'll do. I sit back at the head of the bed and grab the jar. I scoop enough to get my cock slick just as Jack straddles me.

Jack grabs the headboard. The muscles of his bicep flex as he lowers himself down onto me. I guide myself inside of him. Jack takes in a breath and sinks down onto me.

"Fuck, you're so tight."

He grunts. His hand moves to my throat. He squeezes, and my breath gets ragged.

Jack doesn't take it slow. He bounces on my dick like he was born for it.

"You like that?" I ask. My voice is tight in his hand.

He shoots me a sharp look, like I've insulted him. "Yeah. You?"

I shiver. "You feel so good."

His hand gets tighter on my throat, and I choke as he rides me. "You better hold it in. I'm nowhere near done using your cock yet."

Oh. Why didn't I see this coming? It's official. Jack is a power bottom. And I'm so fucked.

He rides me hard and fast. His eyebrows knit, and he shudders on a moan. His breath is hot on my face. "Pound me, you little bitch."

I grip his hips. I have the power to drive us both to oblivion right now.

But I don't.

"Slow down."

Jack doesn't. He's a man on a mission. He's going to rut and hump until we both reach a messy, mind-blowing climax.

But, as Jack should know by now, I always sleep with a knife under my pillow.

I pull the switchblade out now. I sit up, and I position the blade underneath his throat.

Suddenly, Jack stills. *Now I have his attention.*

"I'm going to enjoy you," I murmur, whispering my lips against his. "I'm going to worship your perfect body...even if it kills you."

He swallows hard. His Adam's apple bobs underneath the blade.

His cock, already diamond hard, begins to weep.

He's loving this.

Our Jack has a mild violence kink that needs to be itched, and I'm just the man to scratch it.

"Don't. Move." I graze my lips against his chest. His wiry hair tickles. He shivers.

I kiss his nipples. I drag my tongue over his skin. He tastes like salt and wanting.

"How do you feel?" I murmur.

He closes his eyes. "Like my entire body is one big cock."

I chuckle. "I haven't even touched you there yet."

He swallows. "I know."

I trace the tip of my knife down the scars on his chest.

The tight muscles of his abdomen twitch when I draw it over the ridges of his six-pack.

When the blade touches his cock, he intakes a sharp, quick breath.

I know my knife better than I know my cock. I know exactly how to wield it in a way that won't draw blood...but *will* give just enough pressure to make Jack tingle with anticipation.

His erection looks painful. Blood-blushed and swollen stiff. Using the tame flat side of the blade, I caress the length of him. I pet the metal over the head of him. When I tease the slit with the tip of my knife, a bead of precome surfaces and leaks.

I let out a soft, pleased sigh. "Oh, Jack. I don't even have to get the lube. You're dripping for me."

I don't want to humiliate him, exactly. But he's so cute when his ears go red.

"You're a bastard," he growls. Which in Jack terms, I've learned, is shorthand for *don't stop.*

"Yes. I'm awful." I put my blade to his lips. His hot breath fogs the steel. "Lick it and I'll reward you with my hand."

His face is red. The veins in his neck are standing up.

But that dark gaze doesn't leave mine as he obediently slides his tongue over the length of my blade. I'm mesmerized by the blade indenting his pink flesh as he cleans every centimeter of it, licking his own arousal from it.

"Good boy," I tell him. I snap the blade shut and put it down.

He's all mine now.

I put Jack out of his misery. His erection throbs in my hand. I wrap my fingers around him and slowly trace my thumb over a vein to the slick tip of him.

He sucks in a breath, and I hear it catch in the back of his throat. He swears. It's a glorious sound.

"Go ahead," I murmur. "You can grind again."

He does. He pushes his hips back, riding me, as I pet my thumb underneath the rapidly swelling head of his cock.

We're both inching toward nirvana. But he won't let go.

"*Jack.* You with me?"

"Mm." His throat sounds tight. I'm not even sure he's breathing.

I close my lips over his earlobe. I pull the silky skin of his cock through my fingers.

"Let go, Jack," I whisper in his ear. "It's okay. You're safe here."

"Say that again," he rasps. He's on the edge. I can feel it.

"Let go."

"No. The...the other thing..."

"You're safe."

He whimpers. *That's the one.*

I grip his short hair to hold him close. I press my lips to his, squeeze him as I stroke him, and murmur, "*You're safe. I've got you. You're safe here.*"

"Fuck," he swears. "Gabe—"

Gabe.

Not *Madsen.* Not *sir.* Not *bastard-who-dragged-me-into-this-fucking-mess.*

Gabe.

My name sounds like a prayer coming from his lips, and I want to drink it in, every drop like honey, like a nectar offering to the gods of yore.

He moans into my mouth, and I swallow the sound, shoving my tongue past his lips. Our kiss is hot and messy as our bodies buck together. My orgasm feels like an extension of our kiss, a cresting of euphoria at the same time that

Jack pulses and explodes in my hand. He splatters my stomach, and I keep stroking, full, long pumps, until he's cursing in my mouth and clawing at my shoulders.

My abdomen is wet. My hand is wet. My shoulder is wet, Jack's face buried in the crook of it.

"I've got you," I purr, my voice low and hoarse and raw. "I've got you, tough guy."

39

KENNEDY

My pillow is wet with tears.

I'm my very own Greek tragedy.

Rich, privileged princess runs away from rich, privileged life. Finds a possessive psychopath and a neo-hippie lover-not-fighter who both love her and appreciate her for who she is.

So she ditches them because she *has a lot of feelings.*

There's a knock on my door. I quickly wipe my face, brushing off any evidence of my self-pity.

The door cracks open. Rebecca half waves. I motion her to come in, so she does, closing the door behind her.

"The boys are asleep," she sighs. "Finally."

She's wearing a matching pajama set. I'm wearing Jack's sweater and my panties.

We may be twins, but I think I'm the lone cuckoo bird in the nest.

Until Rebecca plops down in bed beside me. She holds up a joint. "We all have our vices. It might not be...*fucking two guys and admitting it over Thanksgiving dinner. But it's the* best I could do on short notice."

Okay. Maybe there is some family resemblance.

I can't help but smile at that. "Thanks, sis."

She lights, and we take small pulls. We lapse into quiet for a moment. "What's that like?" Rebecca asks.

"What?"

"I mean...is it just sex? Or is it more?"

"If I can fit them both in my cunt, surely I can fit them both in my heart."

We laugh, and I continue. "Gabe is warm. He's playful. We have fun. He's effortlessly open. And full of so much love. An abundance of love."

"And Jack?"

I close my eyes. I consider my words.

"Imagine a big dog. No—imagine a wolf. And this wolf sits at your feet. Walks beside you, no leash required. He sleeps at the foot of your bed. He responds to no one but you. He never leaves your side. And if anyone so much as looks at you the wrong way, your wolf rips their throat out."

"That's Jack?"

"That's Jack. Jack's my wolf."

Sadness. Crushing, crushing sadness.

The thing I love most about him is the thing I hate about him right now.

"This wolf...does he bite?"

A bitter smile at her question. "Sometimes. Other people. But not me. Never me. He'd pull out his own teeth one by one before he bit me."

"So what's the problem?"

"Sometimes, I don't want the wolf. I just want my boyfriend."

Rebecca rests her head on my shoulder. "It sounds like you have a decision to make, Ken. Love the wolf—teeth and all—or send him back to the wild."

I close my eyes. For a minute, I just relish the nearness of my twin. "I'm sorry I called you straight-edged."

She puffs a laugh against my shoulder. "I'm sorry I called you crazy."

We cuddle up. I tuck my hands into the front pocket of Jack's hoodie.

My fingertips brush something soft inside the pocket that wasn't there before. Is that...?

I tug it out. Wrapped around the bolt of velvet is the shimmering golden necklace.

Helen's necklace. When we were sitting in the bar, Jack slipped *me* the necklace.

My heart goes tight, breaks, and explodes in my chest.

Rebecca's breath catches. "What is that?"

The backs of my eyes sting. I choke on a noise, and I can't be certain if it's a laugh or a sob. "It's Jack's way of saying he trusts me."

The doorbell rings.

Rebecca sighs. "The fucking kids better not have ordered cookies again."

"You're literally a walking ad for contraception, do you know that?"

She flicks me off, and I laugh. I'm delirious. I listen to her footsteps as she goes downstairs. For the smallest moment, I allow myself a second of silence. A second of peace.

With me, the necklace, and Jack's trust.

But then I realize...it's quiet. *Too quiet.*

Hold on...

Adrenaline shoots through me, and I'm on my feet.

That wasn't DoorDash.

I rush downstairs, but the second my feet hit the landing, I realize I'm too late.

Anders has my sister trapped with a gun to her head.

His eyes meet mine, and his mouth turns downward.

Out of the shadows, a second man appears. My blood turns to ice.

"Kennedy." Langston purrs my name. His dark hair flops over his face. His smile shows a row of perfectly white teeth. "It's been too long."

40

JACK

One shot. That's all I need.

The sun is blazing above, and it cooks me like an egg underneath all these thick, protective layers. My mouth is chalky, the taste of concrete in the heat.

I adjust my position on the rooftop, belly low to the ground.

I steady the gun, aiming it over the edge.

Through crosshairs, I can see him. Our target stands in the market square. He's positioned himself by an assortment of olives. It's under a tent, which keeps him covered for the most part.

There's a crackling in my earpiece. Faceless voices.

It's now or never.

I can't take it. I don't have a clear shot.

"I've got it," I say into my headpiece.

Are you sure?

"I've got it," I repeat, my voice tight.

The truth is: I want this. Badly.

I want to prove myself. I want to be someone to these men.

We only have one chance. Don't fuck it up.

I exhale. I wrap my finger around the trigger.

My heartbeat slows, and my blood cools.

I can see him through the scope.

You're mine, fucker.

The world slows, and I pull the trigger.

But then the target looks up at me. Her hijab falls away from her head.

I see her face for the first time. That mouth wide in shock. Kennedy's big, brown eyes stare back at me, piercing through the crowd.

The bullet hits her, and she explodes into a cloud of feathers.

I'M GASPING. My lungs hurt. Every breath is too shallow, and I can't get enough air.

I groan and claw at the bedsheets.

Gabe's arm is stuck around me, strong as iron.

"It's okay," he's saying in my ear. "It's just a nightmare."

Have I been screaming? My throat is tight.

Adrenaline makes me its bitch, and I can't control my limbs, thrashing in bed. I just want the images to go away. But Gabe won't let me go. He tightens his grip around me harder. His body is so warm behind me, and his voice is thick and calm in my ear.

"You're okay, tough guy. I've got you."

He puts his hand flat against my heart. I can feel it beat machine-gun fast against his palm. Slowly, Gabe's words start to trickle like cold water through my brain. I squeeze my eyes closed. The howling in my ears subsides.

I'm okay. *I'm okay.*

But I don't feel okay.

"Kennedy," I rasp. "Something's wrong."

"She's fine. She's with her sister."

But just at that moment, my phone rings.

Lo and fucking behold.

Kennedy. On my caller ID.

Gabe and I exchange a look. I answer the call and put it on speaker.

"Kennedy?"

Silence on the other end. My throat goes tight. Suddenly, it all comes spilling out.

"You," I tell her. "I trust you. I pick you. Every time. Whatever I am...whoever I am...I'm yours. I'll spend the rest of my life proving that to you."

Still more silence.

"Ken?"

"That was touching," the voice says on the other end. "Honestly, I didn't think you had it in you."

My blood goes cold.

It's Kennedy's caller ID. It's her phone number. But it's not Kennedy.

"Anders," I whisper.

Beside me, I can feel Gabe staring intently at me, but I can't move. My muscles have turned to stone.

"You have something I want. Now, I have something you want."

"Kennedy."

"You have one hour to come to the Outer Banks and make the trade, or your something-valuable won't be very valuable anymore."

With that, Anders cuts the line.

I drop the phone. I breathe. My heart is a stone lodged in my chest.

"Jack." Gabe's voice grounds me. I turn and meet his gaze.

"They have Kennedy," I tell him. "They want to trade her for the necklace."

Which only means one thing: they haven't found the necklace on Kennedy. *Yet.* I don't know how long we have until they do. Or what they'll do to her when they decide she's expendable.

The thought makes my stomach curl.

Those blue eyes are bright and intense as he watches me from his spot in the bed. My soul anchors to my body again. "Remember earlier when I told you that you weren't a weapon?"

I nod.

"Yeah. Forget all that." He cocks his head, his messy hair flopping to the side. "It's time to soldier up. Let's go rescue our girl."

41

KENNEDY

Jack's voice echoes in my ear.

Whatever I am, I'm yours.

I'm yours! I want to scream back. I'm yours, I'm yours, I'm yours.

But I can't. Because right now...*I'm his.*

His hostage, anyway.

The boat bobs up and down in the low evening swells. The sun is setting, bleeding streaks of red and orange out into the ocean, like someone put a gun to the sun and pulled the trigger.

After Langston and Anders ambushed me at my sister's, they pulled me out of the house, tied me up, and tossed me in the back of the car. Now, I find myself sitting on the deck of *Sweet Charl*, the Caines' family ship. Not one of the crew members so much as did a double take when Anders shoved me across the plank and onto the ship, my hands tied with rope behind my back.

With enough money, you can get away with just about anything.

It's cold out here, the open waters whipping up that

early winter chill, and I'm wearing nothing but Jack's over-sized sweater over a pair of underpants. I tuck my legs against my body to ward off the chill.

I sit alongside the edge of the boat, on a stained wooden bench. If I try hard enough, maybe I can pretend I actually *am* Gabe's snotty, billionaire wife, and this is my honeymoon sunset sail.

I try not to think about my sister, who they left tearstained and tied to a chair in her kitchen.

I try not to think about my mom and dad, who know too much.

I try not to think about Jack and Gabe, who are, no doubt, arming themselves to the teeth as we speak.

Once we're on the ship, they cut the rope around my wrists. Makes sense. What am I going to do—make a grand escape and leap over the edge of the ship to certain death?

I'm trapped, and there's no way out but to endure this.

Langston knows this. He watches me with a slow, sneering grin.

Once, he was attractive to me. Dark, wavy hair. Deep, intense eyes. Perfectly groomed, with soft, flawless skin that has never known a day of hard labor. A solid, spoiled body poured into a dark tailored suit. A ruby ring with his family crest winking on his left hand.

Now, he's just an asshole.

"Kennedy," he says, his voice slow and thick. "Nothing's changed, has it? You get inside men's heads. You make them crazy for you. And then you chew them up and spit them out."

"Not all men. Just you." To make my point, I add, "Nice face."

There's still a mark on his cheek where I sank my teeth into him. I'm honestly surprised he hasn't gotten it smoothed over with plastic surgery. He can afford it, obviously.

It's a near perfect indent of my teeth. A semicircle indentation on his face.

Maybe he's saving it so he can sue me later.

Or maybe he's just a *fucking freak*.

The mention of his scar sends a flicker of anger in his eyes. *Good*. He leans forward and suddenly grabs my chin roughly. His fingers squeeze my jaw, and I wince.

"Does he know you like I do?" he murmurs. His eyes go dark. "Does he know how absolutely broken you are? Will he come rescue you at all?"

"Fuck you," I spit with as much venom as I can muster.

A smile crosses his mouth. "Should we? Once more. For old time's sake."

Fear—real fear—shivers through my chest.

The *click* of a gun clip snapping out of place breaks Langston out of his own fucked-up fantasy. He tilts his head and scowls at Anders.

"Jesus Christ, Anders, what are you doing?"

Anders perches at the back of the ship. He has three guns neatly laid out at his feet, and he's cleaning them, checking them, and filling them.

He also hasn't been able to meet my gaze. I'd like to think he feels an inch of remorse for getting me involved in this, but who knows?

"Getting ready," Anders replies.

"They're two men," Langston huffs. "Not an army."

For the first time, Anders's gaze flickers to me. We exchange a look, because we *both* know.

"Not just any two men," he says. "They're Wolfpack boys."

Anders finishes loading his weapon, tucks it in a holster

at his side, and then peels off the Velcro of his arm brace. He removes the sling and stretches his arm, wincing through the pain.

He has a lot of the same tells Jack has. He's preparing for a life-or-death battle.

I swallow back the knot in my throat and stare out into the bleeding ocean. I slip my hands into my pockets as though to warm them. Quietly, my fingertips brush Helen's necklace.

Jack trusted me with it. And I'll protect it with my life.

I close my eyes and say a silent prayer:

Dear Helen of Troy, from one woman trapped in the middle of a stupid war because of stupid boys and their stupid egos...if you've got any cosmic sway, please protect my men.

42

GABE

In any other circumstance? I'd find the Outer Banks kind of pretty.

The sand is pure white. The shore is empty and tranquil. The moonlight spills out like a cracked egg over the Pamlico Sound, dipping pure white across the rippled ocean.

Like I said, it's nice.

But with our girl kidnapped and trapped in a rich dick-bag's mega-sailboat, I'm filled with the urge to burn the whole place to the ground.

The black water looks like a serpent across the coast.

When I was still in BUD/S training, they woke us up every day and made us do laps through the ice-cold water. To this day, a line of men with machine guns doesn't scare me. But the open water? That sends piss-your-pants-inducing fear through me.

Oh, well. Rip the Band-Aid, then.

We have to get Kennedy. And that's the only thing that matters.

Jack and I suit up in the car. All black to blend in. I hook a knife in my boot. A second blade in my belt. No guns. This is a stealth mission.

"Let's go over the plan," I say. "One more time. I'm the brawn. And you are—?"

"The eyes," Jack says. I can already hear the irritation in his voice.

"And why are you the eyes?"

"Because I can't shoot with my busted arm."

"Right-o. Now. Give me your guns."

If looks could kill, I'd be sand-flea food right now. But instead, Jack relinquishes his guns and hands them over to me.

I know he must feel naked without them. But this is for both of us. I can't have Jack firing a weapon with his arm the way it is. There's nothing worse than stray bullets flying around the place.

The two of us suit up. We steal a kayak and paddle it out to the boat lit up in the middle of the pond. The sailboat stands out like an island in the bay. The water laps at the side of our little boat as, one by one, Jack and I quietly dive into the inky-black ocean.

It's cold as hell, and it knocks my breath out. I gag on salt water on the way up.

It's an easy swim to the boat. Jack lags—I know his shoulder must be killing him, but he won't say as much. We make it to the anchor and cling to the thick chain, treading water and catching our breath.

From here out, we speak only with our eyes and hand signals. We know the codes. We fit back into our military skin maybe too easily.

I climb the chain first. The anchor is so big the chain barely bends under my weight. Barnacles cut up my hands, but I ignore them and press on.

I peek out over the nose of the ship. Two pairs of boots stand guard a couple of yards down. I wait until they're facing the other way, and then I quietly pull myself up.

Taking the first two down is easy. Neither of them sees me coming. All it takes is a hard knock on the skull with the handle of my blade and they're knocked unconscious.

I drag their limp bodies away and hide them behind the thick beam. I glance down the ship. It's dark out here, lit only by starlight and a couple of emergency lights. Caine is expecting us, though. Security guards walk up and down the length of the ship.

I glance back toward the anchor. Jack has pulled himself up, so I grab his arm and lift him the rest of the way.

With my hands, I tell him, *Two to the left, three to the right.*

He nods, and we move forward. We use the shield of the large, billowing sails to hide us. Together, we take out security and staff, slowly creeping toward the back of the ship.

Toward Kennedy, hopefully.

But we hit a snag. Just as Jack rounds the boom, his shadow against the sail gives him away.

One of the security men pounces on Jack before I can stop him. Jack fights back, but he's struggling. He manages to get the guy in a hold and covers his mouth so he won't shout, but this guy won't go down easily. He throws Jack backward, slamming Jack's bad shoulder right against the boom.

Even in the dark, I can see Jack's expression contort in quiet pain.

I rush to his rescue. I spot a winch hooked in one of the pilings, and I snatch it up. In one swift movement, I slam it against the side of the guy's head.

He goes down like a bag of rocks.

We're nearing the end of the line.

I crouch down.

"Need a hand?" I ask.

He nods, so I help him up to his feet.

"You know something?" he says. "We actually make a pretty good team."

I can't help the grin that slices across my face. "That's the most romantic thing you've ever said to me."

The moment is suddenly shattered because—

Floodlights blind us, damaging our view.

I can hear the sound of slow, steady clapping. I squint against the blinding light and have to use my hand as a shield so I can see what we're up against.

Above us, on the raised deck, Caine stands by the curved metal railing.

Beside me, Jack mutters a single word under his breath. "*Shuck.*"

"Good job, boys. But entirely unnecessary. If you wanted an invitation, all you had to do was ask."

I grip the handle of the winch tighter. It's heavy, but I could throw it. Hit him square in the head.

But Jack touches my wrist, and I stop.

Because I see what he sees.

Beside Caine is Anders. Kennedy is trapped in his arms, a gun to her head.

Caine waves us up. "Come on. Let's talk."

43

JACK

I'm dripping salt water on the polished, wood-paneled floor.

Langston orders anyone who is left standing to haul up the anchor. The boat sets sail into the nighttime water. I know it's not a joyride. He's getting us as far away from the shore as he can.

The deeper the water is, the easier it is to sink one or three bodies in it.

We sit in an enclosed dining room, washed with yellow-white lights. Langston and I are seated at a table with white linens. The staff sets out a platter of hors d'oeuvres in front of us. The utensils click rapidly together as the boat shudders and sways.

Someone fills a glass for me and sets it on the table in front of me. I don't touch it.

Caine frowns.

"That's a very nice whiskey," he informs me. "You should drink it."

But I can't take my eyes off Kennedy.

The color has drained from her face. She's terrified, but

she has her mouth pushed into a deep, bitter frown. She may be scared, but she's not going to give Anders or Caine the benefit of seeing her shake.

Good girl.

We're outnumbered, and more importantly, Kennedy is on the line. I'll sit here. I'll listen to his bullshit. But I won't laugh at his jokes.

"What do you want?" I ask plainly.

"The same thing you do. To end this. For good." He pops a small caviar-laden cracker into his mouth. Fish eggs jiggle, and a few tumble into his palm. He swipes up the mess with a napkin. "Now. Show me the gold."

"Let Kennedy go first."

"You don't seem to understand. That wasn't a request. Put the gold on the table, or Anders will shoot you in the head, and we'll take it off your cold, dead body."

"I don't have it."

Now, genuine emotion flickers over his face. Anger. "Jack. You've made a mistake. You had one bargaining chip. This is a trade, and now you have nothing to trade with."

"I'll tell you where it is. But first, you let Kennedy leave. Unharmed. Not a request."

"You must think I'm insane. Don't you? Why would a man of my caliber spend his time chasing mythical artifacts and otherworldly treasures?" He lifts his arms wide with a shrug. "I've always had everything I need. These little jewels...this naughty little hobby of mine. It's the one thing that quickens my heart. It's the only thing that makes me feel alive anymore. I can see it in your eyes. You understand, don't you? The rush of having something so precious. So breakable."

He pulls Kennedy into his lap. He pets her hair.

Anger burns in my chest.

"We can play this game forever. But that would cost me the one thing I can't afford to lose. *Time*. So, I have another solution." He nods to Anders. "Shoot Gabriel in the leg."

"No—" I start, but there's no time.

I hear the gun go off behind me. Gabe shouts. I grit my teeth.

I can hear my own heartbeat pounding in my ears. *This is not going to plan.*

Langston watches me closely. He cocks his head like a dog. "Anders, how long does it take for someone to bleed out?"

"Two or three minutes. Give or take."

"Alright," Langston smiles. "You have two or three minutes to—"

"I have it!" Kennedy says in a rush. She pulls the necklace out of her sweater and holds it up.

It shimmers.

She throws it on the table. Her eyes connect with mine.

"Jack, I'm—"

I shake my head. "I'd have done the same."

Her bottom lip quivers. She rushes toward Gabe, but Anders puts his hand on her chest to stop her.

"Let me help him," she snarls. "He's going to bleed out."

"Kind of the point." Langston yawns.

"*Please.*"

That word gets Langston's attention. He enjoys it. A little too much. He waves his hand in permission, and Kennedy rushes across the room. I tilt my gaze so I can see her. She's crouched down next to Gabe. She's pulled a cloth from one of the tables, and she wraps it tightly around his thigh.

"Mm. Thank God they missed my enormous dick," he groans through his teeth.

"Quiet." Kennedy sniffs.

Langston lifts the necklace from the table and examines it. Greed glitters in his eyes.

"Now," he sighs. "That is a thing of beauty."

The necklace curls up in his palm like a gold snake. He rubs his thumb over it, the pattern shimmering like scales.

"You have what you want," I say. "Let us go now." I hate how close my voice is to begging.

"Yes. Well. Sort of." Langston smiles up at me. "I'm a businessman. Not a soldier. This is all very...macabre. It would be much more efficient for me to have Anders kill all three of you and toss you over the side of the boat. But I believe there's still room for negotiation. A compromise that would suit everyone involved."

I say nothing. He seems to like the sound of his own voice, so I let him continue.

His dark eyes meet mine. "Let's break it down. I would like to keep the gold, which I have rightfully purchased. You would like to go home with Kennedy and have a life of peace and quiet. Is that correct?"

"Sure."

"Now, Kennedy and I...we go back. I don't want to hurt her. Actually, I *want* you two to walk away here unscathed. As far as I'm concerned, there's no reason to dispose of a perfectly good asset, and Anders has done nothing but sing your praises. So here's my proposition. Finish the job. And then I'll let you walk away, completely unscathed."

"The...job?"

He nods. "Kill Gabriel Madsen. Obviously, I can't let him leave. He was part of the original mission. He knows too much. But you...you're a good soldier, aren't you?"

A snarl climbs my mouth. "Go fuck yourself."

When he smiles, he shows all of his perfect, pearly white teeth.

"Pity," he says. "I thought you'd be smarter about this."

He turns and waves toward Anders. Then, the worst sounds I've ever heard in my life—

Kennedy screams.

Anders grabs her by the hair. He yanks her to her knees in front of him, his gun swiftly moving to the back of her head.

I get to my feet. "*Wait.*"

Caine looks at me, his thick eyebrows lifted. A slow, smug smile curls over Caine's mouth.

"Is that a *yes*, then?"

My heart is pounding in my chest. Every beat sounds like one single word, over and over again, drilling its way into my skull.

Kennedy. Kennedy. Kennedy.

"If I do this, you'll let her go unharmed."

"I'm a man of my word."

I don't know that. But I don't have any other choice.

Langston tilts his head over his shoulder and lifts his hand. His guard approaches him. I watch the other man take his gun out, unload a clip, remove most of the bullets, and then snap it back in. He hands the gun to Langston.

Langston looks back at me. "There's one bullet in this gun," he tells me. "So if you shoot me, Anders shoots her. Mutually assured destruction."

"I'm familiar with the concept."

I can feel Gabe staring at me. But I can't meet his gaze. Not yet.

Langston snaps his fingers. "Let's do this out on the deck," he says. "Less of a mess."

44

GABE

Anders pulls me off the floor and lifts me from my own personal puddle of blood. I can't help the yelp that leaves me when I'm forced to put weight on my shot leg. Like a gentleman, he hooks an arm under my shoulders so he can drag me out to my death.

Jack has that look in his eyes I know well. A hard, dead glaze.

It's the look of a man who has closed himself off from any last shred of his humanity so he can finish the job.

They pull me out onto the wooden deck. The weather is shit. It's bitterly cold out here, and the sailboat pitches from side to side in the uneasy chop.

I'm forced to my knees, which takes the breath out of me.

The leg hurts like a bitch, but apparently, that's not going to be my problem for very much longer.

Everyone has followed us out to witness my execution. Jack stands in the center, gun in hand.

I look away. To the water. The bright moon that flickers behind the sail. The boom strains against its natural pull.

The lines groan as they're pulled taut by the wind. I hear Jack's heavy footfalls approach, and a wry grin tugs at the corner of my mouth.

"When I signed up for the Navy, Mom told me I'd die in the dirt," I say. "She'd be proud of me now. Look, Ma! Your boy is dying on a yacht!"

"Gabe—"

Jack's voice, I'm surprised, is choked.

I shake my head. "It's okay. No hard feelings. All part of the job, right?" I give him a wink. "Glad it's you, tough guy."

I have to joke. I don't want to die crying.

I don't fear death. It gets all of us, eventually.

But my body, wired with the human impulse to stay alive, starts shaking all the same.

I force out a grin and look up at Jack. *At least I'm not alone*, I think.

Those strong hands held me once. That stern mouth kissed me.

I meant what I said. *I'm glad it's him.*

"Take care of our girl, yeah?"

Those dark eyes flicker across me. "Take care of her yourself."

What...?

Jack tilts his head so he can address Kennedy. "Kennedy," he says, "take a knee."

Kennedy's irises are wild, her cheeks flushed. She quickly drops to her knees, head bowed.

Jack lifts the gun away from my forehead. Instead, he directs it toward Langston.

The shot goes off, the clack ricocheting across the empty sound.

Langston blinks.

Slowly, he stands. He touches his chest. His stomach.

Then he laughs. He laughs so loudly the sound seems to echo in the air around us. "You missed!"

"No," Jack says. "I didn't."

Langston narrows his eyes.

The last frayed thread keeping the boom in place finally pings free.

There's a loud, animallike groan as the huge metal arm of the ship comes loose. Jack comes to his knees beside me as the boom swings across the deck, jerking the boat from one side to the other in the process.

The quick tack throws everything and everyone off-balance. It knocks men down like bowling pins. Both Langston and his guard go flying over the side of the ship. Anders barely drops to the ground in time, but his gun goes clattering across the polished deck.

Jack and I tumble to the ground. Our eyes meet.

"You get Kennedy," he says. "I've got Anders."

"Copy that."

Blood is rushing through my heart. I'm alive. We're alive.

The team is back.

Jack pushes his fingertips against the deck and launches after Anders.

45

JACK

Everything inside of me crystalizes into one pure, clear purpose:

End Anders's life.

Anders's eyes meet mine. He snatches the gun off the ground and then throws himself belowdecks, vanishing.

I race belowdecks, leaping down the short flight of stairs and hitting polished wood.

There's a galley down here. Dark. Lit only by gas lanterns.

All the doors are shut tightly to keep them from swinging on the water.

I follow the trail of open doors Anders leaves behind him.

I snake my way through the long body of the ship, past the staff quarters, and down into the engine room.

The second my boots hit the floor, I go quiet. The room is small, tight, and loud. Brass mechanics and the churning and grinding of the engine. The whole place is illuminated by small red bulbs.

There's nowhere to run in here.

Carefully, I step around the bulky equipment, hunting for him—

When Anders rounds the corner and throws his body into mine.

We scramble together. He hooks his good arm around my throat. I hook my ankle around his and cut his legs out from underneath him. We hit the ground together and start swinging.

My body takes the hits. In the gut. In the face.

But I don't feel a goddamn thing.

I'm propelled forward by my mission. This man. *This fucking man.*

He betrayed me.

He betrayed the Wolfpack.

He tried to kill Kennedy and Gabe.

Langston was a greedy, entitled bitch. The dirt at the bottom of my shoe. With Anders, it's personal. And now, I'm going to make sure he never gets the chance to hurt anyone I love.

Ever again.

Some inhuman strength rears up inside of me. I overpower Anders, get my knee on his shoulder, and hear a sickening *crack* as I pull hard enough to break his arm. A second time.

Anders lets out a howl. His gun falls from his hand and hits the floor.

I pick it up and get to my feet.

He pants as he sits on the ground, cradling his arm, his back to the wall. I lift the gun to his head, but he doesn't even flinch.

Those empty eyes just stare up at me. Eyes of my former commander.

My former friend.

"Why'd you do it?" I hear myself say. My voice shakes. I need answers this time. "How much money was worth the life of your brothers?"

His eyebrows furrow. "I was tired, Jack. Tired of being a soldier. It was my ticket out. My chance to be something else."

"You are something else," I tell him. "You're the bad guy. And bad guys die."

My grip tightens on the gun. I can feel the trigger under my finger.

One squeeze. That's all it would take.

But my muscles won't obey.

Out of the corner of my eye, red and blue lights flash in the port window.

The coast guard is coming. The real good guys. They could arrest Anders. Lock him up. Do it the right way.

Or I can end it. For good. Right here. Right now.

I can quell this raging fire in my veins with one simple squeeze of the trigger.

The wind lashes across the ship outside, but in that moment, it almost sounds like Kennedy's voice. And Gabe's.

You're not a gun. You're not a killer.

Anders's gaze looks out the port window, and I can tell he's seen the coast guard lights, too. For the first time, I see something I've never seen in Ander's eyes.

Fear. Real, genuine fear.

What does he see in the flash of those twin lights?

An ugly confession? Prison time? Does he see a gruesome conviction in his future? Does he see them removing his war medals from their prized spot over his fireplace?

His eyes meet mine, and he swallows.

"Go ahead," he says, his voice thick and determined now. "Do it. Do what you know how to do."

The gun feels heavy in my hand.

How many times have I thoughtlessly pulled the trigger?

Too many to count.

Not anymore.

I move my thumb over the back of the weapon. I push the safety lock into place.

Anders's eyes go wide, and the color falls out of his face.

"It's like Julius Caesar says," I explain.

"What?"

"*Que soy...ultra...*you know what, shut the fuck up." I tuck the docile gun away and crouch down so I'm level with Anders.

I look him in the eyes when I tell him, "It's over, Anders. I'm not your weapon anymore."

There's nothing but pale fear on his face.

I lock him in the engine room. He's someone else's problem now.

Letting go feels like a victory.

I retrace my steps back upstairs. Gabe has Langston and the security guard tied up with rope, sitting side by side. He has another rope in his hands, which he's looping around a winch.

Kennedy stands by the railing. Her hair whips in the air.

She's gripping the rail so tightly her knuckles have gone white.

"Kennedy." I say her name, and those soft brown eyes meet mine. I can feel my heart—a living, beating animal in my chest. I close the distance between us and take her face in my hands.

Those eyes never leave mine. I trace my thumb over her bottom lip. My throat is tight. All the words I want to say are stuck, the sharp edges stabbing me.

"I'm sorry. I'll never abandon you. Ever again. I—"

"Jack. *I know.*"

She kisses me. She smells like sea salt. The entire world melts away.

The heavy hammering in my heart slows.

When we break apart, her breath shudders. She glances toward the sheltered room and then asks, "Does anyone have eyes on the necklace?"

Gabe's eyes narrow. "Er…"

And then we hear it.

Dripping.

The water pat-pats as it falls from Langston's wet designer suit and hits the deck underneath.

"This is all your fault," he hisses. His voice shakes. "You crazy bitch."

He has the necklace gripped tightly in his wet fingers. In his other hand, he holds a gun. A gun trained directly at Kennedy.

No. This shot can't miss.

I throw my gun toward Gabe. In a single move, he swipes it out of the air, wraps his hand around the trigger, and fires.

Both guns go off at the same time.

Langston falls to the ground. A small red dot grows between his eyes.

Both Gabe and I turn to Kennedy. "Are you okay?"

She touches her chest. "I'm fine. He missed—"

But then the rope behind her back snaps. Kennedy shouts as she goes tumbling over the side of the boat.

"Kennedy!" I try to grab her, but I'm too late. Her fingers slip right through mine as her body sails down toward the dark waters.

I can't swallow the rock stuck in my throat. I am numb. I am empty. Waves crash inside my chest, breaking me apart.

I grip the railing and look over the edge, the worst-case scenarios flying through my brain.

Kennedy has drowned.

Kennedy broke her head against the side of the ship.

Kennedy is gone.

And then, I see it.

There's a pole jutting out the side of the boat, one designed to rig up dinghies. Only instead of a dingy, Kennedy hangs off the pole like a bat. She grips the pole between her legs, her thighs crisscrossed around it. Her body sways with the motion of the ship, hair dangling down.

I can't believe it.

The sound that leaves me is a half-laugh, half-groan of relief. "The Liberty Bell. The fucking Liberty Bell."

"A little help here?" Kennedy calls up to us, and Gabe throws her the rope.

46

GABE

A gull swoops across the cloudless dawn sky, totally oblivious to the bloody chaos below.

My leg hurts like a bitch, I'm woozy from the blood loss, but—

It's over. It's finally over.

Jack, Kennedy, and I sit crammed together on the damp deck cushions. My thigh has been properly patched up, at least, and it's holding for the time being.

The coast guard officers swarm the yacht, taking pictures, talking to staff, trying to put the pieces together.

After they boarded the ship, they corralled as many of us as they could out of the way and took statements. Langston has a sheet covering his body. They escorted Anders back to their boat. He went in handcuffs, stony and quiet, with the look of a man walking to the gallows.

Then, they took apart the boat.

Helen's gold was only a piece of the puzzle. I watch as, one by one, they carry out stolen goods from belowdecks and stash them safely on the coast guard boat.

Kennedy is wrapped in a blanket. Her head rests on Jack's shoulder, and her hands grip the seat below. Our hands press together.

She's safe.

We're safe.

"You okay, angel?" I ask her.

Her fingers entwine with mine. "I am now."

I need medical attention. A shower. A forty-eight-hour nap. My eyelids start to close when I hear—

"Gabriel Madsen?"

I blink awake. "Who's asking?"

A man approaches us. He wears a smart button-up, and his silver, curly hair looks spiderwebbed with mist.

Seeing him is like stepping on a land mine of pure relief.

The man rolls up the sleeve of his shirt and shows off the tattoo underneath. "The strength of the wolf is the pack," he recites.

"Aaron Schilling. You have no idea how happy I am to see you again."

The corners of Aaron's eyes crinkle. "The feeling is mutual. You kept the necklace safe. We're grateful for your service."

"Couldn't have done it without a little help."

I feel Kennedy and Jack's presence beside me. The pull between the three of us is fucking gravitational. My pack of idiots.

My family.

Aaron nods. "We'll sort everything out. For now...well done."

"Careful, Aaron. I have a praise kink."

He gives my shoulder a pat. I exhale and feel my soul leave my body.

All of a sudden, I think, *I want to go home.*

I haven't had a home in a very, very long time. Not since childhood, maybe. But now...

I picture the woods, that stupid chicken, the bed in which the three of us managed to squeeze into, and, *yeah.*

That'd be alright with me.

47

JACK

I have to be stealthy.

I tread lightly across the pine-needle-ridden ground. I lower my bootheel first, then toes. I avoid snapping sticks under my weight. I am panther-like. Quiet.

I get to the hutch and gently push the latch up with my thumb. Slowly, I open the top.

Inside, there are six neat, empty straw nests. I spot my target: a beautiful, brown speckled egg.

The enemy isn't in sight. Now's my chance.

I slide my hand soundlessly inside the hutch. But the second my fingertips touch the smooth shell of the egg—

A flurry of feathers comes flying out of nowhere. The hen gives a warrior cry and stabs her needlelike beak into the back of my hand.

I gently shake my hand to loosen her death grip, but she gets a couple more pecks in before I'm able to extract the egg. I add it to my carton and then size up the bird.

"You're a bitch, Rebecca," I inform her.

She coos something equally insulting in chicken and puffs her chest at me.

With some careful maneuvering and a few more lashes to my hand, I manage to fill up my egg carton. I close the hutch back up and make my way around the chicken pen.

I'm a chicken daddy. Not a title I would've assigned to myself before, but I wear it proudly now. I outfitted Clucky's old pen in the back of our cabin and built a real, sturdy coop.

It's strange the things that bring me peace these days.

Fresh eggs for breakfast. The sound of Kennedy humming while she studies her bar prep. The taste of coffee in Gabe's morning kisses.

The little things.

I enter the kitchen, where I'm greeted with the smell of bacon crisping and a pot of coffee boiling.

"Success?" Gabe asks. He's at the stove with a dish towel over his shoulder, his hair in that sexy just-woke-up tangle, and he's wearing an apron that says, *Peg the egg master.*

I have no idea where he finds these things, and I don't ask.

I set the carton down on the kitchen counter, and he immediately reaches into it, removing a few for breakfast.

"We need to get Rebecca a muzzle. Where's Kennedy?"

Gabe tilts his gaze upstairs. "Soaking in that beauty sleep."

"I'll go rouse her."

"Don't be long." Gabe cracks an egg in the pan. "Breakfast in ten. That's ten minutes, not ten orgasms, by the way—"

I signal a *copy that* and climb upstairs to wake our sleeping beauty.

Except when I enter our bedroom, I find she'd fully immersed herself in animated-princess-sings-to-the-woodland-creatures status.

Kennedy is sprawled out in bed, limbs everywhere. She shares the pillow with Clucky, her face practically buried in the chicken. Clucky is napping happily, her beak tucked into her feathers, but when I approach, she side-eyes me suspiciously.

"Scram," I tell her. I nudge her off the pillow, and she fluffs up her feathers disapprovingly, letting out a displeased squawk before toppling off of the bed. She lands on her feet, huffs, and starts pecking at the strap of one of Kennedy's dresses strewn on the floor.

"Time is it?" Kennedy slurs. She doesn't open her eyes.

"Time to get up." She has a feather stuck to her cheek. I pluck it from her. "I thought we had a rule about birds in bed."

Kennedy stretches her arms above her head. She makes a sweet noise that makes my blood rush. "We do."

"Which is…"

"If hens aren't allowed in bed, neither are cocks."

I catch her chin and force her to look at me. "That's a terrible joke."

A smile plays on her lips. "You're a terrible joke."

I kiss her. She tastes warm and sleepy and, somehow, like freshly baked cookies. She gently teases her tongue along mine, and I make the decision that we're going to be late for breakfast.

I climb into bed, shedding clothes while keeping my lips on hers.

The covers slide off her, revealing the swell of her bare breasts. I fit my body against hers. She's naked, and when I push my fingers between her legs, she's ready for me.

Gabe and I took turns with her last night. Still, she wants more.

My good, greedy girl.

Last night, I pounded her until her thighs trembled. I made her scream. This morning, I'm delicate.

This is her reward. And mine.

I ease inside of her, filling her inch by inch. She gasps against my lips, and her arms wind around my shoulders.

I used to always rush this part. Now, I slow down. I want to savor this precious, wild woman underneath me.

Our tongues tangle with lazy morning kisses. I pin her hand to the mattress and lace my fingers in hers. When I move inside her, it's with slow, measured waves.

Kennedy's eyelids lower. Those thick lips fall open, and every time I push all the way inside of her, I'm rewarded with a small, breathless gasp.

I nuzzle into her thick hair. I kiss her throat and underneath her ear. I want to bury myself in this woman.

"I love you," I tell her, my voice low and heated.

"I love you." Hers is a whisper.

I make love to Kennedy, our pleasure slowly building. I cup her ass, slotting her tightly against me so she can grind her clit on the base of my cock.

She grips my shoulders. Her legs twist in mine, and her toes flex into the back of my calves. I swallow her mouth in my kiss as I feel her body go tense, and clench, and then shake apart. She whimpers over and over each time her body pulls at me with tight, quick pulses. I swell and spill inside of her, and still her body clings, draining me for everything I have.

We collapse, a pile of limbs. Panting. Sweating. Blood humming.

We're tangled so tight my dog tags stick to her skin. I can feel her heartbeat alive in my chest.

"Jack?"

"Yeah?"

"You have permission to wake me up like that every morning."

"Copy that."

I cup her face, stroking her hair. She kisses the tip of my nose.

"Do I smell breakfast?" Kennedy asks.

"You smell cold breakfast. Gabe is going to kill us."

"Mm. At least I got one last ride before I die..."

Kennedy twists her hips upward, sheathing me deep inside her. I groan against the second swell of heat.

"Forget Gabe," I say. "Your pussy is going to kill me before he gets the chance."

I feel her coy smile against my mouth. "I'm starving."

"You worked up an appetite."

She wiggles her hips. "What's on the menu?"

"Eggs...toast...coffee..." My mind is whirring to come up with more breakfast items. Anything to keep her riding my dick. "Um...eggs..."

Her fingers catch on my mouth. Each tiny little gyration inches me further from sanity. "More eggs?"

I grunt around her fingers. "So many eggs."

"Busy chickens."

"*Mmmph.*"

Kennedy grabs my face and crushes her lips against mine. Then she wiggles out from underneath me, twisting to climb out of bed. "Sounds delicious! Let's get up!"

I am up.

Somehow, Kennedy has both completely satisfied me and left me aching.

I hook an arm around her middle to trap her to me. "Already?" I ask.

She twists so she can scratch the top of my head. "Be

good, Big Bad Wolf, and I'll let you eat me alive after breakfast."

I growl low in the back of my throat. That delights her, and she laughs. My heart does a flip at the sound.

"Meet you downstairs." Kennedy pecks a kiss to my lips and peels away, vanishing into the bathroom.

I sit up in bed, give myself a second to let my blood cool, and then put my clothes back on. I smell like sex and Kennedy, and if I could make a cologne out of her scent, I'd wear it every damn day.

Gabe will want to lick her from me. That thought alone is enough to propel my feet back downstairs.

But when I come to the bottom landing, I go still. My blood is humming, and it has nothing to do with the semi.

Something is wrong.

The air is thick with the smell of breakfast and black coffee. But quiet. Which is unlike Gabe, who will talk to Clucky just to hear the sound of his own voice. I don't hear clattering in the kitchen. My eyes flicker to the window. There's a car parked outside. Not ours. The back of my neck tingles as though there's a spider crawling up my spine.

"Gabe?" I ask.

No response.

Someone else is in the house.

This house is a sanctuary. A place of peace. There are no guns allowed in the house, except—

The one stashed in the bedroom, the other taped under the sink, and a third tucked in the secret drawer in the foyer table.

Just in case guns. Good for situations like this one.

I pull out the drawer, slide back the bottom panel, and pick my gun out from underneath. I hold my finger against the trigger as I move quietly down the hall.

I stop at the open doorway into the kitchen. The floor-boards creak, and someone coughs.

Got you, motherfucker.

I throw myself through the entranceway. I grab a handful of shirt and slam the intruder against the wall. My gun connects with his stomach, encouraging him to still. He yelps and drops a cup of coffee. It goes splattering across the floor.

When my eyes connect with his, however, my sharpened instincts leave me like a ghost.

"Kip?"

"God...dammit." He groans. "Do you have to try to kill me every time we meet?"

I lower the gun. The screen door opens and shuts.

"I see you two are getting cozy." Gabe grins. He tosses a fresh egg up in the air and catches it. Then he frowns when he sees the floor. "Aw. I liked that mug."

Kennedy appears, and when she sees Kip, she lights up. "Kip!" She goes in for a hug, but I put my hand on her chest to keep her from stepping on glass.

"My fault," Kip says, crouching down to pick up the broken bits. "I apparently...*breathe* too much."

"What are you doing here?" Kennedy asks.

"I heard fresh eggs were on the menu, and I couldn't resist."

I crouch down with him. I take the broken bits from his hand and finish cleaning up. "It's good to see you," I tell him.

He narrows his eyes at me, but he relents, his frown lifting. He straightens up and rakes his fingers through his hair. "Well, I don't have a car for you this time."

"Damn."

"But! I do have something better."

He motions us to the table. Kennedy sits, and I take my

place beside her. With a flourish, Kip pulls over a thin black box he's set at the center of the table, in the middle of Gabe's place settings.

"Tada," he says. He opens the box. Inside, Helen's necklace glimmers on a bed of soft, dark velvet.

I didn't appreciate how pretty the thing was before. It's breathtaking now, and even Kennedy's fingers lift to her mouth.

Gabe takes off his apron and sits at the table with us. "Aaron has arranged to return the stolen items back to where they belong. And, well, since we *were* the ones to recover Helen's gold, he said it only seemed right that we'd be the ones to hand deliver it."

Gabe is grinning. Kip is grinning. But I find myself transfixed by the necklace.

Kennedy's hand moves over my thigh. She squeezes. "What do you say, Jack?"

They're all waiting on my answer.

Kip coughs. "I'll babysit the poultry if that's what's causing you pause."

A hand squeezes my shoulder.

My anchor.

Gabe's voice is gentle as he asks, "You up for one last mission, tough guy?"

48

GABE

It's a fourteen-hour flight to Turkey.

We're riding a private military craft, which is, frankly, very fancy of us. The only other ones on the plane are the pilots, an attendant, and Aaron Schilling—dressed to the nines as always—accompanied by two government-hired babysitters.

The closer we get to our destination, the tightness in my chest grows. The last time I was here...well. It didn't go very well for me.

But then again, the last time I was here, I didn't have Jack and Kennedy.

Jack is wearing one of the red-printed tropical shirts I got him. It looks good on his broad shoulders. He's grown out some black fuzz across his strong jaw.

Kennedy has a soft, flowing white dress. She's twisted two cute braids into her long hair.

I want to tug her braids in my hands. I want to nibble Jack's scruff. My nerves are bouncing and translating to *horniness*.

Jack seems to sense the vibrating inside of me. He takes

the cushy seat across from me. He sets a glass of whiskey on ice on the flat table in front of me.

"Drink," he demands.

I flash a smile. "Does it come with a side of hand job?"

"Down, boy."

His dark eyes meet mine. There is a promise of *later* in them that allows me to swallow down some of the whiskey.

He's right. As always. It takes the edge off.

We disembark from the plane, drop our minimal luggage off at our cheap hotel, and barely have time to wipe the red-eye from our faces before we're due for our meeting.

As we head to the exit, however, Kennedy slows. "I think I'm going to stay behind," she says. "Check out the city a bit."

Jack's eyebrows knit. "Are you sure?"

She slips her hand to the back of his head. "Yeah. This is Wolfpack business." She presses a kiss to his mouth. "I'll find you after."

Jack nods. Then she turns to me and gives me the same sweet kiss before heading out.

Jack and I escort her to the car and then pay the driver a little extra to keep an eye on her. Now, it's just the two of us.

Jack turns to me. "Ready?"

What a loaded question. Am I ready to get rid of the thing that's haunted me, held my life in the balance, killed people I love?

"Couldn't be readier."

Aaron Schilling picks us up. He's arranged the transaction at a café that overlooks the crystal gulf. Stray cats lazily bake on the sun-warmed sidewalks. I can see the ancient columns stacked in the distance, a beautiful reminder of the city's history embedded in the very stone.

Our contact is already waiting for us. Jack, Aaron, and I

join her at the table outside. She orders a pot of herbal tea for the group. A couple of kids come around to our table to try to sell us knockoff watches, but Sabine shoots them a hard look, and they scatter like cats.

Sabine Onasis is a board member of the Historical Preservation Society. She has a feline grace that makes her timelessly beautiful and a stern turn of her mouth that tells you that if you inform her of said beauty, you'll probably feel the business end of her claws.

She has her brother's sharp cheekbones and his striking honey eyes.

She gets down to business. "Do you have the artifact?"

Jack lifts the box onto the table and opens it for her. She looks inside, presses her lips together, and then nods. Jack closes the box.

"I'm glad to see it's in one piece."

From the tone of her voice, she doesn't actually seem all that stoked about it. I don't need applause, but a little *thank you* would go a long way.

"Wasn't easy, I'll tell you that," I say.

Jack's leg knocks against mine. *Calm down*, he's saying.

"Where does it go from here?" he asks.

"It will have to be examined by our historians. After that time, we'll put it on display in our museum, where it can be enjoyed by the people."

I think about how it almost ended up on Langston's coffee table as a conversation piece, and I shudder.

"What's your price?" Sabine asks diplomatically.

"We're not seeking a reward," Aaron states diplomatically. "This was stolen from you. We're just here to see that it's returned safely. And without retaliation."

That last bit is the important part. Everyone gets it.

Sabine's shoulders seem to relax at that. She takes a sip

from her tea and pauses thoughtfully before continuing. "I am no archaeologist," she explains. "It was my brother's life work. Omar used to say that these artifacts were important because they remind us who we are. We have to know where we came from in order to understand who we are."

"I'm into leaving the past in the past these days," Jack says.

"As am I." She takes the box and sets it down beside her. "But it reminds me of him, and that is priceless. Thank you."

We finish the transaction with handshakes and well-wishes. After everything we've been through, this part feels deceptively easy.

Sabine makes her exit, but I break from the pack to catch up with her.

"Ms. Onasis." She's adjusting her bag over her shoulder, and she looks up at me. "I...knew your brother. Briefly. He was a great man."

For a second, there's a glimmer of emotion in those serious eyes. A twitch of a smile. "He was the best of us."

"He gave me something...here." I unhook the necklace from the back of my neck. The thin gold slithers into my palm with the charm. I hold it out for her. "This was his. He'd probably want you to have it."

Her eyes flicker from the necklace to me, and she shakes her head. "He gave it to you. Honor the gift." She tilts her head and then adds, "Clearly, he saw something good in you, too."

There's a knot in my throat, but this hurt feels good.

Sabine leaves, and the necklace vanishes with her.

A hand clasps my shoulder. "A word?" Aaron asks.

There's a bar inside. The three of us settle around it. It's bright daylight, but it must be three o'clock, like, *somewhere*.

There's a different energy in the air when three Wolfpack men get together. A tightness in the spaces between us. An understanding in the private silences that relaxes the shoulders and slows my heartbeat.

No one has to *pretend* here. Not among brothers.

We get our drinks, and Aaron waits until the bartender moves out of earshot to speak. "You've impressed the higher-ups. If you're looking for more work, we have plenty of it. Missions that never happened, so to speak."

"My favorite kind." I sigh around my glass.

"The Wolfpack would accept you back with open arms. Both of you."

That thought makes my skin tingle, but I don't let it show on my face.

"You could do more work like this," Aaron continues. "For the good of the country."

I anticipated this would come up. Jack must have, too. Neither of us discussed it, but maybe we didn't have to because Jack answers for the both of us. "I've put the gun down for now."

"I understand," Aaron replies politely. He opens up his wallet and takes out a small white business card. "I'll leave this here. In case you change your mind." He puts it face up on the table. "Thank you again for your service. Enjoy the rest of your stay." He finishes his drink, collects the tab, and leaves.

Jack and I linger.

I punch my finger against the card and pull it toward me. It has the wolf's head sketched with geometrical precision on the front. When I flip the card over, there's nothing but a single phone number in clear, crisp font.

"Nice stationery," I comment. "What do you think?"

"I think I'll never go in blind again." He picks up the card and tucks it into my shirt pocket. "Tell Kip to dig."

A smile twitches at the edge of my mouth. "Yes, sir."

Fool Jack once, shame on you. Fool Jack twice, he'll bury you six feet underground.

Jack knocks back his drink. The thick glass hits the bar hard. "Let's go find our girl."

49

KENNEDY

I spend the morning at an outdoor market, fishing through dyed scarves and fresh fruit. Jack and Gabe scoop me up on our way back to the hotel. When we get there, however, our bags are waiting for us outside.

"Are we kicked out already?" I ask.

"What'd you do?" Jack glares at Gabe, who lifts his palms.

"Why is it always my fault?"

The twin doors of the hotel open. A uniformed man greets us with a smile. "Your lodgings have been upgraded," he explains. "The driver will take you to your next destination. Courtesy of the Historical Society."

Then he hands us a note. It reads:

Enjoy the view. Friends of Omar are friends of mine. -Sabine

A car comes to pick us up. The change of plans yanks at my heart. After living with two military guys, going on the run, and getting kidnapped by my ex, I've got easily triggered alarm bells. But Jack moves his hand to mine and gives it a squeeze. "We can trust it," he says.

I trust *him*, so I force myself to relax. We toss our bags in the car and relocate. It's about a thirty-minute drive to our next destination, and I nod off against Jack's shoulder.

There's a weird relief after dropping off the necklace. Like I've removed a heavy weight from my shoulders that I didn't even realize was there.

It's over. It's finally, really over.

I wake up to Jack nudging me gently. "Kennedy. We're here."

I blink the sleep from my eyes, and when I look out the window, my breath catches.

Sabine was right. She can't be an archaeologist.

She's *fucking loaded*.

We're dropped off in Datça at a beautiful, modern villa resting on the lip of the coast.

It's an impressive, blindingly white building that looks like it could've been a fortress in a previous life. We go through the golden doors and enter a huge, flowing space. The stone walls and tall archways make me feel like I'm in a different era. There are wide glass windows everywhere, leading out to the sandy beach and twinkling ocean.

We find the master bedroom, with a king-size bed (the only kind of bed the three of us can comfortably fit in), with tall wooden posts and a billowing canopy.

"Boom!" Gabe says. He tosses his bag down and throws his arms wide. "This is what I'm talking about! It pays to be the good guys!"

I can't help but laugh. His excitement is contagious.

My Jack is quiet. I step next to him and lean my body back against his.

"How're you feeling?" I ask.

He rests his hand at my hip. His fingers dip underneath my hemline, but just to cup my pelvis, his thumb hooked on the outside of my pants. I'm his *comfort pussy*, and occasionally, he'll just touch it to ground himself.

"Good," he says. Then he kisses the side of my head. "Lighter."

Jack is still a man of few words. But his words have meaning. He doesn't hide behind *I'm fine* anymore. Slowly but surely, he's gotten more comfortable opening up, bit by bit.

And I've loved watching him climb out of his shell.

I nestle against his throat and inhale his musk. "Me too."

Gabe's excited shouts carry through the house. "Holy shit! Check out this shower!"

I grin and take Jack's hand, leading him into the bathroom.

He's not wrong. The shower is gorgeous.

It's huge, with turquoise tiles, a rippled glass window, and a ceiling showerhead big enough to fit all three of us.

I start chucking off clothes.

"I don't know about you guys, but I need to test it out. Immediately."

Gabe turns it on to warm it up. The three of us strip and get in. The hot water blasts down on us like rain, and the pressure feels so good on my scalp and skin. It washes me completely clean, and I feel the plane ride, the pressure from the trade, and all the exhaustion and stress leave my body.

I sigh into the heat. Strong hands grip me from either side. Jack and Gabe take turns washing me, rubbing soap over my skin. Their hands dig into my hair, making my scalp tingle.

Under the shower and their hands, I'm reborn.

The heat pulses through me to a needy ache that settles

between my legs. It gets stronger with every pass of their fingertips or every brush of their naked bodies against mine.

They're hard, too, growing for me, but we're lazy in our want. We take our time, savoring each other, until even the most platonic touches feel like a wicked tease. The brush of Jack's beard against my shoulder. A hand resting on my hip. The gentle way Gabe pushes shampoo from my forehead to keep it out of my eyes.

By the time we leave the shower and towel off, the three of us are aching to get into bed.

We swap kisses as we make our way to the bedroom. Gabe and I tumble onto the mattress, our naked bodies kissing, warm and damp still from the shower.

Jack sits in the plush lounge chair across from us.

"Aren't you going to join us?" I ask.

Jack shakes his head. "Not yet. I want to watch."

The hunger in his eyes sends a shiver through me.

If he wants to watch, I want to give him a show.

I pet Gabe's hair. I coax him lower. He takes the cue. His lips trail down the center of my body. His hot breath tickles my stomach. He kisses my thighs, and I clench with anticipation.

Then I feel him. *There*. The sweet kisses. The heat of his mouth.

Gabe licks me, swirling his tongue with such expert precision it makes my eyes roll back. He cups my ass like a chalice, drinking in deep.

I can't help it. I sneak a look at Jack.

His eyes are dark and hungry. He's holding his erection, slowly stroking it.

The sight of him, so hard for me, makes my mouth water.

Gabe gives me one final, long lick that leaves my sex

buzzing. Then he climbs on top of my body and reaches between us.

"You want me inside of you, angel?" he asks.

"More than anything."

I grip his hips as he eases himself in. The thick head of him kisses me between the legs. He opens me, stretching me, and lowers himself inside.

Gabe is so big, and he makes sure I feel every inch of him with slow, purposeful swoops of his hips. I moan and arch, grinding into him to take him fully.

He fills me so deliciously my core warms like a fireplace, growing hotter and hotter.

I grip handfuls of thick, soft hair. He kisses my breasts, my throat, my face.

Sweet, loving worship-kisses.

He makes love to me, and my heart expands, and my toes curl.

I feel blessed under Gabe. I feel loved.

"You're an angel," he tells me. "You're beautiful. Jack—come here. Get a taste of this. She's in her sweet, needy place."

The way they talk about me makes my heart patter in my chest.

Gabe pulls out of me, and I whine at the emptiness. I'm so tight with want that my legs part wider. Begging position.

Gabe sits up. He kisses my thigh and then settles down beside me.

Jack takes his place. I rake my nails down Jack's strong chest, tickling the thick hair there.

Their bodies are so different. Where Gabe is lean and svelte, Jack is brawny and strong.

I'm addicted to them both.

He grabs my jaw and kisses me. His hands are so rough

after Gabe's sweet touches that I feel a heavy pulse between my legs, and I can't tell whether or not I've orgasmed just at his familiar grip.

I whimper and jut my hips up.

"Please," I beg. "I need you so bad."

Jack reaches between us and adjusts. He doesn't waste time—he plunges inside of me, all the way to the hilt.

He thrusts inside of me so hard I tingle all the way down to the soles of my feet.

I cry out, my toes curling into the mattress. Gabe adjusts my body against his, cradling me from behind. He nibbles my ear. Kisses my throat. Cups my breasts, rubbing my sensitive nipples in a way that I feel all the way down to my clit.

I whine and writhe with pleasure as Jack fucks me, deep and hard, while Gabe caresses every inch of my body.

"Do you know how much we love you, angel?" Gabe murmurs into the shell of my ear.

"Yes..." I moan. "I love you...both of you..."

I tilt my head up, and Gabe catches my lips. I barely get a second to breathe before Jack swallows my mouth in his.

Then my boys make eye contact. Gabe reaches out, and Jack meets him halfway, their mouths colliding with a hungry, sweet kiss over me.

I love watching them kiss. It sends a thrilling shiver through me.

They break. Gabe rakes his fingers through my hair. "You want me to fuck him while he fucks you, baby?"

Oh God. The thought makes my cunt pulse. "Yes..."

Gabe gets up. He leaves the bed briefly to get lube from his bag and then returns, climbing behind Jack.

Jack makes a quick, gasping sound, and I love it because

I know how good Gabe feels inside of me and how good Gabe must feel inside of him.

I kiss his throat, and his growl vibrates against my lips. His mouth finds mine, and our tongues tangle.

Jack pins my hand to the mattress. His fingers curl in mine, tightening.

I feel so close to him like this. So close to the both of them. The three of us riding the same wave of pleasure. And this tide...

I don't fight it.

I drown in them. My orgasm swells and breaks. I cling to Jack as I whimper through it. He moans into the crook of my neck, suckling my skin, nibbling, until his hips give a shuddering thrust. I grip his hair. I close my eyes as I savor the feeling of him, his throbbing heat spilling over inside of me.

Gabe sighs—this beautiful, satisfied sound—and I know he's come undone, too.

The three of us collapse together, panting, sweating.

It should be impossible to feel this much bliss, cradled between my two most favorite people in the world.

50

JACK

The ocean air rolls in. It fills the curtains like sails and then glides over us, kissing our sweat-damp skin.

I pet Kennedy's hair, and she melts against my chest.

Gabe rests at my hip. He tilts those blue eyes up at me, like a puppy dog, wanting, so with my other hand, I pet his hair, too.

"Mmm, I love you, too," Gabe purrs, closing his eyes and leaning into my hand.

"I love you," I tell him.

Words that used to be so hard to say.

Now they feel natural. Effortless.

"What if we stayed here?" Gabe offers. "Like, forever."

Kennedy grins. "On the run?"

I grunt. "Bonnie, Clyde, and Clyde."

"I could take the bar here," Kennedy says.

"I'll start a business," Gabe continues. "I'll learn to fish."

"You'd stink!"

"I'd shower. Besides, you'd learn to love it."

I close my eyes and listen to the sound of their voices as

they daydream together. It's not going to happen. We're going to go back home. Kennedy has to pass the bar and protect the good guys. Gabe has to change the world. I have to feed the chickens.

But they've both been very good, and this is the first time I've seen them relax like this in a long time, so I stay quiet, and I let them dream.

~

IT'S four in the morning when I open my eyes. Immediately, I'm wide-awake.

It's a nagging feeling. Like being tapped on the shoulder. Like someone whispering in my ear.

Jack...

I take stock of the room.

Kennedy is snuggled between me and Gabe. The two of them are peaceful, undisturbed. The room is lit with bright moonlight, and I can hear the ocean whispering outside.

I remind myself where we are. Turkey. Under the care of a friend. No one is coming after us. Reflexively, I reach under my pillow, but I find it empty. I don't keep a gun there anymore. I don't have to.

We're safe.

So why is my pulse kicking?

Gently, I peel myself out from the softness of Kennedy's warm body. Her eyebrows knit at the change, but in her sleep, she finds Gabe's warmth and snuggles up closer to him. He wraps his arm around her and kisses the top of her head.

My heart swells in my chest.

They'll be okay for a minute.

I follow my feet and walk out the glass door that opens

to the beach. I should probably put on some clothes, but it feels right to be naked in the dark out here.

Feels like nature is beckoning me.

When my feet break the top layer of cool sand, I feel the day's warmth still lingering underneath. I walk out to the shoreline and take deep, slow breaths. The air is thick with sea salt. It's healing.

I close my eyes. I listen.

It sounds like the very water itself whispering:

You've done enough. You can take off your armor now.

My legs give out. My knees hit the soft ground. I dig my fingers deep into the sand. The warm water climbs the shore and kisses my knuckles.

I know what I have to do.

My limbs work of their own accord. I take my dog tags off my neck and drop them in the water. The tide licks my hands like a loyal dog and drags the metal out with it.

The ocean washes my hands clean.

It doesn't matter what happens now. No matter what...

For the first time in my life, I am loved. I am free.

THE END

THE WOLFPACK WILL RETURN

The story continues...

What is a hunter when he can't hunt? That's what former special-ops soldier, Jack Crossed, aims to find out. He's determined to live a quiet life with Kennedy, Gabe, and their (cute but stupid) pet chicken. Until Gabe gets kidnapped by the enemy. In order to bring him back home, Jack has to pick up the gun once more. Find out what happens next in the **Double Crossed: Bonus Mission** (available in ebook).

Plus, the Wolfpack returns in **Double Bucked**, a MMF military romance with cowboys, spice, and action. New soldiers. New mission. New mayhem.

THANK YOU FOR READING!

Thank you for reading **Double Crossed**!

I hope you enjoyed Jack, Kennedy, and Gabe's story.

(And Clucky, let's not forget Clucky.)

If you enjoyed this book, **please consider leaving a review**. Authors are like fairies, and applause keeps us going!

Can't get enough? You can find bonus materials (including a soundtrack, aesthetic board, and a full bonus novella) on my website at adoracrooksbooks.com/double-crossed.

Find the Wolfpack's next mission in Double Bucked, a spicy military western romance.

ACKNOWLEDGMENTS

The first person I want to thank is...you! Your support keeps my fingers on the keyboard.

I also want to thank my editors for catching all my pesky mistakes. Plus, a big thanks to my ARC team who came through and helped spread the word!

Finally, the biggest thanks to Lizzy, who turned a Wild First Draft into a still-fun-but-actually-readable book. Your invaluable feedback and encouragement helped me find these characters and I'm so grateful for it!

Mission accomplished, team! Onwards to the next one...

XOXO,

Adora

ABOUT THE AUTHOR

USA Today bestselling author Adora Crooks writes romance with heart, action, humor, and steam.

She currently resides in the magical city of New Orleans with her beloved and their two nutty mutts. Adora lives off of coffee, cookies, and book reviews and daydreams about dirty romances with happy-ever-afters.

Sign up to Adora's newsletter to get exclusive deals on Adora Crooks stories, including ARCS and upcoming releases.

https://adoracrooksbooks.com/gift/

Find a full list of Adora Crooks books with tropes and content warnings on her website.

www.adoracrooksbooks.com